Pleasure in the

Erotic Writings by Latin American Women

DAINA CHAVIANO (Cuba)
"Memo for Freud"
Falling in love gives the narrator nightmares in this witty, sharp poem about male/female relationships.

ROSARIO FERRÉ (Puerto Rico)
"Rice and Milk"
A modern-day fable that gives a mythic flavor and a sinister twist to the war between the sexes.

ELENA PONIATOWSKA (Mexico)
"Happiness"
One woman's imaginative soliloquy on the mystery and passion of love explodes in the rhythms of lovemaking in this breathless, erotic rhapsody.

ÁNGELA HERNÁNDEZ (Dominican Republic)
"How to Gather the Shadows of the Flowers"
The tale of an eldest daughter, Faride, whose increasing madness takes the form of an exquisite sexuality . . . and remarkable creative imagination.

Plus dozens more stories, poems, essays, and excerpts
by Latina writers celebrating the erotic life.

MARGARITE FERNÁNDEZ OLMOS is a professor of Spanish at Brooklyn College and lives in Staten Island, New York. LIZABETH PARAVISINI-GEBERT is an associate professor in the Department of Hispanic Studies at Vassar College, and is co-editor of *Green Cane and Juicy Flotsam: Short Stories by Caribbean Women*. She lives in Nyack, New York.

Pleasure in the Word

Erotic Writings by Latin American Women

Edited by

Margarite Fernández Olmos & Lizabeth Paravisini-Gebert

A PLUME BOOK

PLUME
Published by the Penguin Group, Penguin Books USA Inc., 375 Hudson Street,
New York, New York 10014, U.S.A.
Penguin Books Ltd, 27 Wrights Lane, London W8 5TZ, England
Penguin Books Australia Ltd, Ringwood, Victoria, Australia
Penguin Books Canada Ltd, 10 Alcorn Avenue, Toronto, Ontario, Canada M4V 3B2
Penguin Books (N.Z.) Ltd, 182–190 Wairau Road, Auckland 10, New Zealand

Penguin Books Ltd, Registered Offices: Harmondsworth, Middlesex, England

Published by Plume, an imprint of Dutton Signet,
a division of Penguin Books USA Inc. This is an authorized reprint
of a hardcover edition published by White Pine Press.
For information address White Pine Press, 10 Village Square, Fredonia, NY 14063.

First Plume Printing, September, 1994
10 9 8 7 6 5 4 3 2 1

Publication of this book was made possible, in part, by grants from the New York
State Council on the Arts and the National Endowment for the Arts.

Ⓟ REGISTERED TRADEMARK—MARCA REGISTRADA

LIBRARY OF CONGRESS CATALOGING-IN-PUBLICATION DATA
Placer de la palabra. English
    Pleasure in the word : erotic writings by Latin American women /
edited by Margarite Fernández Olmos & Lizabeth Paravisini-Gebert.
        p.   cm.
    ISBN 0-452-27104-5
    1. Erotic literature. Latin American—Translations into English.
2. Latin American literature—Women authors—Translations into
English.   3. Latin-American literature—20th century—Translations
into English.   I. Fernández Olmos, Margarite.   II. Paravisini-Gebert,
Lizabeth.   III. Title.
PQ7082.E74P5713   1994
860.8′03538—dc20   94–17419
                                                                   CIP

Printed in the United States of America
Original hardcover design by Watershed Design

EDITORS' ACKNOWLEDGMENTS

Over the years we have both come to appreciate the value of collaborative efforts; this book has benefitted not only from our own collaboration but from that of others as well. We would like to express our gratitude to those who have encouraged and supported us: Jaime Aljure Bastos, Editorial Director at Editorial Planeta Mexicana for his faith in this collection published in Spanish in Mexico in 1991 as *El placer de la palabra: literatura erótica femenina de América Latina (Antología crítica)*; the City University of New York for the financial support of a PSC-CUNY Research Award in 1988 and a grant from the CUNY-Caribbean Exchange Program; Gordon A. Gebert for patiently solving countless computer problems; and the rest of our families for their help and patience. Our special thanks to the translators whose generous contributions were essential, and whose dedication and creativity are so often underappreciated. And finally, of course, to the authors themselves, many of whom we have had the privilege of meeting personally as a result of our research, whose works we value and admire for their courage and the tenacity of their vision.

🦉 Contents

Pleasure in the Word

Preface

Historically, written language has been the domain of men, the narrators of heroic deeds. So too eroticism, love and sensuality have been masculine reserves where intellectuals, historians, and sexologists wrote—and still write—about women's sexuality and eroticism, telling them how to think and feel and giving them recipes for making love. Women were granted the realm of spoken language to transmit songs and secret codes to their children. Women, especially Latin American women, were placed by their cultures in a tradition of modesty and silence. For them to speak out in public, to make language their own, and to write required acts of daring and transgression, as well as the desire to invent themselves through creative imagination.

Pleasure in the Word breaks through the restrictions placed on erotic literature written by women. The writers whose work appears here leave behind the melancholy and silent landscape that did not allow them to speak or to write. Here they speak out about eroticism, love, and violence. They give shape to the interactions among the real, the imaginary, and the symbolic; they dare to describe pleasure, sensuality, and women's eroticism not as strangers to the language of love but as bold mistresses of their own words.

The well-known Latin American saying directed toward women, "Flies don't enter a closed mouth," is debunked thoroughly in this volume. The texts by Luisa Valenzuela, Isabel Allende, and Cristina Peri Rossi speak with a freedom that surprises with its authenticity, with its courage not to separate love from eroticism or sensuality from violence. These are texts that burst into zones of pleasure and joy, as well as into zones of pain at the violence of love and the violence of a politics in Latin America that censures and represses the possibilities of expressing love and sensuality.

There is nothing as difficult as speaking of love and the body. How can one give shape to the language of desire? How can we speak of the terrifying fear of sexual initiation by a little girl who is raped? How to repeat the delight of a body in repose entering the same dream as its lover's? In this collection of texts about pleasure,

each writer has found her own specific language—everyday, subjec-
tive, or oneiric—that always trangresses the social order that would
confine her to muteness and to denial of the pleasures of the body.
Each selection violates social order, the place of women in society,
and the established discourses that tend to organize and categorize
sensuality, eroticism, and pleasure.

Pleasure in the Word reveals how each creative writer recognizes
her freedom, as well as her daring to love, following only one truth:
"language constructs itself and comes to life through the creation of
fantasies," through the imaginary dreams of women who reveal the
body and desire with illuminating clarity. This is an anthology of
major importance to both Latin American and world literature.
Finally, wise desiring women—not simply desired, pleasured
women—have invented an erotics of language and a constant dialogue between writing and the joyful pleasure that brings forth their
words. Finally, women have an erotic language of their own. No
longer strangers to words, they reveal and revel in pleasure in the
word.

—Marjorie Agosín

Translated by Mary Jane Treacey

SONG OF THE CHALCO WOMEN

First woman:
I, woman in Tetzmetlucan,
anointed my hands with pine oil
anointed them with maguey juice
        And I come here with my skirt the color of prickly pear
with my shirt the color of prickly pear . . .

        I have to see that they're done!
        I long for the ones from
Xaltepetlapan: they're huexotzincas,
and the captives from Cuetlaxtla,
the cuetlaxtla are rogues . . .
        I have to see that they're done!

Second woman:
How is he? Has he come to his senses?
My son, the king Axayácatl, ordered me to call . . .
with this one he wants to pass his hour of harlotry . . .
        With me you'll pass two, my little boy
You will enter your concubine
just being in my house,
        Perhaps your heart wishes it this way . . .
Let's spend ourselves little by little
        What then, will you do it like that, my lover?
We'll go on doing it just like that.

You are truly a man . .
What are you shaking?
Oh, my heart's desire, you are girded with flowers
Your word . . . !

Another woman:
I only raise my worm and hold it straight:

with it I will give pleasure to my little child Axayacatito,
  Ay, pretty little king Axayacatito,
if you are truly a man you will have something to keep you busy
here.
Aren't you potent?
Take my poor ash, go on then and work me.
  Come take it. Come take it, my joy:
Oh my little boy, give yourself to me, my little boy.
Between joys and pleasure we will be laughing
we will come in joy and I will learn.

The old woman:
I am an old woman of pleasure
I am the mother of you all.
I am an abandoned old woman, I am a dried up old woman
This is what I do, and I am a Chalco woman.
  I came to give you pleasure, my flowery vulva
lower palate, lower mouth.
I long for the king Axayacatito . . .
Look at my little flowered pitchers,
look at my little flowered pitchers:
My breasts!

All the women:
Perhaps your heart will fall in vain, Axayácatl:
Here are your dear little hands: Take me with these hands.
Let's give each other pleasure
  In your house of flowers, in your place of rest,
little boy of mine, lay yourself down, be still
oh my little boy, my king Axayácatl.

Translated by Stephanie Lovelady
[Fragment from *Náhuatl Poetry*]
Garibay Kintana and Ángel María, eds.
Mexico: UNAM, 1964.

Introduction

Contemporary Latin American narrative has often been described as "sensuous" and "passionate," and although these terms do not apply exclusively to the sexual or the erotic, their frequent use by literary critics attests to the importance of sexuality in artistic and literary creation in the region.[1]

Unfortunately, the scant critical references to the expression of sexuality in Latin American literature focus almost exclusively on the works of male authors; the creative expression of sexuality and eroticism from a female perspective, and the limits of what is considered to be women's "proper" language and mode of writing in societies where machismo is still very much the norm have not been seriously addressed. Sexuality remains one of the great unexplored cultural myths in Latin America, despite the fact that its study can offer valuable insights into the concerns of women as they relate to their cultural environment.

An excellent example of the relationship between sociohistorical experience and the literary expression of sexuality can be found as early as the colonial era in the writings of the seventeenth-century Mexican nun, Sor Juana Inés de la Cruz (1651?-1695). An examination of her erotic poetry within the unusually rigid social and religious constraints of colonial Mexico unveils this remarkable woman's efforts to reconcile her sexual needs to the demands of the circumscribed morality of the period. In his study of sex and religion in colonial Mexico, Fernando Benítez notes the attempts of the seventeenth-century Catholic Church and the Inquisition to "abolish sex:"

> In the course of one century, the human body, which had been previously glorified as the supreme work of God, and the notion of a divinely-inspired eroticism from which had emanated the eroticism of the people, were

[1] See D.L. Shaw, "Notes on the Presentation of Sexuality in the Modern Spanish-American Novel," *Bulletin of Hispanic Studies* 59 (1982): 275-282. For a more extensive version of this introduction, in Spanish, see *El placer de la palabra: literatura erótica femenina de América Latina*. Mexico: Planeta, 1991. xi-xxiv.

transformed into the most feared, the filthiest, the most shameful and repugnant aspects of human life . . . Everything that had previously symbolized exaltation, playfulness, joy and happiness, became obscene acts which merited punishment by the eternal flames of hell . . . [S]aintliness degenerated into sanctimoniousness, and charity and God's forgiveness turned into prison and punishment.[2]

Sor Juana Inés de la Cruz was able to navigate around the restrictive powers of the Church and the society described by Benítez by means of her tremendous literary talents, her influential connections, and political acumen. Having won international fame and distinction in her lifetime for her poetry, drama, and prose, this exceptional author nevertheless had to endure the hardships of convent life and innumerable personal sacrifices in return for a lifetime of learning and intellectual achievement.

Her passionate poems to the Countess of Paredes are among the earliest examples of female erotic literature in Latin America. Although judged to be extremely daring, the book, published in Madrid in 1689 after the Countess' departure from Mexico, soon became a bestseller, despite the editors' attempt to cushion the poems' erotic impact, defending them as expressions of "pure absent love without attempts at indecency."

Sor Juana's death at the end of the century coincided with the cessation of the Inquisition's attempts to repress and nullify sexuality. For Benítez, the author represents the embodiment of the erotic forces that the Church had struggled so earnestly to combat:

---

[2] Fernando Benítez, *Los demonios en el convento: sexo y religión en la Nueva España* (Mexico: Ediciones Era, 1985), p. 148. [Our translation.] Another excellent source of information regarding women in this period is *Sexuality and Marriage in Colonial Latin America*, Asunción Lavrin, ed. (Lincoln: Univ. of Nebraska Press, 1989). See also Verena Martinez-Alier's *Marriage, Class and Colour in Nineteenth-Century Cuba: A Study of Racial Attitudes in a Slave Society* (Ann Arbor: University of Michigan Press, 1989).

"With Sor Juana gone, silence ensued. It seemed that the terrible struggle to abolish sex had lost its reason for being once that woman who seemed to magnify and incorporate the erotism of all women no longer existed."

Sor Juana Inés de la Cruz remained an extraordinary and isolated figure until well into the nineteenth century, when other women writers begin to defy social convention in their personal lifestyles and to express eroticism with the passion and daring that had been Sor Juana's trademark. Cuban poet Mercedes Matamoros (1851-1906) experimented with erotic themes in her pre-Modernist work, "El último amor de Safo" (Sappho's Last Love) in *Sonetos* (Sonnets, 1902). Matamoros assumes an active, defiant voice that projects itself beyond the parameters of the accepted feminine expression of the era and prefigures the erotic expression of 20th-century Latin American women. Also remarkable for her passionate defense of women's right to demand and achieve sexual fulfillment is novelist and suffragist leader Ana Roqué (Puerto Rico, 1853-1933) whose virtually unknown novel *Luz y sombra* (Light and Shadow, 1903) is a bold portrayal of the consequences of a woman's sexual and emotional frustration.

Modernismo, the first significant Spanish-American literary movement, emerged in the late nineteenth century and is usually characterized as an artistic revolt against bourgeois values and a rejection of the archaic literary traditions of the past. Uruguayan poet Delmira Agustini (1886-1914) is frequently mentioned as the sole female author whose poetry and way of life reflected *modernism's* challenge to literary and social conventions. Agustini's publication in 1914 of a collection of poems entitled *Los cálices vacíos* (Empty Chalices), with its sensual language and erotic themes, could be considered the starting point for contemporary erotic writings by Latin American women. Agustini, like Matamoros before her, expresses a very modern sentiment in her works: the need to define her own emotional and social situation, and to unleash the full potential of her passions in a relationship that is shared mutually and equitably.

As is the case of women authors in other areas of the world, female writers in Latin America had to confront the problem of surviving as individuals in a society that has traditionally been among the most restrictive regarding appropriate social roles for women, where those who defied convention often suffered dire consequences. Thus, many women limited their expression to poems dealing with love and sensuality, with themes that often included the depiction of woman as victim. This focus on the inner, personal reality does not, however, always represent a withdrawal from the external world, nor does it result in a poetry devoid of social value; it should be seen rather as a necessary step for women to penetrate and document the internal territory of their growing consciousness.[3] Honduran poet Clementina Suárez' (1903) delicate, sensual verses examine love from the perception of woman's role as nurturer; Julia de Burgos' (Puerto Rico, 1914-1953) search for personal authenticity and social justice inspired the poem "Río Grande de Loíza," where the themes of eroticism and nationalism are intriguingly combined; the works of Cuban author Carilda Oliver Labra (1922) echoed Burgos' attempts to discover the authenticity of female experience, and to record the struggle for equality in relations between men and women and against the repression of female sexuality. Her poem "I Can't Help It, My Love, I Can't Help It" transcended the strictly literary in order to penetrate into popular consciousness as a text favored by those newly initiated into love. Rosario Ferré's (Puerto Rico, 1942) comments regarding Julia de Burgos' poetry apply to great extent to all these courageous precursors of the genre. Ferré described Burgos' "revolutionary eroticism" as one that "goes against the very foundation of bourgeois society and points . . . towards an unmasking of hypocritical morality and a defense of natural values, such as love and equality."[4]

---

[3] See Margarite Fernández Olmos' discussion of Spanish-American women authors in the *Longman Anthology of World Literature: 1875-1975*, Marian Arkin and Barbara Shollar, eds. (New York: Longman, 1989): 1199-1208.

The introspection of these authors served, therefore, not only to express the intimate and the personal, but also to provide access to the critical and the philosophical. Unfortunately, writers like Suárez, de Burgos and Oliver Labra had to experience a singular and lonely search for the recognition and validation of their sexual and emotional needs. Their solitary quest was made more difficult by its being undertaken without the support of their society or of the women's consciousness movement that would emerge in later years. Like French diarist Anaïs Nin (of Cuban-born parents), who made the intimate the main focus of her literary work, these writers often link eroticism with romantic love and emotion. Nin describes the quandary faced by women of her generation as that of first of all knowing "who we are, what are the habits and fantasies of our bodies, the dictates of our imagination." She argues that women "not only have to recognize what moves, stirs, arouses [them], but how to reach it, attain it," since in the end women have to make their "own erotic pattern and fulfillment through a huge amount of half-information and half-revelations."[5]

Women's writing in the late 1950s and throughout the 1960s reflected the increased social consciousness of the Latin American population; authors like Rosario Castellanos (Mexico, 1925-1974) and Beatriz Guido (Argentina, 1924) expressed their social concerns in works that examine the relationship of women to their culture and to the structures of power. These authors relied on the personal to examine the conflicts and complexities of their respective societies: Castellanos' poetry often identified the repression of women's sexual expression with other forms of political and social dominance in Latin America, and the excerpt in this volume from Guido's *La casa del ángel* (The House of the Angel, 1954) describes a young girl's sexual initiation with strong political and

---

[4] Rosario Ferré, Editorial in *Zona de carga y descarga* (mayo-julio 1973): 3. [Our translation.]

[5] Anaïs Nin, "Eroticism in Women," *In Favor of the Sensitive Man and Other Essays* (New York: Harcourt, Brace Jovanovich, 1976), p. 10.

social overtones.

Alejandra Pizarnik (1935-1972) prefigures the frank and openly erotic stance of Latin American women writers in the 1970s and 80s. Her tragic death by suicide deprived the Latin American literary community of one of its most imaginative and promising members. Pizarnik's works, written mainly in the 50s and 60s, were experimental and strongly influenced by surrealism. Although most critics have emphasized the darker side of her often macabre poetry and prose, the diversity of her artistic creativity is evident in the ample representation she has been given in this collection. At times violently erotic, as in the fictional essay "The Bloody Countess," a work strongly influenced by Jorge Luis Borges, Pizarnik's versatility is manifest in her gentle, sensual poetry and the linguistically imaginative prose piece, "The Lady Buccaneer of Pernambuco or Hilda the Polygraph." Her death in 1972 occurred at a moment of true awakening and evolution for female expression in the region.

The 1970s mark a turning point for women's writing in Latin America. The impact of the international women's movement as well as the political tensions in the continent heightened consciousness and affected the direction of women's writing. Women began to receive long-overdue critical attention, and distinctions in their use of new approaches to express old enduring problems began to emerge: parody and humor to question the nature of power and expose the hypocrisy of traditional notions of gender roles; the affirmation of female eroticism and sexuality; an experimental language that *embodies* new and untried human relationships. It is worth noting that women have expressed their awareness of changes in their writing and of the need, as Luisa Valenzuela (Argentina, 1938) has stated in "Dirty Words," to "unleash the menacing differences which upset the core of the phallogocentric, paternalistic discourse . . . [through a] transformation of that language consisting of 'dirty' words that are forbidden to us for centuries, and of the daily language that we should handle very carefully, with respect and fascination because in some way it doesn't belong to us."

The question remains, however: if sexual oppression is but one of the many reflections of contemporary gender inequality, how do we make the dominant culture more responsive and more representative of women? To transform cultural definitions we need to draw on women's experiences, give them a contextual cultural framework, try to understand the codes of meaning and symbolic transformations contained in social conventions.

As a result, this collection has been assembled with particular emphasis on the affirming qualities of eroticism in women's writing, a category that is constantly being challenged and appropriated by women who recognize its possibilities as a vital resource for change and empowerment. American poet Audre Lorde has written about the "suppression of the erotic as a considered source of power and information within [women's] lives," seeing it as the oppressor's attempt to "corrupt or distort those various sources of power within the culture of the oppressed that can provide energy for change." We have taken as our point of departure her definition of the erotic as "a measure between the beginnings of our sense of self, and the chaos of our strongest feelings. It is an internal sense of satisfaction to which, once we have experienced it, we know we can aspire."[6]

The source of positive energy Lorde describes as the erotic manifests itself in Latin American women's writing in a myriad of forms, styles and themes. Our own definition of erotic literature has been qualified by the results of our research, and must necessarily include works that are not only explicitly or implicitly sexual, but also intensely personal and intimate, and reflective of human sexuality in all its variations: heterosexuality and homosexuality, homoeroticism and autoeroticism. The selections chosen for this collection focus thus on the erotic thread that can be traced at least to the final decade of the nineteenth century and develops into an important literary trend in the 1970s and 80s as women discover their

---

[6] Audre Lorde, *Uses of the Erotic: The Erotic as Power* (Trumansburg, N.Y.: Out & Out Books, 1978), pp. 1-2.

unique creative voices. The approximate chronological ordering of the texts illustrates the evolution that has occurred with respect to the proliferation of themes and styles, and the growing sense of freedom to express in a direct and critical language a woman's most intimate needs and desires. The urgency of the task of finding a female erotic voice is described by Luisa Valenzuela as she distinguishes between the pornographic and the erotic in literature.

> Pornography is the negation of literature because it is the negation of metaphor and nuance, of ambiguity. It seeks a material reaction in the reader, a direct sexual excitement; eroticism, on the other hand, although it can be tremendously brazen and strong, goes through the filter of metaphor and poetic language. Pornography does not enter into literary disquisition.
>
> I think that as women, we have to rescue erotic language because in the final analysis it is dominated by male fantasies. Every one of us must tell one own's truth, trying to express the other's desire, because the last thing that wants to be expressed is desire.[7]

An interesting result of the research for this anthology has been the discovery of several recurring themes and writing strategies. Not surprisingly, the issue of power and powerlessness, and the quest for control over one's self in intimate relationships are concerns that recur in many works by women; the form they take in many Latin American writers, however, is inextricably linked to the historical and sociopolitical realities of Latin American societies.

Thus, for example, in the excerpts from the novels by Beatriz Guido and Albalucía Ángel (Colombia, 1939), both dealing with the violent sexual initiation of young girls, the protagonists'

---

[7] Interview with Luisa Valenzuela in *Historias íntimas: conversaciones con diez escritoras latinoamericanas*, Magdalena García Pinto, ed. (Hanover, N.H.: Ediciones del Norte, 1988), p. 248. [Our translation.]

sexual awakenings are neither ahistorical nor apolitical; both occur within specific historical contexts of political violence and upheaval, and great emphasis is placed on the social and class distinctions between the protagonists and their male victimizers. Even in cases in which the protagonist's transformation into a sexual being is voluntary and based on mutual affection, as in the chapter "The Awakening," from Isabel Allende's (Chile, 1942) novel *La casa de los espíritus (The House of the Spirits,* 1982), the reference in the title applies as much to the growth of the young woman's political consciousness as to her initiation into sexuality.

There are numerous examples of works in which eroticism and sensuality are coupled with a critique of sociopolitical structures. Julia de Burgos' "Río Grande de Loíza," for example, reflects the poet's love for nature in sensual descriptions of the "Man-River" of her youth, but it is also a hymn to her nationalist sentiments for an "enslaved" or colonized Puerto Rico. Likewise, the intensely erotic verses of Ana Istarú (Costa Rica, 1960) not only reflect the poet's quest for liberation from the traditional morality of Latin American society which stresses virginity and chastity before marriage, but also equate the sexual domination and oppression of women to the political oppression of Latin America.

In the short story by the Venezuelan Matilde Daviú (1946), "The Woman Who Tore Up the World," the protagonist identifies with Latin America as she prepares her vengeance against her betrayer: "she felt like an invaded land and began to prepare her defense" in order to save the area from the "sexual enslavement of the Western world." Even children's literature exhibits these concerns: Rosario Ferré's story "Rice and Milk" is actually a parable of female sexual liberation for the young, with sexual symbolism and positive images of female empowerment that seek to correct the androcentric bias of traditional fairy tales. At the same time, however, the story criticizes the exploitative power of the landowning classes.

An ideal example of the Latin American woman writer's combination of sexual and political concerns can be found in Ana Lydia Vega's (Puerto Rico, 1946) "Lyrics For a Salsa and Three

Soneos By Request." Vega's works examine the distortions and contradictions of traditional values, and the absurdities of colonialism in Puerto Rico's consumer-oriented lifestyle. Her female characters are often in the "pink collar" professions, still dependent on male bosses, but, sexually at least, liberated from traditional mores. "Lyrics For a Salsa . . ." reflects the freer sexual attitudes of working women which has been the result of profound socioeconomic changes, as well as the anachronistic *machista* values of men who continue to cling to the past. In one of the story's three denouements or "Soneos" (following a scene describing a frustrated sexual encounter between the characters), politics and sex are humorously combined to reveal their inextricable relationship.

Vega's irreverent humor is another characteristic of many of the writers included in this volume. Even as women examine such serious issues as the appropriation of sexual power and the elimination of age-old taboos proscribing female sexual freedom, they are able to sense the humor and the absurdity of much of what passes for "normal" behavior. Luisa Valenzuela is one of the most skilled artists in this respect, as can be seen in her comical exploration of sex as leisure sport, "The Fucking Game," where the author claims, "One must never forget that this is a game of pleasure and not a competition, and good sportsmanship must prevail above all else;" Alejandra Pizarnik's parody "The Lady Buccaneer or Hilda the Polygraph" demonstrates the relationship between language and sex with ingenious and irreverent puns, neologisms and word play; Mexican novelist María Luisa Mendoza's (Mexico, 1931) *De Ausencia* (Ausencia's Tale, 1974) also displays a keen sense of language and humor regarding the adventures of its protagonist, whom David Foster has referred to as a "Mexican Fanny Hill."[8]

The freedom to explore sexual alternatives is not limited to heterosexual relationships; a significant number of Latin American women authors are daring to explore less conventional sexual alter-

---

[8] David William Foster, "Espejismos Eróticos: *De Ausencia*, de María Luisa Mendoza," *Revista Iberoamericana* 51 (julio-diciembre 1985), p. 662.

natives, boldly questioning the heterosexual norm in openly homo-erotic and autoerotic literary works. Uruguay's Cristina Peri Rossi's (1941) story "The Witness" is a compelling work that explores male reaction to lesbianism and to women who dare assume control of their sexuality; her poem "Ca Foscari" is a homage to homoeroti-cism. Nemir Matos (Puerto Rico, 1949) uses frank and direct lan-guage to describe a lesbian lover, while Cecilia Vicuña (Chile, 1948) in "Beloved Friend" declares one woman's love for another in ten-der and halting tones that reveal universal fears of rejection and the unknown.

Mexican poet Rosamaría Roffiel's (1945) "Gioconda" is an unabashed expression of autoeroticism that describes autosexuality and the pleasures of the female body with joy and confidence; the 1989 publication of her lesbian novel *Amora* places Roffiel in the forefront of feminist writing in Latin America. Likewise, Marjorie Agosín (Chile, 1955) describes with uninhibited delight in "My Stomach," a seventy-seven year old woman's gratification in her physical self.

The quest for power and control over one's sexuality, and the freedom to explore erotic fantasies are themes which gradually progress from veiled allusions in the earliest works presented here to a more open and frank expression in the candid and direct writ-ing of contemporary authors, this despite the fact that centuries of patriarchal and *machista* criteria have left deep roots regarding sexu-al attitudes in most Latin American countries. And although women have become more aggressive in their demands for genital equality and in the pursuit of their sexual needs, those intent on challenging the status quo are still in the forefront, practicing a "revolutionary eroticism" insofar as their struggle to attain a freer expression goes against the grain of traditional literary practice for women. They are literary pioneers within what is still largely a male-dominated field.

Amongst the finest and more representative examples of this type of pioneering work are the poems of Daína Chaviano (Cuba, 1957). Chaviano represents a new vision of male/female relationships devoid of the idealization of romantic love, replaced with a more realistic attitude and a feminist representation of female consciousness. In her poetry, female sexuality is not placed exclusively at the service of a male; no longer is being *for* another the whole of women's sexual construction. Her writing calls for a change in the norms of sexuality and for a critical reexamination of female psychosexual and sociosexual experience. What distinguishes the contemporary Latin American feminist writing of authors such as Chaviano is an Eros dynamic fed by self-knowledge and female affirmation, and the will to attain woman's total potential.

The sexual discourse of contemporary Latin American women authors is innovative and groundbreaking work that uses the dimension of gender to produce a powerful critique of sex and politics. It is a constructive creative process that exposes the cultural constructs of sex and gender in its pursuit of genuine sexual liberation and consciousness, and, ultimately, in the restoration of the total and unrestricted dignity and autonomy of the Latin American woman.

—Margarite Fernández Olmos
Lizabeth Paravisini-Gebert

Pleasure in the Word

❦ Delmira Agustini (Uruguay)

ANOTHER RACE

Eros, blind father, I wish to guide you . . .
I ask at your invulnerable hands
that his magnificent body be poured out in flames
over my limp body strewn among the roses!

The electric petals I unfold today
release the nectar of a garden of Wives:
for his vultures my flesh will surrender
a full swarm of pink doves.

The two cruel serpents of his embrace
receive my great fevered stem . . . wormwood and honey
seep into me from his veins, his mouth . . .

Stretched out thus I am a burning furrow
that can nourish the seed
of another Race, sublimely insane!

Translated by Margarite Fernández Olmos

THE GOBLET OF LOVE

Let us drink together from the egregious goblet
The rare liqueur offered to our souls!
The sumptuous freshness of my roses shall open
Under the indelible shadow of your hands!

You awakened my dormant soul
In the silent grave of the hours:
For you, my life's first blood
In the amphoral light of my dawn!

Your voice embroidered in gold
My melancholy silences: you broke
My great strand of weeping pearls
And opened my horizon to the rising sun.

For you, in my nocturnal birth, dawn
Opened the pink tremor of its tulle:
Thus in the shadows of life I offer you
My soul now unfolded like a blue sky!

Oh I feel myself blossom like a rose!
Come and drink of my sumptuous honey:
I am the proud goblet of love
To be seized by your divine hands!

The goblet raises its splendor in flames . . .
Like a magic spell it would shine in your hands!
Its mysterious perfection demands
Fingers of fantasy and lips of harmony.

Take it and drink, its glory will golden
The idyll of light of our souls:
Let the roses of my dawn wither
Under the indelible shadow of your hands!

Translated by Daisy C. De Filippis

INTIMATE

I will tell you the dreams of my life
In the deepest of the blue night . . .
My naked soul will tremble in your hands
My cross will be borne on your shoulders.

The pinnacles of life are so lonely,
So lonely and so cold! I locked
My yearnings up inside me, lifted myself up
Whole like an ivory tower.

Today I will open that great mystery to your soul;
Your soul can enter me.
The tremors of the abyss are found in silence:

I waver, I hold on to you.
I die of reverie; I will drink in your fresh
And pure fount the truth, I know I
Will find in the noble recesses of your chest

The spring that will vanquish my thirst.

And I know the ineffable miracle of
Reflection produced in our lives . . .
In the silence of the night my soul
Reaches for yours as for a great mirror.

Imagine the love I must have dreamt
in the icy grave of my silence!
Larger than life, more so than dreams,
Imprisoned beneath the unending azure.

Imagine my love, a love searching for

An impossible life, a superhuman life,
You who knows the weight and consumption
Of Olympian souls and dreams on human flesh.

And when before the soul that felt
The azure too small for its wings to wash,
Your soul opened up like a noble horizon
Of sun and dawn, a beach of brightness;

Imagine! To embrace the impossible,
Alive, radiant! The living illusion!
I blessed God, the sun, the flower, the air.
Life itself, because you were life!

If with anguish I bought this happiness,
Blessed be the tear that stained my eyes!
All the scars of the past rejoice
As the sun is born in his red lips!

Oh, you probably know it, my love, but let us go
Far into the night in bloom:
Here what is human frightens, here one can see,
Hear, feel, the throbbing of life.

Let us go further into the night, let us go
Where not even an echo can reverberate in me.
Like a flower of night, there in the shadow
I will open up sweetly for you.

Translated by Daisy C. De Filippis

DEFEATING THE JUNGLE

When you cross the jungle chasing silky
Albescent deer; wild hair, cruel eyes,
Amidst the white flight of your rare greyhounds,
On your stallion of snow, Nemrod of my dreams.

My ear delights in the resonant flight
Of the mysterious soul of your golden Oliphant,
And, as with a sweet, my mouth rejoices in the promise
Of the exquisite prey that will perfume your table.

Translated by Daisy C. De Filippis

🖤 Julia de Burgos (Puerto Rico)

HARMONY OF WORD AND INSTINCT

Everything was a wonder of harmonies
in the first gesture opening before us
heavenly and earth-bound impulses
from the depth of love of our souls.

Even the air cast itself up onto lightnesses
when I fell overcome by your glance:
and a word, still virgin in my life,
pounded my heart, and became flame
in the river of feeling that enclosed you
and the flower of illusion I entrusted to you.

A marriage of new sensations
lifted my dawn into light.
Soft waves buoyed my consciousness
to the blue beach of your morning,
and the flesh became silhouette
at the sight of my freed soul.

Like a shout that is total, soft, and deep
the word burst forth from my lips;
never had my mouth more smile!
nor had more flight entered my throat!

In my soft word, made more tender,
I created myself in your life and your soul;
and I was unanticipated scream passing through
the walls of time which bound me;
and I was spontaneous budding of the instant;
and I was scattered star in your arms.

I gave all and fused myself forever
in the sensual harmony you gave me;
and the expressive rose that opened itself
on the verbal stem of my word,
offered you its petals one by one
as our instincts joined in a kiss.

Translated by Heather Rosario-Sievert

RÍO GRANDE DE LOÍZA

Río Grande de Loíza . . . Undulate into my spirit
And let my soul founder in your rivulets,
To seek the fountain that stole you as a child
And in mad haste returned you to the path.

Wind into my lips and let me drink you,
To feel you mine for a brief moment,
And hide you from the world in myself
And hear voices of fear in the mouth of the wind.

Come down for an instant from the spine of the earth,
And seek the intimate secret of my longing;
Confounded in the sweep of my bird fantasies,
Drop a water rose in my dreams.

Río Grande de Loíza! . . . My source, my river,
After the motherly petal raised me into the world
With you went down from the rough hills
To seek new furrows, my pale desires,
And all my childhood was like a poem in the river,
And a river was the poem of my first dreams.

Then came adolescence. Life surprised me
Fastening to the broadest part of your eternal voyage;
And I was yours a thousand times, and in a beautiful romance,
You woke my soul and kissed my body.

Where did you carry the waters that bathed
My form, in a spike of the newly open sun?
Who knows in what remote Mediterranean land
Some faun on the beach will possess me!

Who knows in what rainstorms of what far lands
I will be pouring to open new furrows;
Or if, perhaps, tired of biting hearts
I will be frozen in crystals of ice!

Río Grande de Loíza! . . . Blue. Dark. Red.
Blue mirror, fallen blue fragment of sky;
Nude white flesh that turns you black
Every time night goes to bed with you;
Red band of blood, when under the rain
The hills vomit torrents of mud.

Man river, but man with river purity
Because when you give your blue kiss you give your blue soul.

My dear Mister River. Man river. The only man
Who has kissed my soul when he kissed my body.
Río Grande de Loíza . . . Great river. Great tear.

The greatest of all our island tears,
But for the tears that flow out of me
Through the eyes of my soul for my enslaved people.

Translated by Grace Schulman

🌹 Clementina Suárez (Honduras)

SEX

Sex,
incarnate rose,
flower of lust
from which my youth bursts forth.

Amphora full
of sensations
and vibrations,

harp that vibrates,
that cries and wails
voluptuousness.

Lily inflamed
on the altar of fire
of red abode . . .

Shameless you were
in your fit of madness
that afternoon

when the divine flower
of life and love,
I gave as offering to his love.

But I bless you
marvelous cavity
because you gave me life

and because in that damaged flower
a new life
I also gave . . .

Translated by Heather Rosario-Sievert

VI

From your warm bed
I rise,
singing.

With a radiant feeling
of the Universe
and of love.

Nothing strikes my countenance
nor my eyes!
I am certain of the size
of my dreams
and I stir them up with happiness.

What tenderness in your caress!
I saw in it the ripening
of all my fruits.

And in this first day
how lightly your eyelids
fall on your eyes.

For my own
innocent happiness
I told you over and over again:

Shut your eyes!
How limpid
I do see them.

Dew drops fall
from your lashes.

Clementina Suárez

You are,
as in the first awakening,
new in time.

You begin the balance
of a precise passion,
that does not rob the rose
of its harmony
or its nostalgia.

I would have to have loved you
and listened
for all of your voices.

As if within my body
you had left a son
still there yet . . .

That to love you
I was already awake,
my lifted face
I could offer to you
with sustained honey.

And more so,
I knew
that dressed in orange blossom,
in blood or in sand,
the modesty of my trefoil
is not disputed.

I can live in you
with unalterable faith.
In the wind or in the water
leaping about like a fish.

Together at last, unclouded,
All this I understand
with more gentle affection,
diminishing
my body in your memory.

But if you have not been able to arrive
and the way of your star
is unsure.

For you to hear me,
I would have to dress myself
like a bride again.

I would have to illuminate
the corners
and find the garments
where the forgotten
leaves its moss.

Not even like that.
Cloven hoof of ash
would stamp out my frenzy.
And never
would we arrive at the star.

You must wake up.
Raise your skeleton
from dream.

Abandon yourself naked
willing
different.

You cannot wait
for the ants
to eat
your eyes.

How to sleep
on the empty beds,
when there is a groan
and an open side
that reclaim your blood.

Birthing I am,
visibly,
and mounting me go creatures
angels and seeds.

Translated by Heather Rosario-Sievert

CONJUGATION

Your body on my body
Suddenly, I feel myself flower . . .

Translated by Heather Rosario-Sievert

❦ Carilda Oliver Labra (Cuba)

I CAN'T HELP IT, MY LOVE, I CAN'T HELP IT

I can't help it, my love, I can't help it
when I go into your mouth, and I linger;
and almost without warning, almost for naught,
I touch you with the tips of my breasts.

I touch you with the tips of my breasts
and with my unshielded loneliness;
and even perhaps without love as a guide
I can't help it, my love, I can't help it.

And my fate as a sheltered fruit
is consumed by your lustful and hesitant hands
like a poison's broken promise.

And though I'd like to kneel down and kiss you
when I go into your mouth, and I linger,
I can't help it, my love, I can't help it.

Translated by Margarite Fernández Olmos

EVE'S DISCOURSE

Today I greet you brutally:
with the blow of a cough
or a kick.
Where are you hiding?
Where are you fleeing with
your mad box of hearts,
and that mess of gun powder you have?
Where are you living:
in the pit where all dreams fall
or in that spider web where
the fatherless orphans hang?

I miss you,
Do you know it?
like my very own being
or the miracles that never come to pass.
I miss you.
Do you know it?
I'd like to persuade you of
I don't know what happiness,
what crazy thing.

When are you coming?
I'm in a hurry to play at nothing,
to call you "My life"
and let the thunder humble us
and the oranges pale in your hand.
I feel like looking at the bottom of your being
and finding veils
and smoke,
that, in the end, die out in the flames.

I truly love you
but innocently,
like the clear-eyed witch where I ponder.
I truly don't love you
but innocently,
like the betrayed angel I am.
I love you,
I don't love you.
We will raffle these words
and the one that wins will be the liar.

Love . . .
(What am I saying? I'm wrong,
I wanted to say here that I already hate you.)
Why don't you come?
How is it possible
that you let me go by without engaging the
fire?
How can you be so austral
and paranoid
and give me up?

You are probably reading the papers
or passing
by death
and life.
You're probably with your problems
with the acoustics and your
groin,
lifeless,
wretched,
busying yourself with ambitions of mourning.
And I who melts you,
who insults you,
who brings you a fractured hyacinth;

I who approves of your melancholy;
I who convenes you
to the halls of heaven,
I who mend you:
What?
When will you murder me with your spit,
hero?
When will you wear me out again under the rain?
When?
When will you call me little bird
and whore?
When will you curse me?
When?
Look, time is passing us by,
time,
time,
and I no longer even see goblins,
and I no longer understand umbrellas,
and I am growing more sincere
and wise.

If you delay,
if you get tied up in a knot and don't find me,
you will go blind;
if you don't return now: scoundrel, imbecile, dimwit,
        idiot,
I will go by the name of Never.

Yesterday I dreamt that a bullet went off
while we kissed
and neither of us let go of our hope.
This is a love
that belongs to no one;
we found it mislaid,
shipwrecked,

in the street.
Between you and me we retrieved it and gave it shelter.
That is why, when we wear each other down,
at night,
I feel the fear
of a mother you left
alone.
But what does it matter?
Kiss me,
again and again
Fit yourself around my waist
so that I can find myself.
Come back;
be my animal,
move me,
I will distill what is left of my life,
the doomed children.

We will sleep like murderers who save themselves,
bound by an incomparable flower.
And the following morning when the cock crows
we will be nature itself
and I will resemble your children in bed.

Come back, come back
Pierce me with lightning.
Pin me down once again
We will play the phonograph forever.
Come, with your infidel's nape,
with your stone blows.
Swear to me that I am not dead.
I pledge you, my love, the apple.

Translated by Daisy C. De Filippis

🍐 María Luisa Bombal (Chile)

Excerpt from
THE LAST MIST

We arrived in the city several hours ago. I can feel it hovering lifelessly around us, behind a dense curtain of mist, making the air heavy and oppressive.

Daniel's mother had the dining room opened and the chandeliers over the long table around which we gathered, stiff and numb, lit. But the golden wine, poured for us into thick crystal goblets, warms our veins; its warmth mounts from our throats to our temples.

Daniel, slightly tipsy, promises to restore the abandoned oratory in our house. By the time dinner ends we have arranged that my mother-in-law will return to the country with us.

My pain of the last few days, a pain piercing like a burn, has turned into a sweet sadness that brings a tired smile to my lips. When I rise, I must lean on my husband's arm. I don't know why I feel so weak and I don't know why I can't help smiling.

For the first time since we got married, Daniel arranges the pillows for me. I wake up at midnight, choking. I toss for a long time between the sheets, but can't manage to fall asleep. I suffocate. I breathe in with the sensation that I'm not inhaling enough air. I jump out of bed, I open the window. I lean out and it is as if my surroundings had not changed. The mist has modulated the angles and muffled the noises, bestowing on the city the warm intimacy of a closed room.

A mad thought takes hold of me. I nudge Daniel, who half-opens his eyes.

"I'm suffocating. I need to take a walk. Can I go out?"

"Do as you please," he mumbles, and lays his head again heavily on the pillow.

I dress. On my way out I grab the straw hat I wore when I

left the *hacienda*. The gate is not as heavy as I had imagined. I start walking up the street.

Sadness again flows to the surface of my being with all the violence accumulated during sleep. I walk, cross avenues, thinking:

"Tomorrow we will return to the countryside. The day after tomorrow, I will hear mass in town with my mother-in-law. Then, at lunch, Daniel will tell us about the work in the *hacienda*. I will immediately visit the greenhouse, the aviary, the vegetable garden. Before dinner, I will doze by the fireplace or read the local papers. After dinner I will amuse myself provoking small catastrophes in the fire, rashly stirring the red-hot coals. Around me, the silence will soon indicate that every subject of conversation has been exhausted and Daniel will noisily rearrange the bars on the doors. Then we will go to bed. And the day following will be the same, and so will a year from now, and ten years from now; and it will be the same until old age snatches away all right to love and desire, until my body withers and my face wrinkles, and I grow ashamed to show myself bare-faced in the light of day.

I wander at random, across avenues, and keep walking.

I feel incapable of fleeing. Of fleeing, how? Where to? Death seems a more attainable adventure than flight. I do feel capable of dying. It is possible to wish to die because one loves life too much.

Between the darkness and the mist I glimpse a small square. As in an open field, I lean exhausted against a tree. My cheek seeks the dampness of its bark. Very close to me, I hear a fountain unstringing a necklace of heavy drops.

The white light of a streetlight, a light transformed by the fog into a vapor, bathes my hands, making them seem pale, lengthening a confused silhouette at my feet, my shadow. And so it is that, suddenly, I see another shadow next to mine. I lift my head.

There's a man before me, very close to me. He is young; a pair of very light eyes on a tanned face and a slightly arched eyebrow give his face an almost supernatural look. A vague but enveloping warmth emanates from him.

And he is fast, violent, definite. I understand that I had been awaiting him and that I will follow him wherever he goes, wherever that leads. I throw my arms around his neck and then he kisses me; his luminous eyes keep looking at me through his eyelashes.

I walk, but now a stranger guides me. He guides me to a narrow, steep street. He forces me to stop. Behind a wall, I glimpse an abandoned garden. The stranger loosens, with some difficulty, the links of a rusted chain.

Inside the house the darkness is absolute, but a warm hand reaches for mine and invites me to follow. We don't stumble on any furniture; our steps echo in empty rooms. I feel my way up the long staircase, not needing to lean on the banister, because the stranger guides each and every one of my steps. I follow, feeling under his power, surrendering to his will. At the end of the corridor, he pushes a door and lets go of my hand. I remain standing on the threshold of a room which suddenly is full of light.

I take one step into a room whose discolored chintz curtains impart on it I don't know what antique charm, I don't know what melancholy intimacy. All the warmth of the house seems to have concentrated here. Night and its mist can beat against the glass panes in vain; they will not filter into this room a single atom of death.

My friend draws the curtains and with a slight pressure from his chest makes me retrace my steps slowly, toward the bed. I feel myself swoon in sweet anticipation, but nonetheless, a curious modesty compels me to feign fear. Then he smiles, but his smile, although tender, is filled with irony. I suspect that no nuance of feeling holds any secret for him. He withdraws, pretending in turn to want to reassure me. I remain alone.

I hear very light steps on the carpet, barefoot steps. He is again before me, naked. His skin is dark, but a light down, to which the lamplight clings, covers him from head to toe in a halo of brilliance. He has very long legs, straight shoulders, and narrow hips. His forehead is smooth and his arms hang motionless alongside his body. The grave simplicity of his pose imparts on him a second nakedness.

Almost without touching me, he loosens my hair and begins to undress me. I quietly submit to his desire, with a throbbing heart. A secret apprehension makes me shudder when my clothes curb the impatience of his fingers. I burn with the desire to be uncovered immediately by his gaze. My body's beauty demands, finally, its share of homage.

Once naked, I remain seated on the edge of the bed. He steps away and watches me. Under his attentive gaze, I throw my head back and this gesture fills me with an intimate sense of well-being. I knot my arms behind my neck, I braid and unbraid my legs, and each gesture bears an intense and absolute pleasure, as if, finally, my arms, my neck, and my legs had a reason for being. Even if this delight were the only purpose of love, I would already feel amply rewarded!

He approaches; my head reaches to his chest, he offers it to me with a smile, I press my lips against him, and rest my head, my face. His flesh smells of fruit, of vegetables. In a new outburst of passion, I throw my arms around his body and pull his chest against my cheek once more.

I embrace him ardently and listen with all my senses. I listen to his breath rise, fly, and fall; I listen to the explosion that his heart reiterates untiringly at the center of his chest, echoing inside him, spreading in waves through his body, transforming every cell into a sonorous echo. I clasp him, I clasp him tighter and tighter; I feel the blood flowing in the veins and feel the force that crouches, latent, within his muscles vibrate; I feel the bubble of a sigh stirring. In my arms, an entire physical life, with its fragility and mystery, boils over and overflows. I begin to tremble.

He then leans toward me and we roll, embracing, to the hollow of the bed. His body covers me like a huge boiling wave, caresses me, burns me, penetrates me, wraps me, drags me swooning. Something like a sob rises to my throat, and I don't know why I begin to cry, and I don't know why it feels so sweet to cry, so sweet the tiredness inflicted on my body by the precious cargo weighing between my thighs.

When I awaken, my lover sleeps stretched out by my side. The expression on his face is placid; his breath is so light that I must lean over his lips to feel it. I notice that, hanging on a very fine, almost invisible chain, there's a little medallion nestling in the chestnut hair on his chest, a trivial little medallion, like the ones given to children the day of their first communion. All my flesh grows tender before this childish detail. I straighten a rebellious lock glued to his temple, I rise without waking him. I dress noise-lessly and leave.

I leave as I came, groping.

I am outside. I open the gate. The trees are motionless and it hasn't dawned yet. I run up the narrow street, across the square, retracing my steps down the avenues. A soft perfume accompanies me; the perfume of my enigmatic friend. All of me has been impreg-nated by his aroma. And it is as if he walked by me or still held me tightly in his embrace or as if he had poured his life into my blood, forever.

And here I am lying next to another sleeping man.

"Daniel, I am not sorry for you, I don't hate you, I only hope that you never hear a word of what has happened to me tonight . . ."

Why, this autumn, this obsession to have the avenues con-stantly swept?

I would let the leaves pile up on the grass and the paths, covering everything with its reddish and crackling carpet which moisture would later turn silent. I try to convince Daniel to let the garden go a bit. I feel nostalgia for abandoned parks, where crab-grass erases all the tracks and where neglected hedges narrow the paths.

The years go by. I look at myself in the mirror and I see, def-initely etched under my eyes, all those little wrinkles that had until now only surfaced when I laughed. My breasts are losing their roundness and their green-fruit consistency. My flesh sticks to my bones and I no longer seem slim but full of angles. But, what does it matter! What does it matter that my body is withering, if it already knew love! And what does it matter if the years go by, all alike. I had a beautiful adventure, once . . . One single memory can help one bear a long life of tedium. It can help one repeat, day in and day out, without fatigue, the same menial everyday gestures.

There is a being I cannot encounter without trembling. I could meet him today, tomorrow, or ten years from now. I could meet him here, at the end of a tree-lined path, or in the city, as I turn a corner. Maybe I will never see him again. It doesn't matter; the world seems full of possibilities, every minute holds a promise for me, each minute has its emotion.

Night after night, Daniel sleeps by my side, as indifferent as a brother. I can shelter him indulgently because many years ago, for one long night, I lived in another man's warmth. I get up, stealthily turn a lamp on, and write:

"I knew the perfume of your shoulder, and since that day I have been yours. I desire you. I would spend my life, lying down, waiting for you to come to press your strong body against my now familiar one, as if you had been its owner since time began. The memory of my clinging to your neck, sighing in your mouth, tears me from your embrace and hounds me."

I write and I tear it up.

Some mornings I am overcome by an absurd feeling of happiness. I have the premonition that an immense happiness is going to descend upon me in the space of twenty-four hours. I spend the day in a sort of exaltation. I wait. A letter, an unexpected event? I don't know, to tell you the truth.

I walk, I venture deep into the woods, and although it's late, I slow down my steps on my return. I give time one last chance for the arrival of the miracle. I enter the drawing room with my heart pounding.

Lying on the couch, Daniel yawns, amidst his dogs. My mother-in-law is winding a new skein of gray wool. No one has come, nothing has happened. The bitterness of disillusionment only lasts a fraction of a second. My love for "him" is so deep that it is above the pain of absence. It is enough to know that he exists, that he feels and remembers in some corner of the world . . .

The dinner hour seems endless.

My only desire is to be alone to dream, to dream as I please. I always have so much to think about! Yesterday afternoon, for example, I left a jealous scene between my lover and me in suspense.

I hate it when, after dinner, they call me for the traditional game of cards. I like to sit by the fire and withdraw into myself to search for my lover's light eyes within the flames. They shoot out abruptly like two stars and then I remain a long while engrossed in their light. The memory of the expression in his eyes is never as sharp as at moments like these.

Some days I am overcome by a deep weariness, and I vainly stir the ashes of my memories to light the spark that conjures his image. I lose my lover.

A fierce wind returned him to me the last time. A wind that brought down three walnut trees and made my mother-in-law cross herself, compelled him to call at our door. His hair was tousled and the collar of his overcoat turned up. But I didn't recognize him and I collapsed at his feet. Then he took me in his arms and carried me in a faint, into the afternoon's wind . . . He has not left me again since that day.

The pale autumn seems to have stolen this ardent sunny morning from summer. I search for my straw hat and can't find it. I search for it calmly at first, then feverishly . . . because I am afraid of finding it. A deep feeling of hope has sprung in me. I sigh, relieved, before the futility of my efforts. There's no longer any doubt. I left it behind one night at the stranger's house. Such intense happiness invades me, that I must hold my two hands against my heart so that it will not escape, light as a bird. Like all lovers, we are joined forever by something besides an embrace. Something material, concrete, indestructible: my straw hat.

Translated by Lizabeth Paravisini-Gebert

🖤 Beatriz Guido (Argentina)

Excerpt from
THE HOUSE OF THE ANGEL

The day of my sisters' first ball I was happy just to watch from my hiding place behind the marble balusters of the second floor.

I can still see them, going down the stairs with strings of pearls across their foreheads, wearing dropped-waist dresses and short underskirts, their lips lightly and surreptitiously painted with colored paper. I was happy not to be a part of the ebb and flow of people that had invaded our gardens and salons, dancing in such a ridiculous fashion, shuffling their feet and clapping hands, as if they were playing pattycake.

I remember feeling that from that evening on my sisters began to grow ever more distant and remote, as if someone had torn them from my side forever. And I was horrified to think that one day I too would dance the Charleston in the arms of one of those men dressed in black, like undertakers or chimmneysweeps. "How much better it would be," I thought, "if they wore light colors: sky blues, pinks, like the gentlemen in that film *Indiscreet Wives*."

I sensed that someday I too would be a part of that world that I found myself spying upon from behind the balusters on the second floor.

"I have seen enough," I said to myself, and went up to the room where we kept the trunks. From one of them I pulled out the puppets that laid forgotten at the bottom. They were puppets made of rags and sticks.

I felt that all my gestures that evening were false: I held the puppets against my chest, but I couldn't think of them as being anything but rag and sawdust, and I realized that there was now something more powerful and enticing that no longer allowed me to bring them to life.

Meanwhile my sisters' ball continued. I wanted to resume my spying on what was transpiring in our salons. For the first time in my life I was drawn to the world of the grown-ups. Yes, I sensed the end of my childhood. And the saddest thing of all was feeling this sense of estrangement from my childhood while I was holding the puppets against my chest. The puppets had been the grand passion of my early years.

So much so that my father himself once took me to see the Trilusa Puppets when they came to Buenos Aires.

Nana dressed me in a white eyelet dress with pink ribbons which I wore over several starched petticoats. We sat, my father and I, behind the rails, on the bleachers. He, giving himself presidential airs, waved to his political cronies as we walked past the Hidalgo Street Committee headquarters. I was thinking of all the things I would have to remember once I was alone in my room that night.

My puppets, as I said, were hand puppets, they had no strings. I used them to dramatize the plots of the pulp romances and dime-store novels I stole from my sisters. They didn't mind, as long as I dramatized stories they had read.

They would sit on the benches in the weapons' room, with Nana as a member of the audience. I had built my little theater in a niche. The best of my dramatizations, one which made my sisters cry disconsolately, was my version of Jorge Isaacs' *María*.[1] Sometimes I had to interrupt my representations because we were overcome by fits of weeping, especially during the scene in which the dying María said farewell to Efraín.

One day Julieta said to me:

"If you do *María* again, I'm not coming."

The puppet that played the role of María was very beautiful. I had made it to resemble me, with hair from my own braids and

---

[1] Nineteenth-century novel considered a masterpiece of Romantic literature in Latin America.

eyes the same color as mine. Efraín looked like Julián.

I never invited Vicenta to these dramatizations. Once I started going to the movies, I began to dramatize the plots of the films I had seen, leaving out the love scenes. I didn't dare have the puppets kiss. Once Nana cried, at the end of *Yesterday's Path*:

"Let's have a kiss! Let's have a kiss!"

I couldn't do it. The puppet playing the leading lady was the same one that played the role of María.

But now that evening awaited me. I started to glide through the salons to the imaginary tune of the "Blue Waltz."

It was played by an imaginary orchestra hidden in the terrace that led to the garden. How beautiful were the ivories and opalines in the glass cabinets! I could see myself in the crystal, in the silver goblets, in the porcelains. I became a lady whose image was reflected infinitely on the draperies, on the miniatures, on the ceiling. I saw myself as a woman whose beauty could stop the duel that was to take place at dawn.

I came to see myself, that early evening, as the cause of the duel: two men were fighting for me.

I didn't dare enter the dining room, the setting for the eagerly awaited dinner; the events of that night were to surpass all my daydreams. Suddenly I heard voices arguing. I climbed the stairs and stopped before my parents' bedroom door. For a moment I feared that my mother would have her way. But in the middle of the discussion my father started to hum "Melenita de oro" as she cried dejectedly. So there was no doubt about it: the duel would take place the following morning at dawn, at four o'clock, as I had heard it would. They resumed their argument in whispers, like earlier that morning: but it grew louder and louder until I could hear my mother laughing and crying at the same time.

"This time I will not forgive you."

"The girls will come down to dinner."

"I will never allow that . . . "

"I command you to send them down. Don't think for a moment that I will stand by as you turn them into prudes like yourself. You have done them enough harm already. Are they or are they not my daughters?"

"Never!" my mother insisted.

The argument was so bitter and painful that I started to fear for my mother.

"There are all types of women in your family," he said after a long silence, "from nuns to the other kind . . . Don't try to tell me that María Celia is not having enough fun in Paris for the three of you?"

"And which one did you marry?" my mother said indignantly.

"Neither one of them, unfortunately," he replied, "a pity . . . especially since María José is so beautiful—and has had so many years of abstinence!"

"That's sacrilege!" answered my mother. "You will be damned to hell . . . After this evening . . . "

"No, don't say that word . . . it's a sin. Remember: what God joins on this Earth man can't untie, or something like that. Isn't that the way it is? Why don't you ask Nana, your prime minister? That stupid . . . old . . . ignorant woman."

"You will be damned to hell," my mother continued to scream. "I must consult with Celina! I want a separation! There must be a way, there must be something, something that can be done!"

I thought of my mother and my Aunt Celina—now Sister María José.

Instinctively, I recalled that November night in school.

Our Aunt Celina—Sister María José—would tuck us in at night and give us her blessing, making the sign of the cross on our foreheads with her thumb.

"Sleep in peace, Ana, I am by your side," she used to say to me. "You can always call me if you need me; call me if you're ever afraid at night."

I slept peacefully, thinking that Celina watched over my sleep.

That November night I woke up in a panic; I felt I was choking in the closed room. Everyone else was asleep; I jumped out of bed and peered into the corridor. The moon was traveling through a thick layer of fog and humidity, illuminating the well in the patio like a beam of light; the clock was striking midnight, more slowly than usual. Suddenly I heard gentle and subdued laughter coming from the terrace. I was afraid. It sounded like childish laughter coming from beyond the grave, as if from a children's cemetery. Nonetheless, an overwhelming curiosity made me climb the steep and winding staircase that led to the terrace.

I was so horrified by what I saw that I thought I would faint. The first one I recognized was my Aunt Celina. She was whirling in the center of a ring of women, her shaved head uncovered, and wearing a flowing nightgown, like the others. Then I began to recognize them, one by one. They were spinning like madwomen despite the heat, the humidity, and the moonlight which made the atmosphere seem heavier. Not all of them had shaved heads. One of them—I didn't recognize her—was combing her hair and peering daringly into the solitary street. Another, the youngest of them all, was pouring a transparent liquid onto very thin and delicate wine glasses. I later learned that it was anisette.

The ones dancing in the ring would stop once in a while to drink from exquisite crystal glasses resting on a silver filigree tray.

Sometimes I think that that night never happened and that my Aunt Celina was not among the dancers. However, as I was going down the stairs my nightgown got caught on the rail. I was afraid I would not be able to tear myself away and they would catch me there on their way down.

That night I felt so sad and forsaken that I awakened Julieta; I laid by her side, but it was so hot that I placed my pillow on the floor by her bed and went to sleep. At dawn the first thing I did was to return to the terrace; I expected to find them sprawled on the floor.

The terrace was dark; the flagstones still retained the heat from the previous day, and the silence made the night feel warmer.

They called us to Mass. I went down the stairs stealthily and entered the church. They were all there. None of them took communion; their heads were bowed so low that their foreheads touched the prie-dieus. Every once in a while the silence was broken by a muffled and gleeful hiccup.

"You will be damned," my mother continued to scream.

I didn't want to listen any longer and walked slowly down the stairs to my room.

"Oh! If only I had a red dress," I thought, "and a feathered hat like that of my mother's sister, the one who owns a fashion house in Paris. Maybe that would somehow help fulfill my mother's prayers. Everything would be like in the photographs of *La ilustración* or *Cosmopolitán*: two men in white shirts and black pants brandishing their swords; a carriage in the distance and in it a lady, crying behind a black veil, like Mary Astor in *The Son of Zorro*.

I locked myself in my room. The moon shone on the angel's terrace. The curtain would soon rise on the last act of the day. As I looked out on the terrace I remembered that the angel was missing its nose. The anarchists had broken it off with a stone on that First of May.

They were coming down Cuba Street from the north, shuffling their feet to the beat of the "Internationale." The women carried their children in their arms, the men clutched hammers and sickles. The shuffling of their feet resounded in the walls of the house, making it shake as if its foundations were giving way.

"The Antichrist," my mother screamed, kneeling on her prie-dieu.

We stood behind the curtains, very still, so as not to be seen.

"They are furious because of the execution of Zacco and Vanzetti," they said.

"Who are they?" I asked.

"Innocents," they told me.

"Tomorrow we will have to lower the blinds and close the shutters. It's going to be a terrible First of May," they replied.

"Who are they?" I asked again.

"Revolutionaries, sinners."

Suddenly they stopped singing as they came to a halt in front of our house. My mother's prayers intensified. The only sound to be heard was the trembling of the rosary beads in her hands.

"We will have to call the police," Nana said, grabbing us abruptly by the arm.

After a few minutes of silence, amid laughter and blasphemies, they climbed over the gate onto the grounds and started to throw stones at the terrace on the lower floor.

It took me a few minutes to realize that they were throwing rocks at the stone angel. I ran in despair to my room but my father stopped me just as I was opening the window.

"You're crazy," he said, holding me against his chest. "They'll go away, don't worry about the angel," he added.

And so they did. The laughter turned into cries and lamentations. The shuffling of their feet resumed and they went away.

I went out on the terrace. The angel had lost its nose and some of its fingers. It was covered with mud and a red liquid; I thought it was blood. I brought a pail of water and, perched on a ladder, started to wash it off. I really thought that it was bleeding; I hadn't seen the tomatoes on the ground.

Nobody paid me any attention when I told them that the angel had lost its nose; they were completely engrossed in the events of the following day.

My father was busy making arrangements for the defense of the Obligado Street Committee headquarters and my mother was worried about the Victoria's Committee.

"It's just like in Mexico!" they said.

"Sinners . . ."

"The Antichrist, the end of the world!"

I looked at myself in the mirror. There was no doubt about it—I could never be the lady in the carriage. I took out my diary and wrote incoherently.

"Tomorrow at dawn there will be a duel on the grounds of our house. It's eight o'clock in the evening. I am afraid. Julieta will soon come in to tell me that Pablo Aguirre has arrived. I await him; I have reviewed my past life, day by day. I await him; I am no longer afraid. I know this will be the most important night of my life. I am so excited about there being a duel in the house, though I know it is a sin. I will have to go to confession . . . I must think only of him. Perhaps tomorrow he will be dead; but tonight he will dine with us. I will soon go down to dinner.

"I wished I looked like my mother's sister, the one who lives in Paris; I would like to dress like her: short underskirts, lips slightly colored, strings of pearls on my forehead, like some women I once saw escaping from a house on fire.

"Maybe if I dressed like that to go down to dinner it would be easy for Pablo Aguirre to see that I have thought about him all day. Otherwise, he will think that I'm nothing but a child who doesn't even know what a duel is. Of course, if I went down dressed like that my mother wouldn't allow me to sit at the table for an instant. I don't think that anything can happen to me while I wear clothes like these (Isabel was so right!); there is nevertheless a voice that keeps on repeating to me: this is the most important day of your life.

"Oh! if only he would address just one word to me during dinner . . . , I don't know, I can't think any more, I am very tired, as tired as if I had spent the day screaming the confession of my sins in the Plaza de las Barrancas, like the Salvation Army people."

I went down to the garden. Sitting on the balcony that opened to the grounds, the one from which you can see Arcos Street, I awaited the arrival of the afternoon papers. I didn't dare to buy *Crítica*—which was forbidden in the house—so I timidly asked for *La Razón*. Pablo Aguirre's photograph was on the front page.

I folded the paper as if I had been caught by Pablo Aguirre himself. And I realized that for the first time in my life I was coming face to face with my own dreams. Pablo Aguirre's photograph in that afternoon paper showed him with the collar of his overcoat turned up, his arms folded, his hair tousled. I thought someone had printed that photograph in the newspaper on purpose to mock me. The caption underneath it read: "This photograph of Pablo Aguirre was taken at the Cemetery of La Recoleta, the day of the burial of his colleague Peñaloza." I held the newspaper tightly against my chest. I don't know what fiendish enticement I thought I saw in those small almond-shaped eyes. Nevertheless, I thought that never again would I be alone; I had chosen a face.

"What are you doing?" Julieta asked, suddenly appearing by my side. "What have you got there?"

How could I explain to Julieta that it wasn't a mere newspaper I was holding against my chest . . . Nonetheless I replied:

"The paper," I said, and tried to run away.

But she caught me, and, as she tore the paper from my hands, she saw the photograph and said:

"What a mug!"

That's how she described the photograph, in such a vulgar and grotesque way.

I took the paper from her and swore never to speak to her again; at least not for the remainder of the day.

I locked myself in my room. I cut the photograph out and pasted it with yellowish glue to a page of my diary. Beneath it I copied the following poem, skipping the verses that didn't interest me:

Haughtily he walks by, look at that man of mine.

🌷

Don't look at his mouth, it has the power to burn

Don't look into his eyes, they can freeze you to death.
When he walks through the plains the river bed trembles,
When he walks through the forest shadows become clear-
ings,
When he walks past them, haughty, firing his gun in jest,
The wild beasts huddle under his somber gaze.

He loves *a woman*, he's master of his fate
And one Spring day death will catch him unaware
crowned with a wreath of vine amid the fruits of the earth.

But my *loving* hand, as it rips his finery,
rewards his firm courage with a sprout of wings.

Julieta returned to get me. I knew that Julieta's entrance
closed a chapter of my life forever, that I could no longer halt the
oncoming events.

"He's arrived," she said. "He's in the library; Papa directed
us to go downstairs immediately. Why did you hide? I didn't mean
to take the paper away from you."

Isabel joined us. I let them go down ahead of me. Our
father was at the foot of the stairs; behind him was Aguirre.

"My elder daughters," he said: "Julieta, Isabel—Pablo
Aguirre, a brave man," he added in a very pompous tone of voice,
"and this is Ana, the youngest."

I raised my eyes to his tie. I didn't have the courage to look
further up. My eyes stopped at his chest, as if there had been a big
circle drawn around his heart: the target for the duel.

"You'll have to excuse my wife, she will not dine with us."
my father said.

But I don't know what strange hope that her presence might
forestall events made her come down to the dining room . . .

"I'm glad . . . " whispered my father.

"My wife . . . , Aguirre . . . , a brave man," once again changing the tone of his voice.

He barely nodded his head in greeting. They placed him next to my mother, across the table from me.

"There'll be no reconciliations, I have already sent the seconds away," my father said, daring my mother with his eyes. "Doctor Peralta will come at three."

Aguirre seemed not to be listening. He was staring through me as if he couldn't see me.

"You can stand guard by the weapons, and there's the guest room if you want to rest. It doesn't make any sense for you to return to town."

"I think I will rest. My brothers and Alberto Laplacette will be here at two," he replied.

"Don't let that business about the two deaths Esquivel has been responsible for bother you. It's very difficult to die in a duel . . . It's all a myth!"

I could watch him at my leisure during dinner. When he wasn't looking at me, my eyes lingered on his profile and on the triangular cut of his beard. His high collar touched the roots of his hair on the nape of his neck. When he wrinkled his brow the lock on his forehead fluttered.

I didn't dare raise my eyes. When I felt his eyes fixed on mine, I looked down. Then I could only see his nervous hands tearing breadcrumbs apart.

My father's voice reached me as if from a dream.

"There'll be no reconciliations," my father continued.

"Death doesn't frighten me," Aguirre answered. "It is enough for me to know that others are following my example and that accusations can no longer be made with impunity. A country immersed in shadows abandoned to the derision of those charlatans," he said incoherently without taking his eyes from me.

I knew then that this was the first person that spoke only to me. I don't know how I managed to remain seated at the table in front of him. Without having to invent time. There, before me, was a man with a triangular face and small almond-shaped eyes, enveloping me with his voice and his gaze.

My mother asked, "Have you stopped to think that you could be killed?"

My father stared at her.

"In times like these, ma'am, politics is neither an art nor a game. And honor is more important than the thought . . . of death."

"What about your soul? What if you were to kill Esquivel?"

"My wife is very sanctimonious, as you can see. I don't know why she turned out that way since there are all types in her family. She's in charge of the girls' education. Of course, it would have been otherwise if they had been boys."

Pablo was not listening. I felt his gaze fixed on mine. I pushed my hair away from my face and smiled at the servant waiting at the table so he could admire my smile. My only fear was that of blushing to the roots of my hair.

How I hated my mother when she said: "The girls may leave the table."

Isabel and Julieta obeyed absentmindedly. I folded my napkin and slowly pulled my chair back; I raised my eyes to his, as he followed my every movement.

"This will be our fifteenth duel; there hasn't been a duel on the grounds in five years," my father continued.

I advanced towards Aguirre; I curtsied slightly without looking at him, and ran out of the room. I reached my bedroom. I undressed. Julieta was already in bed.

"He is young, too young to die," she said, half-asleep.

"Not everyone dies in a duel, some are saved somehow," I replied.

"This one is to the death, I can feel it . . . like Labourdette's . . . , but you were too young then." She knelt down on the floor fingering her rosary beads.

I laid in bed under the ivory-colored mosquito net. I couldn't breathe, I felt I was choking. The bed and the room reeled dizzily. Only the tulle of the mosquito net remained in place.

"Wouldn't you like to have a dress made of mosquito-net tulle?" I asked Julieta.

"Blessed are thou," she answered, "can't you see that I'm praying? . . . among women; don't interrupt me, I can't stop, and blessed is the . . . "

I knelt on the bed and framed my face with the tulle to make Julieta laugh, but she wouldn't stop praying.

I climbed out of bed from under the tulle and opened the windows. Julieta was mumbling incoherent words between her prayers.

The moonlight etched the profiles of the terrace. In the shadows the angel resembled a bat. I looked out to the park and saw three men come in through the Cuba Street gate. Hidden behind the balusters I heard my father's voice greeting them.

"At last!" he said. "Everything is ready. We will stand guard in the weapons' room."

His voice was drowned by the hooting of an owl. I returned to my room; the shadow of the angel was projected on the terrace window. I think it lulled me to sleep. The sound of the water fountain came through the other window. I barely heard my mother's voice when she opened the door and said, "Pray for him . . . for them," she corrected herself.

Later I heard steps in the guest room. I waited. I caressed the scapulary of Our Lady of Carmen on my chest and jumped out of bed. I opened the door to my room, trying not to awaken Julieta, and glided down the hallway to his room. I knocked. When he didn't answer I told myself that something must have happened to him and opened the door. Aguirre had his back to me, he was looking out on the park. Startled by my entrance, he turned around and approached me with a sure step. As I advanced towards him I opened the collar of my nightgown to take the scapulary out—as if to justify my presence—and standing on tiptoe, I placed it on his neck, pulling it over his head.

"Forgive me," I said, and lied, "my mother sent you this for your protection."

"Thank you, thank you very much," he replied, smiling.

I remained nailed to the floor. I couldn't withdraw. And then it was too late. For an hour I did nothing but defend myself. I couldn't scream, however. I didn't even think of screaming. I defended myself desperately, knowing my defeat in advance.

Thus I shortened the time he had left before death.

I rolled on the carpet. I defended myself from behind the solid baroque legs of the bed; I wrapped myself in the brocade bedspreads and waited for him to find me again. When I saw the frames with the yellowed photographs of my family scattered around on the floor and heard Vicenta's voice definitely lost in the distance, I screamed, as I recalled my mother taking communion the previous morning with us trailing behind. I heard my father's voice again making the arrangements for the duel. Then I was able to scream without being heard.

It was a cry of pain, of hate and outrage. I got up with difficulty. He remained sprawled on the carpet. I opened and closed the door behind me without looking back. Then I walked slowly to my room and laid in bed to wait.

At four o'clock I heard steps going down the stairs followed by the same steps crushing the dead leaves on the grounds. I clenched my teeth to bolster my wish: his death.

We heard two simultaneous shots . . . Julieta woke up, startled.

"May God protect them," she said, and I left the room before she could ask me where I was going.

I ran down the stairs like a ghost, as though flying, crossing the park until I reached the duel grounds. I noticed no one around me. I knelt by the body lying on the ground; they had already covered him with a dark cloth. I uncovered the body with one swift stroke only to realize with horror that it was not that of Pablo Aguirre.

My father whispered in my ear, "Have you gone mad? We will speak about this later. And in your nightgown . . . "

Without listening to him I raised my eyes to Aguirre's. He covered his face with his hands; I don't know how much hatred he had seen in my eyes.

What happened later is of no importance. Neither were the months that followed that day. Whenever I opened my eyes, during my illness, I could see his tall silhouette leaning against the door frame; he seemed not to dare to come in.

He became inseparable from my father; he was there when my sisters got married, when Nana and my mother died.

But I had lost forever the shadow of the angel on my window, the Plaza de las Barrancas, the park, the gazebo with the wisterias.

I started to inhabit the wasteland that he had opened for me the night of the duel. I would leave my house in the mornings and not return until dusk. I walked through the city, losing myself in the saddest and most remote neighborhoods . . . But every time I turned a corner he was here, waiting for me. I don't know if he is dead or alive. We could be two ghosts for all I know. We should have died that night; he on the grounds, I on the angel's terrace.

Now I can go out; they're waiting for me.

Translated by Lizabeth Paravisini-Gebert

ᵀ Silvina Ocampo (Argentina)

ALBINO ORMA

Albino Orma was good-looking and left-handed, but he managed well with his right hand.

He told me one day that by pouring ink on a piece of paper and folding it down the middle while the ink was still wet, you could (according to the images you saw on the blots) not only draw conclusions about a person's psychological state, but also know the day and circumstances of his or her death. Since I was interested in sorcery (though he assured me that this was a scientific matter) I agreed to put it to the test. Our romance lasted a week. Sometimes I would not show up for our dates because I had to go out with Irma. One day I went out on Palermo Lake with him in a boat. We rowed to the forbidden island, where we got off. After kissing me he took out of his pocket a piece of paper and a fountain pen. He removed the cap and shook the pen over the paper until there was a large ink stain; then he folded the paper in two and pressed it with his fingers; when he unfolded it we saw a strange image that resembled a bat. He explained to me that life, like the ink blot, was symmetrical, and that there was a close relationship between the early and late experiences of one's life. Life was like that ink blot. Everything repeated itself: if eight years after one's birth one had suffered an accident, eight years before dying one would suffer a similar accident. If nine years after birth the individual had been intensely happy, nine years before death he or she would again be intensely happy for similar reasons. If at the age of three one had tasted for the first time the flavor of bananas, three years before dying one would discover, for example, the similar flavor of the custard apple. If at the age of five one had met a bearded Luis, five years before dying one would meet a bearded Juan or Carlos. With the pretext of finding out more about my lifespan, I confided in him. On the inkblot, as if on a map, I jotted the most salient events of my life, following the contours of that monstrous drawing.

I confirmed, in effect, that there was a strange, almost perfect symmetry between my early experiences and what I realized then, would be my last. That is how Albino Orma discovered my betrayal and my death, which would take place soon (because of which he forgave me). That stage of my life corresponded, according to his calculations, to my sixth year of life; Juan, the boy I had met on the square, corresponded to Albino Orma. While the nannies conversed in animated intimacy, we, Juan and I, hidden behind the bushes, played innocently obscene games. I don't remember very well what these games consisted of, because they were so complicated only a child could understand them. Devastated planets oscillated in my memory when we traveled to the stratosphere in the swings. Fornication was one of the most alluring words in the catechism book. We wanted to discover its meaning through practice. And we did. Juan was as precocious as I was and he covered me with shame when he brandished his sex like a rod against me. I withstood it heroically, but I vowed revenge and got it at the first opportunity.

Revenge sometimes engenders affection. Six years was a short time to live a love as passionate as ours. Albino was saddened; I, however, felt even more intensely the happiness of a life beginning to extinguish itself.

The fruit vendor's daughter used to come by the house with the delivery man and we became friends. We played on the square, and I withdrew from my lascivious little friend, snubbing him. The end of my love for Juan was as close to my birth as the end of my love for Albino from my death.

Out of modesty I will not narrate the details of my experience with Albino Orma; they correspond exactly to my experiences with Juan, the boy on the square. With him I also traveled to heaven on the swings, since love restores us to our childhood.

Translated by Lizabeth Paravisini-Gebert

🖤 Rosario Castellanos (Mexico)

ON THE EDGE OF PLEASURE

I

Between myself and death I've placed your body:
so that its fatal waves might break against you without touching me
and slide into a wild and humiliated foam.
Body of love, of plenitude, of fiestas,
words the winds disperse like flowers,
bells delirious at dusk.
All that the earth sends flying in the form of birds,
all that lakes store up of sky
along with the forest and the stone and the honeycomb.

(Heady with harvests I dance above the haystacks
while time mourns its cracked scythes.)

City of fortune and high walls,
circled by miracles, I rest in the enclosure
of this body that begins where mine leaves off.

II

Convulsed in your arms like a sea among rocks,
breaking against the edge of pleasure or gently
licking the stunned sands.
(I tremble beneath your touch
like a tensed bow quivering with arrows
and sharp imminent hisses.
My blood burns like the blood of hounds
sniffing their prey and ravage.
But beneath your voice my heart surrenders
in devoted and submissive doves.)

III

I taste you first in the grapes
that slowly yield to my tongue,
conveying their select, intimate sugars.

Your presence is a jubilation.

When you leave, you trample gardens and turn
the turtledove's sweet drowse
into a fierce expectation of wild dogs.
And love, when you return
my raging spirit senses you draw near
as young deer sense the water's edge.

Translated by Magda Bogin

NYMPHOMANIA

I held you in my hands:
all mankind in a walnut.

What a hard, wrinkled shell!

And inside, the simulacrum
of the two halves of the brain,
which obviously aspire not to work
but to be devoured and praised
for their neutral, unsatisfying taste
that endlessly demands,
over and over and over, to be tried again.

Translated by Magda Bogin

❦ María Luisa Mendoza (Mexico)

Excerpt from
AUSENCIA'S TALE

Former militia officers with pretensions to dandyism who served in the Dardanelles and the Iser condemn—if not violently at least with firm conviction—the wearing of coattails for formal dinners, theater events, or other ceremonies that without exaggeration can be considered obligatory in daily social life. Coattails are only worn by poor devils with no clue about men's fashions or by newcomers to pseudo-bohemian circles. It's just that the tendency of gentlemen who have held commissions in military campaigns leans towards a relaxed elegance that had formerly been antagonistic to true distinction. But let's not be too inclined to severity in matters of current fashion. We can very well forgive—those of us who understand the vastness of our nation, isolated amidst wheat and corn fields and millions of head of cattle—local ignorance in matters of fashion, though we have noted that smoking jackets are now the trend in London, but worn with matte silk linings, that shiny lapels are unacceptable, not even as a joke—crows' mirrors, my father used to call them—as are felt hats and outrageous spats, that Parisian design has maintained silk-like bindings on the lapels, although cut of the same fabric, that's true. Besides, we all know that only waiters don American-style tuxedos.

The wardrobe situation is in continuous metamorphosis, my dear lady. You can very well understand, given your obvious financial position, that it's been a long time since plush hats were the item of choice to cover the old noggin . . . they're only worn by niggers . . . that a belted overcoat—a coachman's dead giveaway—has been soundly defeated by the perfectly-cut evening cape or the greatcoat. And, begging your pardon, boxer shorts that fall below the knee, and shirt tails reaching below the hip have been relegated to what is impossible, unforgivable to wear.

(how long will my skin last without a final go at it. In what coming day, tomorrow, today even when I get to my hotel room, will it show the imprint of so many stories—stories lived, heard, tangled in the dark lines that seem even more pronounced when I speak and remain in the r's or the m's that brush against them, like fishes heaped on a net, quivering, their mouths open, with scales like knives capable of scraping away the softness, leaving behind only dead flesh, fishes of words? Why in heaven's name this downpour of sadness? Ausencia seemed to absent herself from this game of oneupmanship, not giving logical answers, more than normally forgetful about names, titles, synonyms in French, designer labels, breeds, definitions, qualifiers or nouns of real, independent, and individual existence. More past than pluperfect. Then, distracted by the feast of oysters and white wine, of asparagus and "centurion eggs," as she blushingly called the caviar, making an effort to focus her beam of light, which had nearly faded without warning after spending a sleepless night in order to catch the grand zeppelin, the lady understood that she didn't give a hoot about Reinaldo Olavarrieta, this man from Tabasco who inspired in her such grammatical ideas: ferns, lizard-fish, swamp, new corn, gnats, coconut tortillas, sweat, beans and plantains, hammock, green turtle, crocodile, cocoa, laughter, vice, alcohol, chewing gum, heresy, liberalism, terms of endearment . . . , and that nothing was more absolute than the subtle beige of the restaurant with its private alcove where they lunched on delicious tidbits, or than her mind's hopeless efforts to conjure more words to identify this man from Tabasco with the sexual impulse that her companion left behind like forgotten cards on a game table in a run-down ship detained in a jungle customs station and seized without further inquiries, the police taking away sequined prostitutes and frock-coated card sharps among gringa heiresses of tobacco plantations, vacationing delegates, uneven pairs of faggots caught in the act, or sweet grandmothers accompanying a grandchild with a penchant for mad escapades but without capital or friends to finance them. Ausencia thus resigned herself to one of those floodings of her lacunae, from exhaustion, "you'll have to forgive me, there are moments in which fatigue makes me seem absent-minded," and stopped trying to climb the hill of names. And without further ado she said:)

"I would very much like to eat seafood, Reinaldo, but I very much prefer the catholic diet of green and red, maybe accompanied by a smattering of yellow, a bit of white, absolutely no purple, never any beige, and frankly nothing black; I will take a little something, pink maybe, but I'm only doing it for you who are my compatriot and whose voice, despite what you're telling me, Olavarrieta—a very distinguished and elegant voice, by the way, without any s's—fills me with such an ebb and flowing of nostalgia, familiar airs, revolutionary revolts, profanations of church virgins, and lots of textile-plant money since I assume that's the source of your wealth, or am I mistaken?"

Reinaldo opened his eyes wide, understanding the latter but ignoring, like any intelligent, conceited and solemn being, the former. He let his rambunctious and lusty tropical laugh loose as he listened to this teaser regaling him with such absurd perspicacities which he supposed, not making an effort despite himself, referred to the food in her diet and which, contrary to what his companion, exhausted from the effort of calling green by its proper name, salad—red was for tomato, yellow for mustard, white for bread, purple for beets, beige for butter, black for caviar, pink for salmon— would have expected, did not disappoint him, nor did they make him pick up his hat and take off running to look for someone who spoke Spanish properly, it didn't even make him lose interest, right now the woman looked even more adorable than in the zeppelin, more than in the car that took them at breakneck speed to the La Cupola Restaurant, specializing in sunfish and not in steak alla fiorentina.

Ausencia was not too keen—between little sips of coffee and cognac—on going to bed at dusk with this compatriot of hers who had plunged headlong into a rigmarole of tailoring and high fashion. Reinaldo was not precisely enthusiastic about the idea of taking his pants off that sunset, and then dressing again. He was just back from that, from the nonchalant squeeze-me-tightly-there, with God's help he was retracing his steps to his homeland, where one made love like drinking a mammee juice, even though that pulpy fruit was short of juices, just like he and Ausencia were short of lusting to trot in bed. But despite this sluggish calm in both their loins, Reinaldo proposed and Ausencia accepted.

(it was the rush, the sleepy Sunday, it was the obstinate stiffness of my legs, the unknown, the rustling of my petticoats, the whiteness of the linen below his navel, it was his youth, it was mine. All that panting, all that pricking, first gently and then hard and then nothing but the comings-in and the goings-out and then the cascade in my squeezing neck from his bulging rod. It was that Virginia didn't know about it and I would have to explain it to her, it was that Enedina wasn't absent, nor was Ausencia—I, Virgin, she— each one of us in a room separated only by blood, Virginia thinking of me, I thinking of her, Enedina thinking of both of us, the three of us with him who came that afternoon for a Scotch; he with me in that my bed which then was made for him, only him. It was the exhaustion of our flesh and his electricity which led to so many unknown streets, towers of lace, and ships' sirens, sounds never heard by me who only knew of the chants of gold and the sighs of urine . . . It was his joy, yes, it was the mad generosity of his dark youth, it was the game of The Pussy in the Well—no sense in covering it up now—it was the delight of all those new Sundays, one on, one off, and his voice like a closed mine, his broad-shouldered back, well-muscled and lean under my breast and the charade of my violation of his delicious behindnesses. It was the ceremony of his dancing in the buff for me, veiling himself with an Arabian cloth, with linen that had belonged to the other, the one that "had been," it was the way he raised the banner to let his sex peek out, up, down, sideways, and ending up bursting out laughing with feminine then masculine grace in a naked boxing match which I watched in a trance seeing the fluttering of the dove between his legs, whirling like a kite wanting to fly away but being held tight by a boy's string, as if that dark-skinned appendage had been expressly made by God to gyrate against the pubis and the pouches of pleasure that could barely keep up with its rhythmic adorability as it spun in the air and then the uppercut, the jab, and the final knockout which released that watered-down paste over me and my bed, his bed now, in order to start again...it was that.)

"What are you thinking of, queen, sitting there so pierced with silences?" The blue-eyed youth once undressed had given evidence of slightly twisted knees, not quite knock-knees or bow-legs, just somewhat curved legs, as if the well-made patrician trunk, perfect in all its attributes, weighed more than it should have, giving eloquent evidence of sound nourishment, ablutions, brushes against good fabrics with fine labels embroidered in English, French, in Italian, but never in Spanish, good beds, good daybreaks, good evenings, good horsebacks, good berths in luxury liners, good everything, that is.

(when Gerundio died I could have been better, not decent, no, since we cut that word out and made it into paper cones for salted seeds, but better, yes, free. But I didn't want to, I loved my home too much to stray far from it, my ceilings painted with angels and other sillinesses, my former and present properties for me alone...)

"Sir: my new properties are for me alone. It's like you, Mr. Olavarrieta, you, Reinaldo, for example, sitting here next to me. I don't know you, I don't know much more about you than the language you speak, and you were nonetheless destined for me. You would have to buy a ticket to climb to heaven and let out a scream; your life is a never-ending descending from zeppelins to meet the flashbulbs of the cameras photographing us. And this coming month she'll see our faces, she alone, Enedina, in the Zig-Zags, the monthly magazine she reads looking for me, your photo was in the paper, make believe it's a souvenir . . . Enedina is my maid—if one can call her that—. She lives in a very big house of mine, with a door that sometimes—once—resounds like thunder . . . You have no idea. You're the type that springs to life after three o'clock, worried about properties you don't inhabit, like me, and concerned about the statement you make in your elegant clothing, as if the smoking jacket were the answer. I was thinking of my silences, do you understand?"

"No, beauty, I don't understand."

"It's just that going to bed with a man it's not what you'd call something out of this world. We women jump into bed with the ease that men boast of but don't actually feel. We like feeling you down there, ah, how we like it!, but it doesn't go beyond that, a matter of doing what one must once one said one would. The bad part is the memories, the damned piling up of what happened to you before, there, a thousand years ago . . . I don't remember."

"Tell me, Ausencia, speak to me . . ."

"You know? One day we buried my father. His name was Gerundio Batista and he was a miner between the blue of the Spanish sky and the dark night of Sonora. I was still very young in those days, but for five years I'd been threading elusive Sundays: a lover at the plant, no less, and a lover at the mine. I drew lots for them on weekends, without working myself up about it. The truth is that houses of many rooms are very tempting. He 'was' a gringo, but with Arab blood, the other 'had been' Mexican. My 'was' and my 'had been.' Was for him, had been for him."

"Tell me."

"I broke the rules of every day, of every hour. Once my father died I was covered in tinsel and coins. On the desk in his study I learned to sign with the constancy of a millionaire, I collected and bestowed, I acquired and gave away, I took and distributed: the kind of first class deed that is never forgiven by those who only open their mouths to let out their bile—the damnable habit of damning everyone to hell—. If I had not thought of anything beyond the giving and taking, I would not have gotten even with the devil, but would be, on the contrary, in the same boat as all the rich people in the vicinity . . . I wore mourning for twenty days, complete mourning, with veil and gloves. I wore half-mourning for twenty days, white collar and cuffs on a black dress, I wore white without fail for twenty days, white from head to toe, including my curls. I covered three years in sixty days. On the sixty-first day I gave a farewell tea party for a mining colleague who was leaving for New York on personal business. On the sixty-second day society sent me the normal invitations to shindigs and what nots . . . His name was D. H. Haller, you know?, and I loved him. My first long awakening into sex. His chest tangled with white hairs, his power . . . but I'm getting sidetracked . . . "

"Tell me."

"I could go on and on telling you the story of a beautiful life since I've never held back before, but the truth is that women chroniclers of their coituses invent fifty percent of their tales, and the true bed-hoppers are the quiet ones. I only narrate my life story to my lovers, in their own manner and style, tailoring my tale to their image, since in their "tell me Ausencia," they know what they want to hear. It's different with women; other women's tales leave them cold, since they have their own: jazzed up stories if they haven't had much luck and want to boast of their non-existent whoring; and discreet, cleaned-up tales if on the contrary they have run wild horizontally. In other words, whores act like real ladies in front of their friends, and vice versa. That's the way it works, and it's the same with age. All women take years off their age, and the moment one turns forty a woman finds herself celebrating birthdays in a world of contemporaries who'll be thirty-nine forever. I don't have to tell you my story: you're not my lover, not even my acquaintance, a fleeting fuck doesn't count, it fades away, like the face of the customs officer who reads your vital statistics, stamps your passport, and is forgotten. Besides, cheer up, you would end up boring me, everything has been boring me for centuries. And besides, you're not remotely similar, you're not my type, if only you looked like them . . . "

Ausencia began to cover the tip of her foot with the listless parsimony of the idle woman who gets out of bed after reading the theater listings in the paper and choosing the play for the evening. She had just finalized her plans and chosen her adventure. If puddle jumpers could buzz from Paris to Mexico in three hours she would take the eleven o'clock express to Balbuena—now an airport. But she was not in such a rush to move. There was Duvivier awaiting her in downtown Rome, and a whole long week before getting to the port and choosing an ocean liner, and countless sleepless nights, and the memories, and time stretching ahead of her in a wretched row of long and identical days. There was the clockwork care of her eyelids that were beginning to sag under their own weight, and which she pressed half an hour mornings and evenings under compresses of chilled tea, rose water, camomile, salt, and banyan flowers. There was just what no longer appealed to her: life, and no other choice but to await old age.

Translated by Lizabeth Paravisini-Gebert

🌷 Alejandra Pizarnik (Argentina)

WORDS

We wait for the rain to stop. For the winds to come. We speak. For the love of silence we utter useless words. A pained, painful utterance, without escape, for the love of silence, for love of the body's language. I would speak; language has always been an excuse for silence. It's my way of expressing my unspeakable weariness.

This fatal order of things should be reversed. Words should be used to seduce the one we love, but through pure silence. I have always been the silent one. Now I used those mediating words I have heard so much. But who has so often praised lovers over those loved? My deepest leaning: to the edge of silence. The mediation of words, the lure of language. This is my life now: self-restraint, trembling at every voice, tempering words by calling upon all the cursed and fatal things that I have heard and read about the ways of seduction.

The fact is I enumerated, analyzed and compared the examples gathered from my readings or from mutual friends. I could show that I was right, that love was right. I promised him that if he loved me, a place of perfect justice would be his. But I wasn't in love with him; I only wanted to be loved by him and no one else. It's so hard to talk about. When I saw his face for the first time I wanted it to turn toward mine out of love. I wanted his eyes to fall deeply into mine. Of this I wish to speak. Of a love that's impossible because there is no love. A love story without love. I speak too soon. There is love. There's love in the same way that I went out the other night and observed: there's wind tonight. Not a story without love. Or rather, a story about substitutes.

There are gestures that pierce me between the legs: a fear and a shuddering in my genitals. Seeing his face pause for a fraction of a second, his face frozen for an immeasurable moment, his face, such a dead stop, like the change in one's voice when saying *no*. That Dylan Thomas poem about the hand signing the page. A face that lasts as long as a hand signing a name on a sheet of paper. I felt it in my genitals. Levitation: I am lifted, I fly. A *no*, because of that *no* everything comes undone. I have to give an orderly account of this disorder. A disorderly accounting of this strange order of things. While *no* goes on and on.

I speak of an approaching poem. It comes closer as I am held at a distance. Weariness without rest, untiring weariness as night—not a poem—approaches and I am beside him and nothing, nothing happens as night draws near, passes by and nothing, nothing happens. Only a very distant voice, a magical belief, an absurd, ancient wait for better things.

Not long ago I said *no* to him. An unspeakable transgression. I said no, when for months I've died waiting. When I begin the gesture, when I began . . . . A shaking shudder, hurting, wounding myself, thirsting for excess (thinking sometime about the importance of the syllable *no*.)

Translated by Suzanne Jill Levine

THE LADY BUCCANEER OF PERNAMBUCO
OR HILDA THE POLYGRAPH

to Gabrielle D'Estrées and to Severo Sarduy

The highway robber was the spitting image of the douche bag in person.

Reader, I am very strict when it comes to manners. Good diction is precisely what leads me to the precise expression of a profuse state of confusion.

The purpose of these statements, which serve as liminary words or as an intro into the vagina of God, is to pry open a gaping gap into my flashy formality. Like a swimmer diving head or ass first into a pool—with or without water—what I write, for shit's sake, doesn't matter a frig.

Naked as a shrewmouse, Oedipussy Chew Flower laughed at the superfluous advice nobody gave him.

Suddenly he felt like a stroll through this text and telephoned Shithead, and Shithead called me.

In case the reader's forgotten the crash pad where pregnant Chew pads about, Shithead informs us that it's the same as before: the boutique of Coco Panel who fully clothed (though not necessarily well-dressed) looks like a naked fat man. As to Dr. Chew, he's naked (and comes and goes talking to Michelangelo). The sinologist was dragging his feet since he had spent the whole night galloping on a rocking-horse.

Chew wasn't cheerful, in the black devil's Alabama the truth be told. And smoking his cigar, he went up in smoke. Thus yesteryear's pirate Apocalypso Morgan was eclipsed when stripped by his Fata Morgana.

Damn this Job of writing! I abandon myself to my brown study, to no avail. I abandon myself, to no avail.

Remember, pregnant reader, that our pad is always Coco Anel's rococo bootique.

Now then: the rapist of the fair lad of yore, Fleur d'Oedipe Chew, was Mumu Pistachio. While Cono-nut was the kidnapper of Mrs. Clean. But don't seek in vain, dear reader, these fishy characters since the tasty Mrs. and Mumu were roasted on an open spit by a horde of two 122-year-old lady cannibals, from the Bubu tribe of Dent-Africa.

Damn this Lot of living! I abandon myself to my brown study and lookee here, in a lickety-split those two stewed-asses are off ravaging and ramping Dent-Africa way. Hold it—we're really in fricative mode on Checkerboard Square. The thug besieged by mutineering Bubu pigmies joins the unanimous cry of "Long Live Alice in Wonderland!" But Pancho Panel doesn't shit in his pants. Like a solid turd, he stands firm. Besides, he travels with a transistor radio hidden in the ear of his luxurious Kangaroo Benz. The radio emits slippery morphemes like:

"Screw 'im, Coco, screw 'im!"

and

"You've got the rights to the first fuck, Schmuck!"

And so on.

When Coco Panel confronted the thug with a senseless multineering pig-melon,[1] she shook sauceressly her earrings, inherited from a splendid cretino—Pietro Aretino—for the purpose of amazing the pigmied plesbeian who screeched and squeaked as when in Penambuco I stuffed the buco of the oso who ate my ossobuco.

Reader, don't you know I'm getting bored too?

40,000 mini-plegms braked the Harley-Davidson motorcycle (gift of André Pieyre de Mandiargues) and they fell flat on their asses turning over a fishbowl filled with axolotls, quetzals and ocelots (gift of Octavio Paz), of shrewmice (gift of Pabts and Trnka), and of the photographs of famous hetaerae (gift of the lady dwarves of Circe's circus to whom Martha Moia gave heuristic diction lessons).

Let me continue.

---

[1] Prosciutto with melon — Trans.

A tiny Bubu warrior takes 132 steps and advances half a millimeter—do you know, kids, who that little guy is? Oh beasts! Oh budding flowers! I deduce that you also don't know the response to this questionance: does Adela pick a bunch of daffodils or is it the bunch of daffodils that picks Adela?

The mini-warrior (I'll tell you, ignoramuses) is the emperor.

The emperor prostrated himself to the tune of the "Emperor's Waltz," grabbed the microphone, fell inside, was wormed out of the microphone & pigmied himself with laughter when the last minister telegraphed him in the pig-morse code:

"That broad who storks about brandishing Aretino's trinket looks like a minaret stained with claret and with what Your Majesty imagines."

The emperor dried his diapers and whiskers (gift of Gogol) which he had wet in pigmied jocundity; with the flick of a wrist he whisked down his windpipe a shot of whiskey tasting of raspberry and, neither prudish nor prurient, he asked to speak. Someone handed him a little box. He spoke then to the great good-for-nothing:

. . . .
. . . .
. . . .
. . . .

"Who the hell are you?" croaked the monster from the "mannerist" pocket of her sumptuous Kangaroo Benz.

"I'm the Divine Mask of Sader, King of the Pigmist-Hysteria-Snot-Motel (central farting; the dream come true of one's own douche; pingmy-pongmy playpen; boobliography reference room; virgin hairs; foreplayground; buns & Guelph ribbons by Marta Sabelline; and so on and so forth).

"On top of the so on and so forth, I want to finish. Just like this? Without flinging a wad of adjectives at those who appreciate in a writer his descriptive and didactic faculties? Here they go:

The beautiful, ill-starred, Dent-African, ultimate *Rex Pigmarum*.

THE END

Postcript, 1969. "She was known among the disciples of Orgasm, author of a relentless bootlicking of the madhouse; my masturdebating readers know the title."

Postcriptie, 1969 & 1/2. "I have added nothing to this new edition. My repeated readings of Baffo, Aretino, Crébillon *fils*, the anonymous memorialists (the Russian princess, the German opera singer), afforded me the understanding of their joy. Some folks—I'm the first—reproach me for my "realism": situating in Dent-Africa a story about Dent-Africa. They're right, verisimilitude does make my narrative unbearable. But, will there never be a brave spirit? 28,000 anonymous protesters couldn't make me budge an inch. The truth is dearer to me than Platonov,[2] who suffered more than anyone the tragedy of a pigmy destiny.

Translated by Suzanne Jill Levine

[2] A character from Anton Chekhov — Trans.

THE BLOODY COUNTESS

The criminal does not make beauty;
he himself is the authentic beauty.
—Jean-Paul Sartre

There is a book by Valentine Penrose which documents the life of a real and unusual character: the Countess Bathory, murderer of more than six hundred young girls. The Countess Bathory's sexual perversion and her madness are so obvious that Valentine Penrose disregards them and concentrates instead on the convulsive beauty of the character.

It is not easy to show this sort of beauty. Valentine Penrose, however, succeeded because she played admirably with the aesthetic value of this lugubrious story. She inscribes the underground kingdom of Erzebet Bathory within the walls of her torture chamber, and the chamber within her medieval castle. Here the sinister beauty of nocturnal creatures is summed up in this silent lady of legendary paleness, mad eyes, and hair the sumptuous color of ravens.

A well-known philosopher includes cries in the category of silence—cries, moans, curses, form "a silent substance." The substance of this underworld is evil. Sitting on her throne, the countess watches the tortures and listens to the cries. Her old and horrible maids are wordless figures that bring in fire, knives, needles, irons; they torture the girls, and later bury them. With their iron and knives, these two old women are themselves the instruments of a possession. This dark ceremony has a single silent spectator.

I. THE IRON MAIDEN

. . . among red laughter of glistening lips and
monstrous gestures of mechanical women.
—René Daumal

There was once in Nuremberg a famous automaton known

as the Iron Maiden. The Countess Bathory bought a copy for her torture chamber in Csejthe Castle. This clockwork doll was of the size and color of a human creature. Naked, painted, covered in jewels, with blond hair that reached down to the ground, it had a mechanical device that allowed it to curve its lips into a smile, and to move its eyes.

The Countess, sitting on her throne, watches.

For the Maiden to spring into action it is necessary to touch some of the precious stones in its necklace. It responds immediately with horrible creaking sounds and very slowly lifts its white arms which close in a perfect embrace around whatever happens to be next to it—in this case, a girl. The automaton holds her in its arms and now no one will be able to uncouple the living body from the body of iron, both equally beautiful. Suddenly the painted breasts of the Iron Maiden open, and five daggers appear that pierce her struggling companion whose hair is as long as its own.

Once the sacrifice is over another stone in the necklace is touched: the arms drop, the smile and the eyes fall shut, and the murderess becomes once again the Maiden, motionless in its coffin.

II. DEATH BY WATER

> He is standing. And he is standing as
> absolutely and definitely as if he were sitting.
> —Witod Grombowicz

The road is covered in snow and, inside the coach, the sombre lady wrapped in furs feels bored. Suddenly she calls out the name of one of the girls in her train. The girl is brought to her: the Countess bites her frantically and sticks needles in her flesh. A while later the procession abandons the wounded girl in the snow. The girl tries to run away. She is pursued, captured, and pulled back into the coach. A little further along the road they halt: the Countess has ordered cold water. Now the girl is naked, standing in the snow. Night has fallen. A circle of torches surrounds her, held out by impassive footmen. They pour water over the body and the water turns to ice. (The Countess observes this from inside the coach.) The girl attempts one last slight gesture, trying to move closer to the torches—the only source of warmth. More water is poured over her, and there she remains, forever standing, upright, dead.

III. THE LETHAL CAGE

> . . . scarlet and black wounds burst
> upon the splendid flesh.
> —Arthur Rimbaud

Lined with knives and adorned with sharp iron blades, it can hold one human body, and can be lifted by means of a pulley. The ceremony on the cage takes place in this manner:

Dorko the maid drags in by the hair a naked young girl, shuts her up in the cage and lifts it high into the air. The Lady of These Ruins appears, a sleepwalker in white. Slowly and silently she sits upon a footstool placed underneath the contraption.

A red-hot poker in her hand, Dorko taunts the prisoner who, drawing back (and this is the ingenuity of the cage) stabs herself against the sharp irons while her blood falls upon the pale woman who dispassionately receives it, her eyes fixed on nothing, as in a daze. When the lady recovers from the trance, she slowly leaves the room. There have been two transformations: her white dress is now red, and where a girl once stood a corpse now lies.

IV. CLASSICAL TORTURE

> Unblemished fruit, untouched by worm
> or frost, whose firm, polished skin
> cries out to be bitten!
> —Baudelaire

Except for a few baroque refinements—like the Iron Maiden,

death by water, or the cage—the Countess restricted herself to a monotonously classic style of torture that can be summed up as follows:

Several tall, beautiful, strong girls were selected—their ages had to be between 12 and 18—and dragged into the torture chamber where, dressed in white upon her throne, the countess awaited them. After binding their hands, the servants would whip the girls until the skin of their bodies ripped and they became a mass of swollen wounds; then the servants would burn them with red-hot pokers; cut their fingers with scissors or shears; pierce their wounds; stab them with daggers (if the Countess grew tired of hearing the cries they would sew their mouths up; if one of the girls fainted too soon they would revive her by burning paper soaked in oil between her legs). The blood spurted like fountains and the white dress of the nocturnal lady would turn red. So red, that she would have to go up to her room and change (what would she think about during this brief intermission?). The walls and the ceiling of the chamber would also turn red.

Not always would the lady remain idle while the others busied themselves around her. Sometimes she would lend a hand, and then, impetuously, tear at the flesh—in the most sensitive places—with tiny silver pincers; or she would stick needles, cut the skin between the fingers, press red-hot spoons and irons against the soles of the feet, use the whip (once, during one of her excursions, she ordered her servants to hold up a girl who had just died and kept on whipping her even though she was dead); she also murdered several by means of icy water (using a method invented by Darvulia, the witch; it consisted of plunging a girl into freezing water and leaving her there overnight). Finally, when she was sick, she would have the girls brought to her bedside and she would bite them.

During her erotic seizures she would hurl blasphemous insults at her victims. Blasphemous insults and cries like the baying of a she-wolf were her means of expression as she stalked, in a passion, the gloomy rooms. But nothing was more ghastly than her laugh. (I recapitulate: the medieval castle, the torture chamber, the tender young girls, the old and horrible servants, the beautiful mad-woman laughing in a wicked ecstasy provoked by the suffering of others.) Her last words, before letting herself fall into a final faint, would be: "More, ever more, harder, harder!"

Not always was the day innocent, the night guilty. During the morning or the afternoon, young seamstresses would bring dresses for the Countess, and this would lead to innumerable scenes of cruelty. Without exception, Dorko would find mistakes in the sewing and would select two or three guilty victims (at this point the Countess's doleful eyes would glisten). The punishment of the seamstresses—and of the young maids in general—would vary. If the Countess happened to be in one of her rare good moods, Dorko would simply strip the victims who would continue to work, naked, under the Countess's eyes, in large rooms full of black cats. The girl bore this painless punishment in agonizing amazement, because they never believed it to be possible. Darkly, they must have felt ter-ribly humiliated because their nakedness forced them into a kind of animal world, a feeling heightened by the fully clothed "human" presence of the Countess, watching them. This scene led me to think of Death—Death as in old allegories, as in the Dance of Death. To strip naked is a prerogative of Death; another is the incessant watching over the creatures it has dispossessed. But there is more: sexual climax forces us into death-like gestures and expres-sions (gasping and writhing as in agony, cries and moans of parox-ysm). If the sexual act implies a sort of death, Erzebet Bathory need-ed the visible, elementary, coarse death, to succeed in dying that other phantom death we call orgasm. But, who is Death? A figure that harrows and wastes wherever and however it pleases. This is also a possible description of the Countess Bathory. Never did any-one wish so hard not to grow old; I mean, to die. That is why, per-haps, she acted and played the role of Death. Because, how can Death possibly die?

Let us return to the seamstresses and the maids. If Erzebet woke up wrathful, she would not be satisfied with her *tableaux vivants*, but:

To the one who had stolen a coin she would repay with the same coin . . . red-hot, which the girl had to hold tight in her hand.

To the one who had talked during working hours, the Countess herself would sew her mouth shut, or otherwise would open her mouth and stretch it until the lips tore.

She also used the poker with which she would indiscriminately burn cheeks, breasts, tongues . . . .

When the punishments took place in Erzebet's chamber, at nighttime, it was necessary to spread large quantities of ashes around her bed, to allow the noble lady to cross without difficulties the vast pools of blood.

V. ON THE STRENGTH OF A NAME

> And cold madness wandered
> aimlessly about the house.
> —Milosz

The name of Bathory—in the power of which Erzebet believed, as if it were an extraordinary talisman—was an illustrious one from the early days of the Hungarian Empire. It was not by chance that the family coat-of-arms displayed the teeth of a wolf, because the Bathory were cruel, fearless and lustful. The many marriages that took place between blood relations contributed, perhaps, to the hereditary aberrations and diseases: epilepsy, gout, lust. It is not at all unlikely that Erzebet herself was an epileptic: she seemed possessed by seizures as unexpected as her terrible migraines and pains in the eyes (which she conjured away by placing a wounded pigeon, still alive, on her forehead).

The Countess's family was not unworthy of its ancestral fame. Her uncle Istvan, for instance, was so utterly mad that he would mistake summer for winter and would have himself drawn in a sleigh along the burning sands that were, in his mind, roads covered with snow. Or consider her cousin Gabor, whose incestuous passion was reciprocated by his sister's. But the most charming of all was the celebrated Aunt Klara. She had four husbands (the first two perished by her hand) and died a melodramatic death: she was caught in the arms of a causal acquaintance by her lover, a Turkish Pasha: the intruder was roasted on a spit and Aunt Klara was raped (if this verb may be used in her respect) by the entire Turkish garrison. This however did not cause her death: on the contrary, her rapists—tired perhaps of having their way with her—finally had to stab her. She used to pick up her lovers along the Hungarian roads and would not mind sprawling on a bed where she had previously slaughtered one of her female attendants.

By the time the Countess reached the age of forty, the Bathory had diminished or consumed themselves either through madness or through death. They became almost sensible, thereby losing the interest they had until then provoked in Erzebet.

VI. A WARRIOR BRIDEGROOM

> When the warrior took me in his arms
> I felt the fire of pleasure . . .
> –The Anglo-Saxon Elegy (VIII Cen.)

In 1575, at the age of fifteen, Erzebet married Ferencz Nadasdy, a soldier of great courage. This simple soul never found out that the lady who inspired him with a certain love tinged by fear was in fact a monster. He would come to her in the brief respites between battles, drenched in horse-sweat and blood—the norms of hygiene had not been firmly established—and this probably stirred the emotions of the delicate Erzebet, always dressed in rich cloths and perfumed with costly scents.

One day, walking through the castle gardens, Nadasdy saw a naked girl tied to a tree. She was covered in honey: flies and ants crawled all over her, and she was sobbing. The Countess explained that the girl was purging the sin of having stolen some fruit. Nadasdy laughed candidly, as if she had told him a joke.

The soldier would not allow anyone to bother him with stories about his wife, stories of bites, needles, etc. A serious mistake: even as a newlywed, during those crises whose formula was the Bathory's secret, Erzebet would prick her servants with long needles; and when, felled by her terrible migraines, she was forced to lie in bed, she would gnaw their shoulders and chew on the bits of flesh she had been able to extract. As if by magic, the girl's shrieks would soothe her pain.

But all this is child's play—a young girl's play. During her husband's life she never committed murder.

VII. THE MELANCHOLY MIRROR

> Everything is mirror!
> —Octavio Paz

The Countess would spend her days in front of her large dark mirror; a famous mirror she had designed herself. It was so comfortable that it even had supports on which to lean one's arms, so as to be able to stand for many hours in front of it without feeling tired. We can suppose that while believing she had designed a mirror, Erzebet had in fact designed the plans for her lair. And now we can understand why only the most grippingly sad music of her gypsy orchestra, or dangerous hunting parties, or the violent perfumes of the magic herbs in the witch's hut or—above all—the cellars flooded with human blood, could spark something resembling life in her perfect face. Because no one has more thirst for earth, for blood, and for ferocious sexuality than the creatures who inhabit cold mirrors. And on the subject of mirrors: the rumors concerning her alleged homosexuality were never confirmed. Was this allegation unconscious, or, on the contrary, did she accept it naturally, as simply another right to which she was entitled? Essentially she lived deep within an exclusively female world. There were only women during her nights of crime. And a few details are obviously revealing: for instance, in the torture chamber, during the moments of greatest tension, she herself used to plunge a burning candle into the sex of her victim. There are also testimonies which speak of less solitary pleasures. One of the servant said during the trial that an aristocratic and mysterious lady dressed as a young man would visit the Countess. On one occasion she saw them together, torturing a girl. But we do not know whether they shared any pleasures other than the sadistic ones.

More on the theme of the mirror: even though we are not concerned with *explaining* this sinister figure, it is necessary to dwell on the fact that she suffered from that sixteenth-century sickness: melancholia.

An unchangeable color rules over the melancholic: his dwelling is a space the color of mourning. Nothing happens in it. No one intrudes. It is a bare stage where the inert *I* is assisted by the *I* suffering from that inertia. The latter wishes to free the former, but all efforts fail, as Theseus would have failed had he been not only himself, but also the Minotaur; to kill him then, he would have had to kill himself. But there are fleeting remedies: sexual pleasures, for instance, can, for a brief moment, obliterate the silent gallery of echoes and mirrors that constitutes the melancholic soul. Even more: they can illuminate the funeral chamber and transform it into a sort of musical box with gaily-colored figurines that sing and dance deliciously. Afterwards, when the music winds down, the soul will return to immobility and silence. The music box is not a gratuitous comparison. Melancholia is, I believe, a musical problem: a dissonance, a change in rhythm. While on the *outside* everything happens with the vertiginous rhythm of a cataract, on the *inside* is the exhausted *adagio* of drops of water falling from time to tired time. For this reason the *outside*, seen from the melancholic *inside*, appears absurd and unreal, and constitutes "the farce we must all play." But for an instant—because of a wild music, or a drug, or the sexual act carried to its climax—the very slow rhythm of the melancholic soul does not only rise to that of the outside world: it overtakes it with an ineffably blissful exorbitance, and the soul then thrills, animated by delirious new energies.

The melancholic soul sees Time as suspended before and

after the fatally ephemeral violence. And yet the truth is that time is never suspended, but it grows as slowly as the fingernails of the dead. Between two silences or two deaths, the prodigious, brief moment of speed takes on the various forms of lust: from an innocent intoxication to sexual perversions and even murder.

I think of Erzebet Bathory and her nights whose rhythms are measured by the cries of adolescent girls. I see a portrait of the Countess: the sombre and beautiful lady resembles the allegories of Melancholia represented in old engravings. I also recall that in her time, a melancholic person was a person possessed by the Devil.

VIII. BLACK MAGIC

> . . . who kills the sun in order to install
> the reign of darkest night.
> —Antonin Artaud

Erzebet's greatest obsession had always been to keep old age at bay, at any cost. Her total devotion to the arts of black magic was aimed at preserving—intact for all eternity—the "sweet bird" of her youth. The magical herbs, the incantations, the amulets, even the blood baths had, in her eyes, a medicinal function: to immobilize her beauty in order to become, for ever and ever, *a dream of stone.* She always lived surrounded by talismans. In her years of crime she chose one single talisman which contained an ancient and filthy parchment on which was written in special ink, a prayer for her own personal use. She carried it close to her heart, underneath her costly dresses, and in the midst of a celebration, she would touch it surreptitiously. I translate the prayer:

Help me, oh Isten; and you also, all powerful cloud. Protect me, Erzebet, and grant me long life. Oh cloud, I am in danger. Send me ninety cats, for you are the supreme mistress of cats. Order them to assemble here from all their dwelling-places: from the mountains, from the waters, from the rivers, from the

*gutters and from the oceans. Tell them to come quickly and
bite the heart of _____ and also the heart of _____ and
of _____. And to also bite and rip the heart of Megyery,
the Red. And keep Erzebet from all evil.*

The blanks were to be filled with the names of those whose
hearts she wanted bitten.

In 1604 Erzebet became a widow and met Darvulia.
Darvulia was exactly like the woodland witch who frightens us in
children's tales. Very old, irascible, always surrounded by black cats,
Darvulia fully responded to Erzebet's fascination: within the
Countess's eyes the v tch found a new version of the evil powers
buried in the poisons of the forest and in the coldness of the moon.
Darvulia's black magic wrought itself in the Countess's black
silence. She initiated her to even crueller games; she taught her to
look upon death, and the *meaning* of looking upon death. She incit-
ed her to seek death and blood in a literal sense: that is, to love
them for their own sake, without fear.

IX. BLOOD BATHS

> If you go bathing, Juanilla,
> tell me to what baths you go.
> —Cancionero de Upsala

This rumour existed: since the arrival of Darvulia, the
Countess, to preserve her comeliness, took baths of human blood.
True: Darvulia, being a witch, believed in the invigorating powers of
the "human fluid." She proclaimed the merits of young girls'
blood—especially if they were virgins—to vanquish the demon of
senility, and the Countess accepted the treatment as meekly as if it
had been a salt bath. Therefore, in the torture chamber, Dorko
applied herself to slicing veins and arteries; the blood was collected
in pitchers and, when the victims were bled dry, Dorko would pour
the red warm liquid over the body of the waiting Countess—ever so

quiet, ever so white, ever so erect, ever so silent.

In spite of her unchangeable beauty, Time inflicted upon her some of the vulgar sins of its passing. Toward 1610, Darvulia mysteriously disappeared and Erzebet, almost fifty, complained to her new witch about the uselessness of the blood baths. In fact, more than complain, she threatened to kill her if she did not stop at once the encroaching and execrable signs of old age. The witch argued that Darvulia's method had not worked because plebeian blood had been used. She assured—or prophesied—that changing the color of the blood, using blue blood instead of red, would ensure the fast retreat of old age. Here began the hunt for the daughters of gentlemen. To attract them, Erzebet's minions would argue that the Lady of Csejthe, alone in her lonely castle, could not resign herself to her solitude. And how to banish solitude? Filling her dark halls with young girls of good families who, in exchange for happy company, would receive lessons in fine manners and learn how to behave exquisitely in society. A fortnight later, of the twenty-two "pupils" who had hurried to become aristocrats, only two were left: one died some time later, bled white; the other managed to take her life.

X. THE CASTLE OF CSEJTHE

> The stone walk is paved with dark cries.
> —Pierre-Jean Jouve

A castle of grey stones, few windows, square towers, underground mazes; a castle high upon a cliff, a hillside of dry windblown weeds, of woods full of white beasts in winter and dark beasts in summer; a castle that Erzebet Bathory loved for the doleful silence of its walls which muffled every cry.

The Countess's room, cold and badly lit by a lamp of jasmine oil, reeked of blood, and the cellars reeked of dead bodies. Had she wanted to, she could have carried out her work in broad daylight and murdered the girls under the sun, but she was fascinated by the gloom of her dungeon. The gloom which matched so keenly her terrible eroticism of stone, snow and walls. She loved her maze-shaped dungeon, the archetypical hell of our fears; the viscous, insecure space where we are unprotected and can get lost.

What did she do with all of her days and nights, there, in the loneliness of Csejthe? Of her nights we know something. During the day, the Countess would not leave the side of her two old servants, two creatures escaped from a painting by Goya: the dirty, malodorous, incredibly ugly and perverse Dorko and Jo Ilona. They would try to amuse her with domestic tales to which she paid no attention, and yet she needed the continuous and abominable chatter. Another way of passing time was to contemplate her jewels, to look at herself in her famous mirror, to change her dresses fifteen times a day. Gifted with a great practical sense, she saw to it that the underground cellars were always well supplied; she also concerned herself with her daughters' future—her daughters who always lived so far away from her; she administered her fortune with intelligence, and she occupied herself with all the little details that rule the profane order of our lives.

XI. SEVERE MEASURES

> . . . the law, cold and aloof by its very nature,
> has no access to the passions that might
> justify the cruel act of murder.
> —Sade

For six years the Countess murdered with impunity. During those years there had been countless rumours about her. But the name of Bathory, not only illustrious but also diligently protected by the Hapsburgs, frightened her possible accusers.

Toward 1610, the king had in his hands the most sinister reports—together with proofs—concerning the Countess. After much hesitation, he decided to act. He ordered the powerful Thurzo, Count Palatine, to investigate the tragic events at Csejthe and to punish the guilty parties.

At the head of a contingent of armed men, Thurzo arrived unannounced at the castle. In the cellar, cluttered with the remains of the previous night's bloody ceremony, he found a beautiful, mangled corpse and two young girls who lay dying. But that was not all. He smelled the smell of the dead; he saw the walls splattered with blood; he saw the Iron Maiden, the cage, the instruments of torture, bowls of dried blood, the cells—and in one of them a group of girls who were waiting their turn to die and who told him that after many days of fasting they had been served roast flesh that had once belonged to the bodies of their companions.

The Countess, without denying Thurzo's accusations, declared that these acts were all within her rights as a noble woman of ancient lineage. To which the Count Palatine replied: "Countess, I condemn you to life imprisonment within your castle walls."

Deep in his heart, Thurzo must have told himself that the Countess should be beheaded, but such an exemplary punishment would have been frowned upon, because it affected not only the Bathory family, but also the nobility in general. In the meantime, a notebook was found in the Countess's room, filled with the names and descriptions of the 610 victims in her handwriting. The followers of Erzebet, when brought before the judge, confessed to unthinkable deeds and perished on the stake.

Around her the prison grew. The door and windows of her room were walled up; only a small opening was left in one of the walls to allow her to receive food. And when everything was ready, four gallows were erected on the four corners of the castle to indicate that within those walls lived a creature condemned to death.

In this way she lived for three years, almost wasting away with cold and hunger. She never showed the slightest sign of repentance. She never understood why she had been condemned. On August 21, 1614, a contemporary historian wrote: "She died at dawn, abandoned by everyone."

She was never afraid, she never trembled. And no compassion, no sympathy or admiration may be felt for her. Only a certain astonishment at the enormity of the horror, a fascination with a white dress that turns red, with the idea of total laceration, with the imagination of a silence starred with cries in which everything reflects an unacceptable beauty.

Like Sade in his writings, and Gilles de Rais in his crimes, the Countess Bathory reached beyond all limits the uttermost pit of unfettered passions. She is yet another proof that the absolute freedom of the human creature is horrible.

Translated by Alberto Manguel

Alejandra Pizarnik

IN THIS NIGHT, IN THIS WORLD

to Martha Isabel Moia

in this night in this world
the words of the dream of childhood of death
that is never what one wants to say
the native tongue castrates
the tongue is an organ of cognition
of the failure of every poem
castrated by its own tongue
which is the organ of re-creation
of re-cognition
but not of resurrection
of something like negation
of my horizon of maldoror with his dog
and nothing is promise
among the expressible
which is the same as lying
(everything that can be said is a lie)
the rest is silence
except silence doesn't exist

no
words
don't make love
they make absence
if I say *water*, am I drinking?
if I say *bread*, am I eating?

in this night in this world
extraordinary the silence of this night
what is happening with the soul is that it's not seen
what is happening with the mind is that it's not seen

what is happening with the spirit is that it's not seen
where does this conspiracy of invisibilities come from?
no word is visible
shadows
viscous enclosures
where the stone of folly hides
black hallways
I have gone through them all
oh, stay among us a little longer!

my person is wounded
my first person singular

I write like someone with a knife raised in darkness
I write like I am saying
absolute sincerity would continue being
the impossible
oh, stay among us a little longer!

the wearing out of words
deserting the palace of language
cognition between the legs
what did I do with the gift of sex?
oh my dead ones
I ate them up I choked
I can't stand not being able to stand it

muffles words
everything slides
toward the black liquification
and maldoror's dog
in this night in this world
where everything is possible
except
poems

Alejandra Pizarnik

I speak
knowing it's not about that
always it's not about that
oh help me write the most dispensable poem
        the one that can't be used
        even to be useless
help me write words
in this night in this world

Translated by María Rosa Fort and Frank Graziano

DEATH AND THE YOUNG WOMAN (SCHUBERT)

Death and the young woman
embracing in the woods
devour the heart of music
in the heart of nonsense

a young woman carries a seven-arm candelabra
and dances behind the sad musicians
who play on broken violins
around a green woman clasping a unicorn and a
                         blue woman clasping a rooster

at the bottom
and in the sad region
are the small dwellings
seen by no one
made of wood, damp
and sinking like ships,
was this, then, the ideal of space?
creatures in sweet erection
and the blue woman
with the eye of happiness focused straight
on the conjurer's season of dead loves.

Translated by Daisy C. de Filippis

Elena Poniatowska (Mexico)

HAPPINESS

Yes, my love, yes I'm next to you, yes, my dear, yes, I love
you my love, yes, you plead with me not to tell you so often, I know,
I know, these are big words, spoken once and for all life, you never
call me love, my paradise, my love, my heaven, you don't believe in
paradise love, yes my love, take care of me, I don't ever want to leave
these four walls, let me stay in your arms, surround me with your
eyes, cover me with your eyes, save me, protect me, love, happiness,
don't go away, look there is that word again, I bump into it constantly, give me your hand, later you'll say, but I want to feel it now, say it
now, look, the sun, the heat comes in and these tenacious branches
from the ivy with their tiny hard leaves that sneak in through the
warmth of the window and grow in your room and *intertwine* with
us, and I need them, I love them, they bind us together, because,
love, I need you, you are needed, that's it, you are needed and you
know it, my needed man who hardly ever says my name, next to you
I don't have a name and when you say this and the other, my name
is never present and you reject my words, happiness, love, I love
you, because you are wise and you don't like to name things, even
though happiness is there, *watching*, with its happy name floating in
the air, on top of us, in the twilight of the afternoon, and if I say its
name it vanishes, and then shadows come and I say to you, love,
give me back the light, then your fingertips travel my body from my
forehead to the tip of my toe, along a path selected by you, examin-
ing me, and I lay motionless, on my side, with my back toward you
and you retrace your fingertips along my sides from the tip of my
toe to my forehead, stopping suddenly at my hip and say, you have
lost weight and I think of a skinny horse like the one Cantinflas'
musketeer used when he hung his feather blanket on its bony rump,
because I, my love, I am your old nag, and I can't gallop anymore
and I await you watchfully, yes, I watch you, telling you, don't leave

me, you have nothing to do but to be with me, with your hand on my hip, no, we won't leave this place, tie me up, put your shirt on me, you laugh because it looks so big on me, don't laugh, go and get lemonade from the kitchen because it's hot and we are thirsty, go on, go, no, wait for me, I'll go, no, I'll go, well you go, wait, don't get up, now it's my turn, I already went running for the lemonade and I'm here again next to you, as you lie on the bed, free and naked like dusk, drink some of it, drink the bright light, don't you realize, I don't want the sun to go away while we drink happiness, I don't want the sun to go away or for you to stop stretching out like that, in the timeless afternoon and evening that come in through the window, our window, look, cover it with your hand, so the night will stay out, a window should be there forever, although you can cover the sun for me with a finger, yes, my love, yes, I'm here, your window to the world, cover me with your hand, dim me like the sun, you can make the night, you breathe and the air ceases to flow through the window, how happy we are, look how warm you are, the window has remained motionless like me, static forever, cover me with your hand, Oh! how I forget it all!, the window protects our only exit, our communication with the stars, I love you, my love, let's go to heaven while the neighbor does the wash in the yard, in her yard, a laundress's yard, while here in your yard no one washes and there is wild ivy in the sink, it's tall and the wind makes it sway because it can't blow clothes on an empty clothesline, you remember, in October a sunflower grew there, small, emaciated, but I felt it swirl over my womb, in my tossed hair, disarranged, sad and yellow like a small abandoned garden, a tiny garden in the outskirts of the city climbing through the thatch and coming here and enter-ing through the window to this house of crumbs, a white bread house, where I am in the heart of tenderness, a golden house, round as hope, ring around the rosie, house of happiness, have pity on us, surround us with your lime walls, don't open your door, don't toss us out in the open, we have filled you with words, look, look, say again: my love, my paradise, my paradise, my love, the heat rises and I don't know what to do anymore to silence my heartbeats and I don't move, you see, don't say I look like a locust, a grasshopper, don't say I look like a dressed flea, I don't move any longer, you see, why do you tell me: be calm, if I'm not doing anything, I only ask you if you want to sleep, and you bring me close to you, I embrace you and I pin myself to your mouth like a medal, and I know you don't want to, you don't want to sleep, you only want us to be still, still and tame while the heat rises from the earth, and grows, throbbing us, I love you, my love, we are the couple, the archetype, I lean against you, I lay my head like a medallion on your chest, I inscribe myself on to you, like a love word coined in your mouth, there are flames on your lips, heat that suddenly melts my being, now on the Pentecost holy day, but we'll never die, right? because no one loves each other as we do, no one loves each other like this because you and I are we and no one is stronger than the two of us, here, locked up in your chest and in mine, let me see you, you are inside of me, look at me with my eyes, don't close them, don't sleep my love, don't go away into sleep, your eyelids are closing, look at me, let me see you, don't leave me, don't let the sun go away, I don't want it to dim, to set, don't yield like the light, the sun, leave everything as it was over my medlar skin, look, you can see me now better than ever because the afternoon is coming to an end, because you are leaving me also, and here I am telling you: don't leave me, be with me forever, strong as the burning sun I stared at as a child with my open eyes, until I saw black, black like the routine ending of fairy tales with the princess living happily ever after with many, many children, don't sleep, don't sleep I'm telling you, anxiously, constantly, with no afterwards, because there is no afterwards anymore for us, even if you leave me, but you'll never leave me, you'll have to come to pick me up, to put the pieces back together once again on the bed and here I am in one piece, and you can't leave me because you would have to return and you would miss a part of me forever, like the missing piece from a puzzle that ruins the entire picture, all the life you had given me and you can't take away from me because you would die, you would go blind and you wouldn't be able to find me limping, crippled, maimed by you, without words, mute, with the word final sealing my lips, the final ending of all stories, there is no longer a story, I don't tell you stories, endings, nothing counts anymore, things get transformed, there's no longer an extra hour on earth, look, the window screen has holes, I can see the two butterflies on the wall with their papier-maché wings, yellow, pink, orange, and the cotton candy and that small wooden bird you bought on the street the Friday everything began, the yellow Friday like the tiny bird black and shocking pink that pecks us ever since, a child's toy, like the paper butterflies that fly round the park until the real ones leave their cocoons, like the ones you crucified in the other room, big ones, with their marvelous blue transparent wings, you pierced them with a pin, one on top of the other, with a pin that hurts me and I asked you how you did it, well, doing it, and you strung up happiness, you petrified it there on the wall, happy, again this word, I repeat it, it comes back, it returns and I repeat it, and you get irritated and you tell me, there goes the donkey off again to the wheat field, to the greedy blossom of happiness, don't you understand, no, I don't understand, help me to pull out the weeds, help me to walk through God's wheat fields pinned down with the needle without the other butterfly, you say now we are all alone pinned down with the needle, without the other butterfly, that no one belongs to anyone, that what we share is sufficient, and enough, and is even miraculous, yes, yes, yes, my love, it's miraculous, don't close your eyes, I do understand, don't be silent, don't sleep, open up and look at me, you're tired and in a short while you'll fall asleep, you'll enter the river, and I'll remain on the bank, the bank we walked together, do you remember, under the eucalyptus, walking to the pace of the river, under the leaves, under the swords of light, I'm open to all wounds, here, I brought you my young spreading womb, I give you my teeth big and strong like tools and I don't feel ashamed of myself anymore, I lie, yes, I do feel ashamed, and I tell all the nuns I like roses with thorns and all, under the black skirts, while they play with their rosaries, and the wind and the light can't vibrate between their legs, leave this place birds of ill omen, get out, tiny threads of life, withered corner cob-

webs, full of dust, get out, narrow, half-opened doors, go into mourning, spying crevices, get out brooms, let me sweep the world with all of you, you that swept out so many colored papers from my soul, and you love stay, I wish I had met you when I was older, spinning near the hearth my longings for you, even if you had never arrived, and singing to myself the same old song, when I was young he would fall asleep under my window, even if it weren't true, because now you came early, before I had time to get up, and you put your hand on the slit of the door, and you moved the latch, and I liked your pants with their bulging pockets, your pockets that seem to carry inside of them all of life's accidents, and your own thoughts, like little balls of wrapped caramel candy, your thoughts, tell me, what are you thinking my love?, tell me what are you thinking right now, just right now when you stay like this as if you were with yourself, alone, forgetting that I'm here with you, my love, what are you thinking? I always ask the same, do you love me?, you're falling asleep, I know you'll fall asleep and I'll get dressed without making a sound, and I'll close the door carefully, to leave you there wrapped in the warm red and ocher of the afternoon, because you have fallen asleep and you don't belong to me anymore and you didn't take me with you, you left me behind, today in the afternoon when the sun and the warm light were pounding through the window, and I am going to walk a lot, a lot, and the neighbor will see me from her door, with her disapproving look because only from time to time do I venture through this path, I'll walk up to the eucalyptus trees, until I'm exhausted, until I accept that you are a sleeping body over there, and that I am another one here walking and that together the two of us are
hopelessly,
hopelessly,
madly,
desperately,
alone.

Translated by Carmen C. Esteves

❦ Ilke Brunhilde Laurito (Brazil)

GENETRIX I

In the beginning was the Womb.

The dark breast fed the world
and darkness conceived the pre-dawn day.

And then came light.

And the sea became an embryo of fish,
the air, a germination of birds.
The earth, on different gestating levels,
fertilized as flower, fruit, reptile, and beast.

In the gravitation of space,
the Sun:
an egg on fire.

GENETRIX III

SHE:
An animal with smooth skin,
without scales or feathers
But with hands and legs.

Between feet and forehead,
the fertile trunk
fructifying thighs,
buttocks

breasts.
In the middle
of the thick forest,
in a covered
cave
the beast awaits.

GENETRIX V

Open sky: the ceiling.
The floor—the earth's ground.
Four architectural winds
of walls and foundations.
The house (the universe).
A small volcano
in the middle of the clearing.
Around her
the domestic animals
warm themselves
and SHE
falls asleep
with a docile snake
intertwined between her legs.

GENETRIX VI

"It is not good for you to be alone,"
crackles
the fire's voice

AND SHE
Perceives in her dream
a strange animal,
in her image and likeness
(but of shallow chest,
and unexpected protrusions)

There was the snake
—the same, only violent—
furious prisoner
between the tense thighs,
rigid and ready to leap
with is effective poison.

Translated by Paula Milla-Kreutzer

🍐 Luisa Valenzuela (Argentina)

DIRTY WORDS

Good girls can't say these things, neither can elegant ladies or any other women. They can't say these things or other things, for there is no possibility of reaching the positive without its opposite, the exposing and exposed negative. Not even the other women, the ones who aren't so lady-like, can utter these words categorized as "dirty." The big ones, the fat ones: *swearwords*. These words that are so delicious to the palate, that fill the mouth. *Swearwords*. These words that completely spare us from the horror gathered in a brain almost ready to explode. There are cathartic words, moments of speech that should be inalienable and that have been alienated from us from time immemorial.

During childhood, mothers or fathers—why always blame women—washed our mouths with soap and water when we said some of these so-called swearwords, "dirty" words, when we expressed our truth. Then came better times, but those unloving interjections and appellatives remained forever dissolved in detergent soapsuds. To clean, to purify the word, the best possible form of repression. This was known in the Middle Ages, and in the darkest regions of Brittany, France, until recently. Witches' mouths—and we are all witches today—are washed with red salt to purify them. Substituting one orifice for the other, as Margo Glantz would say, the mouth was and continues to be the most threatening opening of the feminine body: it can eventually express what shouldn't be expressed, reveal the hidden desire, unleash the menacing differences which upset the core of the phallogocentric, paternalistic discourse.

No sooner said than done, from the spoken word to the written word: just one step. Which requires all the courage we can muster because we believe that it is so simple; however, it isn't because writing will overcome all the abysses and so one must have an awareness of the initial danger, of the abyss. We must forget the washed mouths, allow the mouths to bleed till we gain access to the territory in which everything can and *should* be said. Knowing that there is so much to explore, so many barriers yet to be broken through.

It is a slow and untiring task of appropriation. A transformation of that language consisting of "dirty" words that was forbidden to us for centuries, and of the daily language that we should handle very carefully, with respect and fascination because in some way it doesn't belong to us. We are now tearing down and rebuilding; it is an arduous task. Dirtying those washed mouths, taking possession of the punishment, with no room for self-pity.

Among us, crying is prohibited. Other emotional manifestations, other emotions no, but crying yes, prohibited. We can, for example, give estrus free reign and be happy. Jealousy, on the other hand, we must maintain under strict control; it could degenerate into weeping.

Why so much fear of tears? Because the masks we use are made of salt. A stinging, red salt which makes us beautiful and majestic but devours our skin.

Beneath the red masks, our faces are raw and the tears could well dissolve the salt and uncover our sores. The worst penitence.

We cover ourselves with salt and the salt erodes us and protects us at the same time. Red salt, the most beautiful of all and the most destructive. Long ago, they scrubbed our mouths with red salt of infamy and we remained branded forever. Witches, they accused us, they persecuted us, until we learned how to take possession of that salt and we made beautiful masks for ourselves. Iridescent, skin-toned, translucent with promise.

Now if they want to kiss us—and sometimes they still do—they have to kiss the salt and burn their lips. We know how to respond to kisses and we don't mind being burnt with them from the other side of the mask. They/us, us/they. The salt now joins us, the sores join us and only weeping can bring us apart.

We mate with our masks on, and sometimes the thirsty come to lick us. It is a perverse pleasure: they become more thirsty than ever and it hurts and the dissolution of the masks terrifies us. They lick more and more, they moan in desperation, we moan with pain and fear. What will become of us when our stinging faces outcrop? Who will want us without a mask, in raw flesh?

They won't. They will hate us for that, for having licked us, for having exposed us. And we wouldn't have even shed a tear nor allowed ourselves our most intimate gesture: the self-disintegration of our mask thanks to the prohibited weeping that opens furrows in order to begin again.

Now our mask is the text, the one that we ourselves, the women, the keepers of textuality and texture, can dissolve if we care to—or not. Reconstruct it, modify it, make our own those words that for others were dirty—dirty in our female mouths, of course—and use that which was meant to stigmatize us in order to arm, as always, our defensive shells. Between two hard covers. Reflect our images in the book, in the text, the other face of the female body, even though it may not be conspicuously female, even though it may elicit the doubtful compliment that we have all probably heard at one time.

"But what an excellent novel (or short story, or poem): it seems like a man's writing!"

At one time, perhaps, we would have been flattered by such nonsense. Now we know. It *seems*, but it is not. Because what we have ultimately come to learn best is to read, to read and decipher according to our own codes.

For a long time now we have been writing bit by bit, each time more fiercely and with greater self-awareness. Women in the arduous task of constructing with materials inscribed by the other. Constructing not from zero, which would have been easier, but rather transgressing the barriers of censorship, destroying the canons in search of that authentic voice which can't be destroyed by anything, not soap nor rock salt, not the fear of castration, nor tears.

Translated by Cynthia Ventura

Excerpt from *The Efficacious Cat*
THE FUCKING GAME

This is a game I invented to pass the time with company. Anyone can learn it: it is simple, does not mess up the house, and distracts one from daily preoccupations. It is best played in pairs and is easier if the components of each pair belong to sexes that are sufficiently differentiated.

It is convenient, although not indispensable, to have a bed handy and to play in semi-darkness. Mid-court shots are absolutely forbidden.

As there are no winners or losers, fucking hardly ever creates disputes.

The game is over when one of the two—or more—participants collapses in exhaustion; which does not mean the player has been defeated, in fact just the opposite. Those that extend themselves the most are the better players.

Rules:

—The faking of sensations is prohibited.

—One must take care that the other partner also participates in the game.

—Great mirth and the elimination of overbearing behavior are required.

Mode of play:

One of the players should assume the more or less active role. That is, they will begin the game by stretching out a hand over their opponent trying to lodge it into the other player's more secluded parts. This first movement will begin to heat up the game, especially if the other person at first resists playing. Once the hand is located and warmed up, player number 1 will move his or her entire body near player number 2 and both will begin to practice a type of mouth to mouth respiration that we will call kissing. This is a very healthy exercise that oxygenates the lungs and inspires further play.

At no time should one forget that hand that has been

advancing without having to reach for the dicebox. On the contrary, one ought to try to introduce at least one finger into the dicebox of the opponent, rotating—the finger, that is—with caution.

At this point in the game, player number 2 should begin to act, if they have not been too stunned to do so before now. To carry this out, the player should also stretch out one hand or two and proceed to unbutton or unzip below the waistline of player number 1. At last he or she will find something surprising. Upon not finding it, refer to the test that we offer below and do not emit immoderate screams, which are in bad taste in this game and break the mood. They should, however, ponder warmly over what has been found, without permitting extended lapses of time between mouth to mouth respirations.

One must never forget that this is a game of pleasure and not a competition, and good sportsmanship should prevail above all else. Therefore, it is best to reserve for the end the culmination of the fucking game—known as the orgasm—and not proceed to it before entering into the second phase.

In the second phase the players, without quite knowing how or when, should have become completely naked. Neither modesty nor prudence have a place in this game. We will reserve these two qualities for the kidnapping game which will be explained in another installment.

To play the fucking game it is best not to think and simply allow oneself to be invaded by joyful tingles and diverse sensations. The moment has arrived to stretch out on the bed and shift the mouth to mouth respiration to other parts of the body.

All good players ought to have reached this point without getting too baffled—something that can ruin the game—murmuring the particulars of each play as they proceed.

Once in a horizontal position the voice can be raised and it is no longer necessary to emit intelligible words. We have arrived at the point in which the two players truly enter into contact, as they produce the partial penetration of one by the other. Each should then carry out an oscillating motion combined with a rotation that turns the partial penetration into a total and very pleasurable sensation.

This is the hardest part of the game, and consists of attempting the greatest number and variety of positions without breaking contact. The game is enriched in direct proportion to the imagination and the enthusiasm displayed by each one of the participants.

The game ends with moans and sighs, but can be recommenced as often as desired. Or as often as possible.

Warning:

Unfortunately, as fucking is also a task undertaken to propagate the species, it is advisable to conduct a thorough study of the necessary precautions that must be carried out in order to impart a truly sporting character to the game.

GASTROPARENTAL TEST

Before attempting the fucking game it is advisable to take the following test to form couples with like or opposite tastes, whichever may be desired.

a) Read with care the following definitions:

PAPAR: to eat soft food without chewing.
MAMAR: to suck milk from breasts.

(Petite Illustrated Larousse)

b) Answer sincerely the following questions:
—Are you a man or a woman?
—Who do you love best, your father or your mother?
—Do you prefer to papar or mamar?

Translated by Margarite Fernández Olmos

Rosario Ferré (Puerto Rico)

RICE AND MILK

Once upon a time there was a very blond and fair-skinned young man named Rice, who for the last five years had been looking for a bride without any luck. For three days the bride-to-be had to answer all his questions:

> How can one saw a wave?
> How can one shear a mirror without scissors?

Only if she could answer would he make her his wife, sole heir to his sugar cane plantation.

Rice was not only very fair, he was also very rich. He was the richest young planter in the whole province. When he rode his horse down the streets of the town, the passersby would sing:

> Rice is looking for a bride
> who should be as fair as milk,

and Rice would answer them:

> who must knit, who must purl
> gather, stitch and interlace
> her needles at a perfect pace.

One day Rice rode in front of a house where a beautiful girl from out of town was staying for a visit, whose name was Milk. She was standing at the window, watering a basil pot, when Rice asked her:

> Maiden of the basil pot
> How many leaves have buds in your shrub?

And the girl answered him:

> Young man with the dark eyes
> How many stars shine in the sky?

For the first time in his life, Rice was unable to answer. He looked at her in surprise, and then rode on down the road. That very afternoon, when he arrived at his house, he sent for the girl to come and visit him.

As soon as Milk heard she was to see Rice that evening, she began to sew a gown made of the finest blue silk, which changed colors as she walked. If she went out on a sunny day, it made her vanish into thin air; if she went walking under the rain, it made her turn all gray.

When the dress was finished, she tried it on. It covered her like a shroud, from shoulder to ankle, so that it was impossible to guess her shape. She only left one small opening, an eyelet through which she would show her hand at the right moment, so that Rice could kiss it.

That night Rice gave a great feast at his house. When they were all seated at the table, he decided to question the girl once more, and he told her:

> Maiden of iridescent silk
> ask for any delectable dish,
> a nightingale's heart, a cinnamon star
> a crescent of pink macaroons,
> and if it isn't served on the spot
> I promise I'll make you my spouse
> and give you the keys to my house.

The girl looked at him sadly, because she wasn't interested in Rice's money, but only in his love. Suddenly she was afraid, because even though his request seemed harmless enough, it had been made in such angry tones that Milk wondered what he really meant. But she answered bravely:

> Young man with dark eyes,
> if you can serve me a slice of baked ice
> I'll be your wife.

Rice immediately ordered the cooks to put a slice of ice in the oven, but the minute the fires in the kitchen were lit it melted, and when the servants brought the tray to the table, all the guests could do was ladle warm water onto their dishes. Then Rice ordered the cooks to build a huge bonfire outside the house and to put a block of ice ten feet long and ten feet wide on a spigot. They turned and turned the spigot as slowly as possible, but it was to no avail. The block of ice melted, and the water dripped and put out the fire. That very night, Rice proclaimed that Milk had won, and so he would take her to be his bride.

The wedding day came along, and Milk walked up the aisle still wearing her gown of iridescent silk. When she stood in front of the altar, it made her blend with the smoking candles, and when she walked out of the church it made her look as if the sun had dissolved her into thin hair. Rice held her hand tightly, as though afraid to let her go.

That evening Milk locked herself up in the bridal suite, with the excuse that she had to make the marriage bed ready. She took off her silk dress and sewed up all its openings tightly. Then she filled it with honey and laid it out carefully on the bed. Then she cut several locks from her hair and slipped them on top of the dress under the bedsheet, before hiding herself as well as she could behind the drapes. When Rice came into the room, he thought Milk was asleep. He sat on the bed, and the first thing he did was look for Milk's hand to kiss it, but he couldn't find it. Then he took out a knife hidden under his jacket, and, without lifting the coverlets, plunged it deep into his bride's body. As the honey spilled all over the bed and the floor, some drops fell on his lips. Then Rice let out a wail and cried:

Oh Maiden of iridescent silk!
If I had known you were this sweet
I never would have slain you.

The next day, Rice's friends found him lying on the bed, with a long knitting needle buried on the left side of his chest. When Milk, now dressed in widow's weeds, went back home to her family, the people of the town sang as she rode by:

Rice at last did find a bride
who was just as fair as Milk,
who could knit, who could purl
gather, stitch and interlace
her needles at the perfect place.

Translated by Rosario Ferré

FABLE OF THE BLED HERON

She wants to cry out before her mirror,
hurl forth her wail upon its burnished shield.
Diamond hard and sperm-like it runs down her face,
and joins the ebb and flow of the universal river
that brings the moon to term over her legs.

She wants to deliver herself unto herself
as restless in death as she was terrible in life
her arms entwined and budding around her chest
like new sprung boughs,
her hips full grown and splitting in half
like ripe melons cleft by time
into twin gourds of equally edible
flesh, so that from their cool, red soul
a shower of black seeds may fall to earth.

She wants to enter into the magic circle
of her embroidered frame;
etch her words onto the glass surface
with the acid flow of her sex,
a cool cut of the cunt,
a clitoris spire cut,
a wave of patterns cut inside the stone.
Right now she's deep into her needlework,
she weaves her words patiently, picking up
the strand of glycerine that shines most
dangerously, deep inside the design,
and her syllables interlace their threads
to tell the details of her story:

"At night they name me maiden mother
when they praise me with their garnet tongues,
it's not my body they sing, but my shadow,

not my faithful flesh but my hallowedness,
the malignant perfume of my sickness.

For my body—"would blossom into semen."
For my eyes—"would rather read a poem."
For my hands—"like the wings of the soul,
each palm must have five fingers."
For my face—"give me
the dark side of the mirror,
rather than let them look upon it!"

"They make love to my twin sister every morning
in a pure, lustless fashion
they bathe in the icy current of her arms;
her light curves on their wrists
like a murderer's blade
and severs the veins cleanly,
they lie down by the banks of her face
as by an Alpine lake
and dream on their own reflections.

"They advise my twin to look upon herself
with a clear conscience,
they carry her all over on a dais
wreathed in ivy and swathed in folds
of passionate brocade, they kiss the ivory soles
of her feet, *Yseault aux blanc pieds*,
they promenade her up and down the street
crowned with diamonds and daggers.

"Venus of Kostenki, Cycladic idol
from faraway Lespugues, her twin souls
ensconced in one sole body, her heart
irreverently playing a duet
requiring two players and four hands

or dancing the quadrille on the sidewalk,
to the ripple of the rhythm
of the steel two by fours,
as she sails down her own coast.

"All to mother, Void to widow,
Wager to wife,
None to sister and Orfan's daughter,
she defiles everything she touches:
wounds open afresh,
milk curdles,
wine turns rancid,
dogs go insane,
honeycombs wilt,
bread will not leaven.

"Portal of her mother's tomb,
her body is a perfect causeway;
snow storms will not close it, nor will heat;
milk is her most terrifying calamity
it floods in daily, in great gushes,
and sows new faces, arms and elbows
within her warm furrows.
Legs and shoulders grow there like vines
around each other,
eyes come up from the deep
and detach themselves from Oblivion
where they lay sealed for ages;
she has awakened them,
and brought them forth into the light.

Her womb is a chaos of vegetation
Amazon armada armageddon
hands, faces, arms
all growing

and feverishly multiplying,
fathers, brothers, sons,
a vine of sinews nurtured by her blood
and someone else's
until the wind polishes her foliage.

"Her belly is a shadow box
where generations are at play;
a platonic cavern where voices echo
into players, where thoughts, gestures
and words collide and frolic with each other
like migrating flocks of birds.

Who will dare question her supremacy?
In her name cities have been demolished
and oceans polluted,
temples have been hewn from live rock,
epics and symphonies composed,
guided missiles detonated
with a simple gesture of her index finger
pressed on the golden triangle of the sun.
Her face has been conceived a hundred score,
mother, sister, daughter
—the mold was patented and refined—
(yet never redesigned in a millennium).
Her body was a restless tower,
a turmoil veering in the wind,
arrogant and worthy of any man's heir
that takes his lost paradise for granted.

Who will dare name her victorious
when death is her dweller and proprietor?
Who will admit her to the vestal arbors
where revelers sing the mysteries of the tongue
and drink from the Castalian springs

when she's ignorant of her origin and of her purpose
and lives darting from branch to branch
like a bled heron
suspicious of her own lightness
unable to soar without the Mistral at her back?

Her face is a salt mine from which few return,
her will is an iron needle
which seams her to transparency.
She is Dido on her pyre of perfumed oaks
pining for the swift sailing Aeneas
beneath the bastions of Carthage,
Galatea besieged by Polyphemus
on Sicily's azure coast,
Phaedra abandoned by Theseus
beside the labyrinth's infernal void.

Woe to my name as well as to my fate
if I should go on breathing beneath her eyes,
or trust that treacherous mirror
which men hold before my face
when they wish me her image and likeness
—Better Medusa, my head seething with serpents!

Better assail her classical perfection,
grind it to dust, demolish it
as she sits primly on her throne
holding on to her wooden spoon
with both hands,
intent on being economical
when her husband throws the house out the window
at every business transaction.

She has cleft in two, in one fell swoop
her reason for existence from her reasonableness;

refused to become logical, inductive, analytical
and at every thrust of her silver knife
essays to console and give sustenance.

Nothing is more devastating than a mother's heart
returning from the dead.
Howling winds are not more deadly,
her face and hair in turmoil
as she holds out both her eyes
on the palms of her hands
and struggles to retrieve what she has lost.
Words, motions, gestures of days past
children flying by like flocks of geese
migrating from spring to fall,
her arms full laden with crimson ovaries
that have ripened and fallen to pod.

She strides into her lover's chamber
as she would onto a public beach
with no door, ceiling or windows,
the keel of her ship carefully trimmed
and her troops well provided for,
ready for conquest.

Passion is her only master:
she sits naked before his mirror
this side of the river of life
and her soul chatters with her cunt
from lark to lark;
high-priest Anubis, the crooner of quasars,
becomes her favorite vocalist
as she hums on his ancient melodies.

She unveils daily before her admirers;
makes them feel the weight of her breasts,

lets them spy on her soul
through the secret keyhole in her ear.
They pursue her heart
down the mangroves of her belly
and listen to the rush of its joy
under her silent navel.

She plucks her eyebrows and shaves her armpits
as though she were peeling oranges,
she sits under the mane of the sun
and suddenly falls to earth
like a flayed grapefruit.

She walks, perspires and applies herself
with vigour to the task
of survival, drinks sparingly
eats a spartan fare,
lives of her own flesh,
quaffs the sea's ale, the planet's loam
fresh off the loins of the earth,
consumes the clitoral compost of ages,
dresses up her own rib
for tomorrow's elegant repast,
limes and inseminates herself
so well, so efficiently
distributed on the refectory table.

She gives birth
and nurses what she births,
in her cunt the Holy One is three
consubstantially.
Her womb is a hive of activity
full of humming verbs
only she will conjugate.
Her orgasms fling open a thousand doors

down endless passageways
through which she drifts and vanishes
each time her soul comes
to ecstasy.

Polyphemus' sister
she too has an all seeing eye
under the sails of her skirts.
With it she examines the world and herself;
the fear of having to be born
and of beginning to die.
She rises in its orchard at break of day
and at twilight lies next to its burning bush
as Venus, the moist planet, swings into her ken.
When it floods, she weighs anchor
and heads out to sea, as any sailor would
worth his salt.

She inhales its scent as if it were ether
and fits it to herself in times of travail,
perfectly conscious and aware
that a knot in time is a knot of life
when one gives birth to oneself."

Her story ended, she rises from her chair.
Her embroidery frame falls from her lap
and its magic circle is shattered
into a thousand fragments.
Her twin has swooned upon the splintered glass,
her veins emptying into a cloud of dust.
Mother, sister, daughter
come to the brim of that mirror
which no longer holds her fast;
she bleeds through a thousand wounds
which have turned into words.

Her blood is whiter than ether
or nitroglycerine.
She signs her name at the foot of the poem
before vanishing into thin air.

An English version by Rosario Ferré
August 1991

❦ Marjorie Agosín (United States/Chile)

MY STOMACH

Naked as in silence
I approach my stomach.
It has been changing like a summer
moving away from the sea,
or like a dress that grows wider by the hour.
My stomach
is more than just round,
because when I sit
it spreads out like a
flame,
then,
I touch it to remember
everything in it:
the salt and the happiness,
the winter's fried eggs
the milk I couldn't swallow in my youth,
the Coca-Cola that stained my teeth
the homesickness for a glass of wine
or a dish of potatoes fried in olive oil.

And in remembering,
I feel how it grows
and reaches each time more
ceremoniously for the ground,
it's even affectionate with my feet and my toes
that could never have belonged to a princess.

I rejoice
in having a stomach as wide as the
hats my grandmother wore
in summer.

This Sunday, the seventh,
at seventy-seven years of age,
my stomach
is still my own,
and proudly promenades along the seashore.
Some say I am old and ugly now,
that my breasts are mistaken for my gut
but my stomach, here by my side, keeps me company,
and it is not fat that's overflowing,
only bits of flesh baking under the sun.

Translated by Daisy C. De Filippis

Marjorie Agosín

WHAT WE ARE

Love stops being what it used to be,
believe me, there's no need to pretend
to be asleep
between bodice and nightdress
nor to invent a penis
blasting off
in the darkness
of the marital crypt

We're no longer so epical
as fornicating, iconoclastic
a little bit the ladies out for
a good time, like young men for example,
with a casual screw
after lunch
and that's that.

Translated by Daisy C. De Filippis

PENIS

And so much has been written about breasts
breasts like hills
breasts of water
breasts where spring will bloom
and now
let's take on the penis
a penis like a wrinkle
a penis like a bowed head
a penis paying homage
to the enchantment of a slit.

A penis shaken with urine
tired of so much coming and going
a penis like the day's catch in the oven
or a broth of skinned chickens.

And now do you understand why it's time
to change the tune?

Translated by Daisy C. De Filippis

Cristina Peri Rossi (Uruguay)

THE WITNESS

I grew up among my mother's friends. I don't know how many there have been, nor can I claim to remember them all, but I haven't forgotten many of them, and though I may not have seen them again, or though they may visit the house only sporadically, I know who they are and have fond memories of them. I did not play with other children but rather with my mother's friends. The truth is that I am quite a lonely guy, and I prefer the company of machines to that of others like me. Machines, or my mother's friends. To begin with, they surface one at a time. For long periods of time my mother will have a single friend who practically lives in our house, sharing with us the food, the video sessions, the television shows, the outings, the games and the evenings at home. They have always been very tender towards me.

"I really enjoy not having other men around the house," I told my mother once, thanking her for not having blighted my childhood with the screams of a violent father or a demanding lover. Women are so much sweeter. I get along much better with them. I would not have liked sharing the house with other men; but I found it enchanting to share it with my mother's friends.

I think my mother felt the same way. Since she and my father separated—when I was very young—the house was only visited by women, and that was very comforting. I assume my father also found it so. The first one I remember was a rather dark-skinned girl with a high-pitched voice and bright black eyes. My mother was very young then, and I was only three years old. We went on a lot of outings together; I slept in my room, and the two of them slept, together, in my mother's room. But sometimes I would get up at night and appear in the master bedroom. Then one of them would take me in her arms and cuddle me, and I would fall asleep between them, cradled by the warmth of their naked bodies. Another one, however, had long blond hair, and it gave me great pleasure to run my fingers, like summer butterflies, through it. My mother used to comb her hair very carefully, sliding the tortoise-shell comb down her silky hair, which reached almost to her waist, while I watched. (I regretted many times not having been born a girl, so that my mother could brush my hair with the same fervor and absorption; I regretted being a short-haired boy and thus being excluded from something that afforded them so much pleasure.) There was another one, however, who was more masculine in appearance; she had broad shoulders, a robust body, a low voice, and seemed to be a very strong woman. She used to buy me lots of toys: she gave me a bicycle, several puzzles, and was always proposing competitive games, daring me to jump, box, swim. I did not have the same affection for her as I had for the others, but I enjoyed her horseplay and beating her at chess. The excessive attention she gave me used to bother my mother, and I think that they once argued about it, but I put my mother's fears to rest, telling her that I certainly preferred her, that she was more beautiful and more intelligent.

The most recent one was a young actress. She had starred in a movie, which I did not see, since my mother did not deem it appropriate for me. We had to protect her, that's what my mother told me. She had had an unhappy childhood and now she needed to learn a lot of things before continuing her career: we were going to give her a home and the knowledge she lacked.

My mother was a very generous woman. She was always helping someone, and she brought me up to do likewise. We have helped a lot of women, even though they have since disappeared from the house. In our house they find a roof, food, warmth, books, music, and affection. You could tell right away that the actress needed protection: even though she was cheerful, amusing and very likable, she was not very consistent and seemed to lack method.

"You will learn to study with my son," my mother told her. And indeed, from the beginning my mother assigned her tasks: she had to do English and French exercises, and she recommended a series of books from our library for her to read.

It was beautiful to watch them together, listening to opera, trying out each other's clothes, exchanging dresses. Sometimes the actress would wear a blouse and skirt of my mother's; at other times, my mother would wear the actress's pants, English hat, and white scarf. I learned from my mother that the actress had abandoned her home, which had not been a real home, and that now, in our house she had finally found a refuge.

"The company will do you good," my mother told me, "you're growing lonelier by the day."

And indeed, I enjoyed her company. Helena had big blue eyes, she was tall and thin, and her long and white neck was like the stem of a wine glass. I grew very fond of her. I let her come into my room—where not even my mother was allowed—and showed her my drawings; she listened to my favorite albums. I liked looking at her. She had agile and subtle movements, not awkward like mine (I've grown a lot lately and can't control my limbs very well); she spoke in a soft, delicate and very suggestive voice, and when she came near me, I felt vague stirrings. I especially liked to look at my butterfly collection with her. She seemed enraptured by the drawings of the butterfly wings, and she soon learned to classify them. We went on a couple of excursions to the countryside, looking for rare species, while my mother waited for us in the car reading one of her books.

My mother also taught her to cook, and she would sometimes surprise us by preparing one of our favorite dishes.

At night they slept together in my mother's bedroom. I tried to delay that moment, because I had grown accustomed to Helena's presence and had no desire to go to sleep. But once my mother announced it was bedtime it was very difficult to dissuade her to let me stay.

In the mornings, before I left for the institute, I went to my mother's bedroom to say goodbye. The door was always closed; I would knock softly, and when I heard that my mother was awake, I would push the door slightly and enter the darkened room. It was difficult to discern the figures in the dark, but my eyes would soon pinpoint the two bodies, one next to the other. Helena was always asleep, being obviously the heavier sleeper of the two. I would quietly kiss my mother and leave. But once I went in without knocking and saw Helena half-asleep, wearing a sheer gown; her cleavage showed precociously through the fabric, and I glimpsed her thighs, firm and resplendent, through the sheets.

The discovery dazzled me. That day at the institute I couldn't concentrate, I was distracted and restless, something that quite surprised my professors.

I returned home nervous and excited, hoping to find Helena there. She was, in effect, in the kitchen preparing a dessert, and it pleased me just to be near her, jumping and prancing around her to get her attention.

"Be still," she told me, laughing.

I adored her laughter. She was playful, daring, a bit childlike. My mother's laughter, on the other hand, was grave, low, mature. The laughter of a woman who can be severe.

After dinner, the two of them remained in the living room, sharing a book. I paced my room nervously, unwilling to study or to play with the machines. I wanted to be with Helena, but at this time of day she belonged to my mother.

I went to the bathroom and masturbated. I did it thinking of Helena's breasts and my mother's legs. Oh, my mother's legs. Earlier, when I was little, my mother used to walk around the house almost naked, displaying her beautiful white legs. They are full, luminous, like two Roman columns. Not even Helena's legs could compare to my mother's. Now, since Helena has been with us, my mother has stopped lounging almost naked in my presence.

After a while, I heard the door to the master bedroom close. They had obviously gone to lie down together in bed for a while. It both pained and gave me pleasure to imagine that moment. I could picture, like on a screen, my mother taking off her white silk blouse, and Helena shedding her black velvet pants. I could see them comparing their breasts, their thighs, their pubis. All this in silence, so as not to awaken my curiosity. Everything in silence, pretending they were asleep.

I did not need to spy through the keyhole. I knew the scene even though I had never witnessed it. The door to their room remained locked, closed to me with them inside. I was the excluded one, the rejected one, the absent one. I imagined a thousand and one schemes to intervene, to interrupt the scene playing itself out inside my mother's bedroom, but I knew I was too cowardly to avail myself of any of them. I didn't feel I had the courage to interrupt my mother, and I wasn't sure I would be able to withstand the vision of the two symmetrical bodies laying on the bed.

That night at dinner I had no appetite and felt somewhat hostile. I managed to annoy my mother, who exclaimed:

"I would like to know what is the matter with you. You are in an unbearable mood."

But Helena intervened on my behalf. She winked at me, smiled, and touched my leg with her foot under the table. Her complicity comforted me. I briefly held her foot with mine and spilled my glass of wine on the table deliberately to annoy my mother.

That night, when I went to my room, I could hear them arguing in the living room. My small fit of ill-humor had managed to disturb them and, satisfied with that small measure of revenge, I closed my door.

A week later I won the Drawing Competition organized by the institute. I was thrilled, and returned home eager to bring the good news to my mother. I opened the door with my key and found no one at home. It's true that I had returned home earlier than anticipated, but I was excited about the prize and wanted to share it with her. The house was in silence. I was on my way to my room when I saw a light in my mother's bedroom. I approached the closed door, and called.

"I have a migraine," my mother answered without opening the door. But I heard movements in the room, a rustle of clothes and sheets.

I assumed that Helena was inside. I was overcome by anguish, my eyes filled with tears.

"I'll be right out," my mother announced, sensing, perhaps,

that I had not moved from the door.

I think I blushed. My mother was on her knees, half-dressed, looking on the floor, like a dog, for the clothes she needed. It annoyed me to find her in such a position. "Go away!" she ordered me, imperiously, but I stayed. Her feet were bare, and she was only wearing a black lace camisole. I saw her beautiful white legs, the opulent breasts barely covered by the netting, the inflammation of her lips, her untidy hair. Next to her, still lying on the bed, was Helena. She started to laugh foolishly. She was naked and tried to cover herself with the sheet when she saw me.

I pounced on top of them. I am very tall, and my bulk pushed my mother onto the bed. In her surprise, she let out a ferocious and muffled cry.

"Go away!"

I held them both on the bed. Helena was laughing stupidly, disconcertedly. My mother, on the other hand, was surprised, and could not manage to understand the meaning of my eruption in the bedroom, something that violated the tacit accord that existed between us. I held them both down with my arms, and I also let out a grave, dull and anguishing scream.

Helena had started to cry. I don't like women who cry. I never saw my mother cry; she never allowed herself such weakness before me. I suddenly felt contempt for Helena for being so weak.

"Kiss her!" I ordered her. Helena sat on the bed, covering herself with the sheet, while I held my mother down, and she looked at me with an expression of surprise on her tear-stained face.

Suddenly I pulled the bedsheets away. It was a fast and violent gesture. Helena's body emerged from under the bedclothes, long and narrow, the marked bones on her shoulders, her nipples like purple grapes, the very dark pubic hair, the red toenails. I also saw my mother's broad neck, still covered with pink stains, the white and milky arms.

"Kiss her!" I ordered.

Sobbing, Helena approached my mother timidly. She kissed her on the mouth. It was a weary, flustered kiss, but I insisted.

"Kiss her!"

My mother struggled to break loose from my grasp, but she is not a strong woman, despite her height, and couldn't break free.

"Now," I ordered her, "grab her breasts."

Helena looked at me incredulously.

"Do it!" I bellowed.

I realized she was afraid. Slowly, hesitatingly, Helena brought her hands to my mother's breasts.

"You're crazy!" she cried, trying to break my hold on her.

"Once before you tried to rid yourself of me," I answered her. "This time, you won't succeed," I added.

Helena's trembling hands cupped my mother's breasts.

"The nipples," I indicated. "Squeeze her nipples."

Helena's eyes were full of dread.

"Do it," I suggested.

Helena barely touched her.

"More," I indicated.

Her fingers then squeezed my mother's nipples firmly.

"That's good," I said, approvingly.

"Lie on top of her," I added.

"What?" mumbled Helena, bewildered.

"Lie on top of her!" I yelled.

I had suddenly thrown my mother on the bed. I liked seeing her like that, half-naked, lying down, with the black lace and nylon camisole barely covering her belly, her waist, the lower part of her chest. A few curling hairs escaped through the lace.

Very softly Helena laid down over her.

"That's good," I whispered.

Her body, thinner and firmer, covered my mother's. I saw Helena's shorter hair, her rounded buttocks, her bare feet. My mother's body was barely underneath Helena's. Their arms rested on the pillow, and their foreheads touched. Now I could see four breasts, four legs, two united torsos, like a prodigious double statue, like two Siamese twins joined by an umbilical cord.

Then, I quickly lowered my pants and climbed the pyramid

they formed from behind.

Standing over them, I was the third figure in the triptych, the only one moving convulsively. I planted myself firmly on my thighs and pressed the women's two bodies under my weight. I quickly penetrated Helena from behind. She screamed. My mother, on the bottom, lying on the bed, panted.

I burst like a broken flower. I exploded. Then, exhausted, I left the room. I left them quickly. Before I closed the door, I said to my mother.

"Don't worry about me. Now I really am a man. The one that was lacking in this house."

Translated by Lizabeth Paravisini-Gebert

Cristina Peri Rossi

CA FOSCARI

I love you like my mirror image
my other my likeness
from slave to slave
        partners in the subversion
        of domesticated order
        I love you this and other nights
with our identifying marks
interchanged
        like we happily exchange our clothes
        and your dress is my dress
        and my sandals your sandals
like my breast
is your breast
        and your ancestresses are mine
        We make love incestuously
        scandalizing the fish
        and the good citizens of this
        and all parties.
        In the morning, at breakfast
        when things start slowly awakening
        I will call you by my name
        and you will reply
        joyfully,
my other, my sister, my likeness.

Translated by Lizabeth Paravisini-Gebert

🐦 Renata Pallotini (Brazil)

WOMAN SITTING ON THE SAND

Look at him, showing off, but then of course, why shouldn't he: twenty two, a tanned body, sun-bleached blond hair. Well-muscled, soft smooth skin on his stomach, his back, inside the curves of his arms. Body hair of perfect length, perfectly placed; enough to give him somewhat of an untamed look, and the hair not too long, but full enough, crowning his conqueror's head, like that of a young lion. But then he is a winner. Winner at what? I don't know. All I can say is that, on a surfboard, his legs taut and gleaming in the sun, he is hard and firm, like a fine-tuned copulation. And it gives me the same kind of pleasure. I am not kidding; as he penetrates the heart of a foaming wave, as if he were kissing a chalice, he brings me to an orgasm. Absolute, perfect, like none I had experienced for a long time, or ever. I suddenly sit up, straighten myself up on the sand on the beach, legs together: he takes me in, and I fly with him, with this young man, primitive and strong.

I'll go even further: not even in bed (since we do have our nights—after all, who's paying for his fortnight's stay in this beautiful hotel?), not even in bed can I reach the slippery, heedless, and moist delight that I experience these mornings, alone on this beach, watching him charge deliberately at the sea, and then plunge like a madman into the wave, first over it, and then inside it, first over me and then inside my body.

There he is, showing off: with a group of young men and women; I wonder who he's trying to impress. He bent his upper body and his muscles bulged under his skin. Now he has straightened himself up and his bulk covers the sun. He's talking about me. I can tell he's talking about me. They're having ice cream; he lifts the ice cream toward me from afar, as if he were offering it to me, and then smiles, because he knows I can't have any ice cream. It's not easy to stay in shape at fifty, and ice cream is an enemy. He laughs with the others, I can read his cruel lips, the lips of a healthy fool: "She doesn't eat ice cream because it's fattening."

The cruel lips of a healthy fool, ah, but how well they travel my body, those lips. He truly earns his daily ice cream, his surfboard, and his sleep. In all fairness, he does have talent. I even have to acknowledge his patience, because one certainly needs patience to kiss the same hidden parts of a despised body night after night for fifteen days, to kiss a body for which one feels absolutely no attraction.

I, on the other hand, am attracted to his body. I kiss it all over, often, especially in the afternoon when, after his he-man lunch and my innocuous salads, we lay down, and he sleeps while I look at him, desiring him like a glass of milk, like a breath of air. I am always starved, and my deep emptiness wants to be filled, fulfilled. I wake him up then, kissing him more than I should, and he grumbles and pushes me away. But to repulse me, he must touch me. I am beside him, in any case, and he touches me in a clumsy way and it is all so casual and so deliberate, that as he pushes me away, he embraces me, and I wrap myself around him, and we move together toward the inevitable moment, the inescapable moment when I am able to juxtapose two images that had been separate, and the final pleasure comes, like reaching the peak of a mountain flooded with light: warm light, a glaring bluish radiance, and then the rancid perfume of something already dying.

But never like at the beach, looking at him from afar, penetrating the sea. Holding my body steady with my two hands on the sand, I can manage to appear as casual as if I were just sunning myself. Yes, that woman—"look at that woman! Hey, man, how do they do it? She must be at least fifty, fifty, and look at those thighs, those breasts! But anyhow, what really does it?—exercise, diets, massages, not to mention plastic surgery, frequent plastic surgery I should say, a nip here, a tuck there, and all is well, the cellulite gone, the breasts firm, firm but with the taste of ripe fruit, I'll tell you something, they're the women to have if you can learn to appreciate them, a lady who knows how to fuck, a woman who knows what she's doing, not a professional—after all a whore is nothing but a whore—but women like these, decent women who haven't slept with many men, women who as a rule haven't had a real good fuck, who are disgracefully overdue, and that's what makes them so good, they're treasures, because they think anything you give them is wonderful, they moan really easily, and you, besides getting your rocks off, come out thinking you are the best, and maybe you are, after all, no?"—Yes, that woman sunning herself . . .

Sunning herself. Well, yes. I am burning the sun, scorching the sun, melting the sand. Here I am, divorced, not well-loved, midway through my life. I lived, I lived, but I knew nothing about life. And suddenly, this kid. A physical problem, a psychological dilemma, a diversion, what do I know. I only know what I've had, what I have, what I want to continue having as a mortal pleasure.

Did I say mortal? Yes, I did. Why do I cling to this delectable lad, why do I continue to sink into the sand, sinking into the sand like a stake being hammered from the top, and all for this explosion, and what is this explosion? A draining that cleanses me and as a result calms me down.

He just sat down, the rascal. He finished his ice cream, buried the stick in the sand, and is talking to one and all, glistening with sweat and tanning lotion, a concession he has made to my whims, indulging my pleasure in taking care of his body, allowing me to rub it all over him.

And what is it that I want, my God? That he come in when he wants, eat as much as he can, sleep to digest his food and then help himself to me (or I to him, is that more accurate?). I won't tell him about the pleasure I feel when he is in the sea, erect, frolicking—that, I won't do. It's not only obscene but quite humiliating. I won't do it, and if I did, I know I'd lose this sweet secret which belongs only to me and to the sand that welcomes me. I won't do it. I pay for the daily expenses, the surfing, the paraffin wax, I close my legs, I contract my nipped and tucked abdomen . . . but I'm discreet and no one on this beach will hear my moans.

His words are the worst part of it: such harsh words, and what is more, deliberately chosen to hover between an insult and a come-on. An insult whispered in the ear during love-making can mask itself as a come-on, and sometimes it is. I know very well, however, that for him, in the comings and goings of his hard body, "my tasty jewel" is a sort of whip with which he avenges himself a second before offering me his pleasure and my own. But I cringe and accept it, submissively. I, who could be his mother.

Those words be damned.

Yesterday he threatened me, saying he was going to take off, that he was fed up with me. His very words. Sometimes I think I'm going to die without him, without his morning surfing, without his penetration, of sun, of wave, of brilliant spark and foam.

Nonetheless, physically, it would be easy. If I were to get up from the sand now, take my towel, and without looking back, walk on the beach, now, toward the avenue, what would happen?

Nothing. He is amusing himself with the other young men (oh, with the young men rather than with the young women!). He hasn't seen me.

If I took a shower, dressed myself in clean white clothes, combed my hair, made myself up . . .

He's still there, it is as if I could see him, I can see him from the window now. He thinks he has offended me and he's pleased. In another half hour he will come to the restaurant on the top floor looking for his *feijoada*. What if I paid the bill, packed my bags and left, went back home, giving up this fleeting, momentary pleasure in exchange for a head held high, the head of an animal, a female, a bitch, a dog, an animal of the female gender, the best shepherd, the best guide-dog, the best guard-dog. I won't die from giving up being in heat.

He's still on the beach.

The plane leaves in a quarter of an hour. The plane leaves now, it's just leaving. I fasten my seatbelt and lift my head. Resistance is the message. Courage the motivation. The plane takes off. The sand is left behind.

I didn't die. My survival is both that of the female and the human being.

I am a woman.
I am.

Translated by Paula Milla-Kreutzer

Renata Pallotini

A MESSAGE FROM SUMMER

I search in your body for the light that was.
Not something in your body itself
but of the slow stars
contained in thought.

This liquid emanating from under your arms
is a taste we had in the tongue.
Nothing is for nothing.

The navel of an animal is always sweet.
Connected intimately to the womb,
it is a tunnel and a root.
The navel is the knife
in the center of the mysterious
body.

I drink a translucid liqueur,
in a navel surrounded
by the hairs that define
a specific animal.

But nothing is for nothing
and what is behind the lair of your sex
is only what I loved once
in another century.

Translated by Paula Milla-Kreutzer

MY PLEASURE

My pleasure is a dream in your body.

The image arouses in you a night of ferns
and dark pillows hidden long ago.
I close my eyes and see you among the leaves
and you desire me as one desires life.
You have been walking toward this moment
and the path feels centuries warm.
You ask me nothing: the body is a ready answer.
Deep and oily like damp bridges
moving from stair to stair in the secret twilight.

And we kiss consciously
kissing every angle of those kisses
until blood alters the volume of things
and a repressed joy reaches the color of fire.

Your pleasure is my body's mirror
stretching itself like a silver thread
wound around my neck
saying
words.
There is a heavy smell in this room.

Translated by Paula Milla-Kreutzer

CRUEL TESTIMONY NUMBER 2

(Early deflowering)

"It was your uncle who did you?"
"No, it was my brother."
"Did you enjoy it?"
"I beg your pardon?"
"Did you enjoy it?"
"Afterwards he took me out
for pizza. I enjoyed it."

Translated by Paula Milla-Kreutzer

🖤 Albalucía Ángel (Colombia)

Excerpt from
THE SPOTTED BIRD PERCHED HIGH ABOVE
UPON THE TALL GREEN LEMON TREE . . .

Alirio was the best *tiple* player in the region and was famous
for his missing toe. In the afternoons, after he finished his work on
the stables, he sat by the path that led to the paddocks, and the others would ask him, play *Esperanza*, and he would get inspired and
play anything from *pasillos* to *bambucos* until it grew dark, or until it
was time for the Christmas novena.

Let's go look for sandpiper nests, he proposed to her that
day, and she went, unconcerned, since on her previous vacation
they had gone to the cane fields searching for nests; and he had
explained to her how the sandpipers get really furious if one goes
near the chicks and many times they had to dive to the ground
because the sandpipers flew straight at them, their wings outspread,
with something like spurs in their claws and their eggs were beautiful, like those of guinea hens. Was it here that you got bitten by the
rattlesnake?, and he said yes, it grabbed my big toe, and before I
knew it I felt the cramps and since I was cutting grass I grabbed the
machete and whoozz!, I chopped it in half with the machete, all in
the wink of an eye, and she asked, did you cut your own toe . . . ?
Of course. If I hadn't chopped it off, I would have been history in
ten minutes, those blasted things are deadly, there's no antidote
around here: shall we sit here?, and he arranged a pile of fresh hay,
because it was a bit wet from the morning dew. He covered it with
his poncho. Are you cold . . . ? And Ana said yes, because the sandpipers had to be caught before the break of dawn, and she had not
worn anything over her nightgown and had come out barefoot so
that her brother couldn't hear her and bug her to take him with her,
and then he proposed, come here, lie down under the poncho, and
he tucked her under it, and laid down next to her. Aren't we going
to look for nests? In a little while, it's still early, and they remained
lying there and she could smell his scent, which was a mixture of
the smell of the stable and Alhucema Negret, which she knew well

because it was the same perfume Flora wore, are you wearing Alhucema? she asked him, since he was so quiet, and Alirio exclaimed, you're so smart! How did you know?, and he took a bottle of perfume out of his pocket and offered to rub a little on her, you'll see how the cold goes away, but she said no, because it'll tickle, but he said don't be silly, it's such a fun game, and she said well, ok I guess, but watch it, and he began to rub her and pinch her here and there. Bumble bee, bumble bee under the barn, when it comes out, it goes buzzzzzzzzzz!, what a pretty little belly you have, and Ana said, you're getting fresh, but he said, come on, I'm only playing, the problem is that you prefer Nebridio to me, I've seen you, and she said well Nebridio is my age and my mother lets me play with him. So what's wrong with me . . . ? I'm not looking for trouble, don't think I don't know my place. I am a farm-hand and you're the boss's daughter, but that doesn't mean I can't tell you how pretty you are, right?, and he started asking her questions about school, about who her friends were, and she told him about Irma and Pecosa and he roared with laughter as he listened to her stories, and then he said, come sit here, and he squatted down, but Ana said she was very comfortable where she was and he said, let's play horsey, didn't you like to play horsey?, yes, when I was three years old, and how old are you now?, almost thirteen and I'm not the asshole you think I am, and he said, Holy Mother! what ugly language, and came back to lie down. He wrapped himself well in the poncho, until even his moustache disappeared under it, and then, suddenly, without knowing why, she decided to tell him about Montse. Did you know I killed a girl once? Ahhhhhh?, Alirio jumped, and she said, well, yes, but it has remained a secret and you have to promise me that you will never ever tell anyone, I swear by this Cross, Alirio said and he made her get comfortable, come here, cuddle up with me, now tell me how that happened . . . ? and now at last he was being serious, no longer mocking her, since every time she told him a story he burst out laughing, as if she were a comedian; you have to promise me you won't ever tell a soul, no matter how many years go by, and he said, I swear to God. But when she started to tell him that Montse was six and she was five, he made a you-must-be-joking gesture and started to smile, and she stopped right then and there. If you don't believe me I won't tell you anything. But he said, don't be so touchy, of course I believe you, don't be like that, go on, and it was just like she wanted things to be, with him treating her like a grown up, begging her over and over again to go on with her story. Are you cold again? and he started to rub her very slowly. No, it's just that I shiver when I remember, and he said, poor thing, come here . . . and how did you kill her . . . ?, while he looked at her and petted her, and she started the story from the point when her mother had warned them don't climb that wall, that it was too high, but Montse insisted, come look at the hens. She didn't refuse, and they climbed up to the railing, and then Montse screamed and Ana saw her almost in the air and managed to grab her thighs but Montse was heavy and very slippery and she let go, and she fell on the pavement, face down, and there she remained, dead, with her arms spread out, until some men who worked down below, in the pharmacy, picked her up and brought her up the stairs between them, and Alirio caressing her, and she clearly seeing their white gowns soaked in blood: your mother, where is she . . . ?, they asked her, and she started to feel a tingling warmth on her legs and his body rubbing against her, what a horrible thing, and she not daring to say anything because if she moved he would stop petting her and the shaking had gotten worse and he climbed on top of her to keep her warm but all the rubbing was to no avail. Don't tell anyone, and he said, no, of course not, rest assured, what a horrible thing, tell me, tell me more . . . and she seeing the blood dripping down the staircase, and Montse's face, I don't know . . . I don't remember anymore, because the man from the pharmacy was suggesting they cut off her dress but it was a sticky mess, and he was slowly opening her legs, searching with his fingers and she didn't let out a peep, because she had to tell him: I didn't kill her, she explained to them persistently, of course you didn't, her mother said, don't be silly, and they took her out of the room, I killed her . . . ! it was me . . . shrieking because he was poking inside her. Don't do that, it hurts! No, no, it doesn't hurt, I'll be very gentle. But he was penetrating her violently, and she could feel his sweating hands on her tense body, no! I don't want to . . . ! but with a calm voice he said: tell me more about your friend, was she as pretty as you are . . . ? and he stopped for a moment. I like to hear your stories, it doesn't hurt, see? and he moved slowly, but that really hurt and she said, I don't want to! but he said I'm not hurting you, be still, and he covered her mouth to make her stop, do you like it like this . . . ? it's so good, and it was like she was being cut open with a knife, and he saying it's so nice, and wouldn't stop, and the world spun around with every one of Alirio's thrusts, and he started to moan and to breathe heavily: Alirio . . . ! Marco's voice came from the orchard, and she prayed for someone to come, but Marco's voice faded away. Oh please Lord, help me get away . . . ! She made an enormous effort, but suddenly something jolted her like an electric charge, everything became blurred and she lost track of things: and when she came back to her senses, Alirio was still on top of her, not saying a word. Very still.

Alirio!, and this time it was Pancho, whistling like when he called the horses to the trough, and Alirio jumped up, don't move, but Ana couldn't have even if she had wanted to because she felt as if she had been put through a mill. He put his poncho on, adjusted his belt, I have to go cut hay, are you coming tomorrow to look for nests?, and she said yes, and he took off running, disappearing into the canes, and she heard him whistle, and she listened carefully for noises but couldn't hear anything, no cows mooing, only the flowing waters of the Leona. I'm going to bathe, she decided, and she rose with a great effort, because her body felt battered and bruised, and then she understood what had happened to Saturia that time, when they thought that Lisandro, the Montoya's farm-hand, was beating her. When she got to her feet, she was covered in blood: he ripped my insides!, and she started running wildly, not thinking of the pain or the weariness.

🌸

She couldn't get the blood out and then she decided it would be best to bury her panties in the garden, where the soil was loose; there wasn't much blood on the nightgown and she left it to dry while she bathed in the brook, which was cold as ice. The thorns of Christ . . . ! Sabina would say if she caught sight of her like that; it would be best to crawl behind the garage and go in through the garden, and she stretched out on the grass, shivering, but it wasn't the cold, because she felt like an oven inside. What if the same thing that happened to Saturia happens to me?; and she imagined herself binding her stomach with an inner tube, and the baby being born in a corner of the bathroom, because Saturia hadn't said a word to anyone and her mother hadn't even noticed what was going on until they heard the screams, and later Saturia had another baby and for three dollars she would let the cattle-drivers fondle her. She would do it in the hay fields with any passerby, I once heard Sabina telling Flora; fifteen years old, and look at her . . . ! and then she buried her face in the ground because the grief was too much for her to bear, and she broke into tears, into heart-breaking sobs, and she cried and cried until slowly she was overcome by sleep, and she dreamt of Montse, who was not Montse but her sister, who was a year ahead of her in school and whom Father Medrano left in detention each Thursday because she staunchly refused to sing when they played *Cara al sol*,[1] I won't sing, oh no?, we'll see about that, Little Miss Know-It-All, and he kept her until five o'clock, and nobody could understand what was going on, until the grandmother explained that it was that her parents were Spanish refugees from Catalonia; and Montse asked her, are you going to the morning rosary?, and she pushed her into the procession, which was starting to traverse a city with high towers and very small squares surrounded by trees that she had never seen before, and Juan José's scream woke her up: they're looking for you, Ana!, and then he stopped, facing the brook, not daring to say more when he saw her sprawled on the grass like that, naked.

Translated by Lizabeth Paravisini-Geber

[1]Hymn of the Falange Española, a Spanish political group which joined forces with Franco during the Spanish Civil War. —Eds.

🌶 Cecilia Vicuña (Chile)

BELOVED FRIEND

Visitors
can't imagine
what they unleash in me.

C. doesn't know I dream
of caressing her
invisibly
While she spreads sweet potato jam
on her bread, she seems
to be toying with chalices
and consecrated stones.
Her way of raising her knife
to scoop up her butter
is a gesture! where
oceans are balanced,
where chilled women
find comfort—
wavy and consequential
as a streak of radar.

When she lifts her skirt
to show me her silvery panties
I see undulant herds of hips
multiplying the roundness
in noisy perfection

If only she'd stay still
so I could live in her,
breathing and slumbering
on those plains.

Her thigh's so shadowy,
her hair glistens so,
it seems to speak another language.
What I say is so clumsy,
but how can I say:

        "You're so beautiful."
        "I'm so happy
          you've come."

When I bring up
the book
of Renaissance paintings
where we examine
Italian primitives
I would like
to say:

        "I meet you in this city."
        "You are these hills."
        "You painted them."

Your fingers mimic exactly
the curving fins
of that allegorical siren—
but that's not quite it . . .
you are a country
of Lorenzetti cities.
Sometime
we'll return to that city.

Don't suffer because
in this painting
two women caress each other.
Sometime
I will caress you.
Don't worry because you're

growing older;
you move to another tempo
and so do I.

Nourish yourself
on the story you tell me
of the wine glass
crossing the threshold.
Draw nourishment, draw luster from it;
don't stop dreaming of the painting
by the Fontainbleu master
in which a woman
grasps another woman's nipple;
for centuries
no one will let your nipple go.

I want to suffer,
to bury myself in you,
to strangle you and dig a deep hole
where earth would slowly
begin to cover you, and I want to see
your colors begin to rot under the coffee-
        colored earth.
Don't you love the combination
of violet and coffee-color?

I didn't mean
to mention death,
but since you dread it so,
how can I help it?

We don't have much time
to talk.
I wish I were a man,
I'd seduce you and make

you leave home and forget
everything, but
I don't like that idea.
Isolated, solitary,
men are always outside,
needing nothing more urgently
than to be inside,
to feel a bit of warmth,
the tidal flow.

I'm tired of you,
of your quibbles of conscience,
you never let yourself go—
and you'd better not—
when you do
I'm afraid your heart's going to shatter

                                  to flower
                                  to hurt you.

It's a lie—I'm not tired of you,
I'm tired of myself.
I just want to be able to see you,
watch you fall in love with someone else,
and never notice me.

After you've been wearing
a flannel shirt and wool socks
for a week,
making yourself old and ugly,
to die a little,
I want to be there
when you come to life again
in a glory of moist, dark eyes.

I want to be an Indian

hidden in the hills
and never come down to the valleys
because everything hurts.

To be enlightened by my own lights.

You were born
of a cross
between Death and your mother.
Not even as a baby
could you have been rosy.
People who make love with you
think they'll never get back,
they'll sink, you'll
knit a damp web to their shoulders
and—since you most likely
have connections with craters—
you'll hurl your lovers into volcanoes,
never to emerge
unless you take pity.

I'm afraid of you
because you can't see me
as I see you,
can't love me
as I love you,
can't even want
to caress me
and live with me awhile,
arranging my hair into Gothic
          inventions,
or asking me to stir tea
with the tip of my nipple.

Your human side's

not as fine
as your bestial nature.
Some think you are sovereign
of arrogant, menacing
regions,
but those who've seen you
feverish
or at menstrual times
love you
against your will—
if you have a will.
Only intensity
gives your life power.
Death finds its undoing
in hairy fountains
and hot glances.

What wouldn't Death give
to keep you from having
those round eyes

those breasts
those thighs
those ankles.

What wouldn't Death give
to wrap you up and
tuck you away
forever.

Translated by Anne Twitty

Gioconda Belli (Nicaragua)

ON SUNDAY'S PAINFUL LONELINESS

Here I am
naked,
lying on the forlorn sheets
of this bed where I yearn for you.

I see my body,
smooth and pink in the mirror,
my body,
once such avid terrain for your kisses,
this body full of memories
of your boundless passion
on which you fought sweat-soaked battles
on long nights of moans and laughter
and noises from my inner hollows.

I see my breasts
which you cocooned with a smile
in the palm of your hand,
which you squeezed like tiny birds
within the five bars of your jail
as a flower burst within me
and held its hard corolla
against your sweet flesh.

I see my legs
long and slow veterans of your caresses,
rotating fast and nervous on their hinges
to open for you the path to damnation
toward my very center,
and the soft vegetation of the mound

where you engaged silent battles
crowned with delight
heralded by volleys of artillery
and primitive thunder.

I see and I don't see myself
in this mirror of you that stretches painfully
over this Sunday's loneliness
a flesh-colored mirror,
a hollow mold seeking its other hemisphere.

It is raining heavily
on my face
and I think only of your faraway love
as I shelter,
with all my might,
my hopes.

Translated by Lizabeth Paravisini-Gebert

🕊 Isabel Allende (Chile)

Excerpt from
THE HOUSE OF THE SPIRITS

The Awakening

Around the age of eighteen, Alba left childhood behind for good. At the exact moment when she felt like a woman, she locked herself in her old room, which still held the mural she had started so many years before. Next she rummaged through her paint jars until she found a little red and a little white that were still fresh. Then she carefully mixed them together and painted a large pink heart in the last empty space on the wall. She was in love. Afterward she threw her paints and brushes into the trash and sat down to contemplate her drawings, which is to say, the history of her joys and sorrows. She decided that the balance had been happy and with a sigh said goodbye to the first stage of her life.

She finished school that year and decided to study philosophy for pleasure and music to annoy her grandfather, who believed that the arts were a waste of time and who constantly preached the virtues of the liberal or scientific professions. He also warned her against love and marriage, with the same insolence with which he insisted that Jaime should find a decent girl and settle down because he was turning into a hopeless bachelor. He said it was good for men to have a wife, but that women like Alba could only lose by marrying. Her grandfather's sermons went out the window when Alba set eyes on Miguel one unforgettable rainy afternoon in the cafeteria of the university.

Miguel was a pale student, with feverish eyes, faded trousers, and miner's boots, in his final year of law school. He was a leftist leader, and he was afire with the most uncontrollable passion: justice. However, that did not prevent him from being aware that Alba was watching him. He looked up and their eyes met. They stared at each other, dazzled, and from that moment on they sought out every possible occasion to meet on the leafy promenades of the nearby park, where they walked with their arms full of books or dragging Alba's heavy cello in its case. On their initial encounter, she noticed that he wore a tiny insignia on his sleeve: a raised fist. She decided not to tell him that she was Esteban Trueba's granddaughter. For the first time in her life, she used the surname that was on all her identification cards: Satigny. She quickly realized it would be best not to tell the rest of her fellow students either. On the other hand, she could boast that she was friends with Pedro Tercero García, who was very popular among the students, and with the Poet, on whose knees she had sat as a little girl and who was now known in every language and whose poetry was on the lips of all the students and scrawled in graffiti on the walls.

Miguel talked about revolution. He said that the violence of the system needed to be answered with the violence of revolution. But Alba was not interested in politics; she wanted only to talk about love. She was sick and tired of her grandfather's speeches, of listening to his arguments with her Uncle Jaime, and of the endless electoral campaigns. The only political activity she had ever engaged in was the time she had gone with other students to throw stones for no apparent reason at the United States Embassy, for which she had been suspended from school for a week and which had nearly given her grandfather another heart attack. But at the university politics was unavoidable. Like all the young people who entered that year, she discovered the appeal of nightlong gatherings in cafés, talking about the necessary changes in the world and infecting each other with the passion of ideas. She would return home late at night, her mouth bitter and her clothes reeking of stale tobacco, her head burning with heroism, convinced that when the time came she would give her life for a noble cause. Out of love for Miguel, and not for any ideological conviction, Alba sat in at the university with the students who had seized a building in support of a strike by workers. There were days of encampments, excited discussions, insults hurled at the police until the students lost their voices. They built barricades with sandbags and paving stones that they pried loose from the main courtyard. They sealed the doors and windows, intending to turn the building into a fortress, but the result was a dungeon that was harder for the students to leave than it was for the police to enter. It was the first time Alba had spent a night away from home. She was rocked to sleep in Miguel's arms between piles of newspapers and empty beer bottles, surrounded by the warm closeness of her comrades, all young, sweaty, red-eyed from smoke and lack of sleep, slightly hungry, and entirely fearless, because it was all more like a game than a war. They spent the first day so busy building barricades, mobilizing their innocent defenses, painting placards, and talking on the phone that they had no time to worry when the police cut off their water and electricity.

From the very first, Miguel became the soul of the occupation, seconded by Professor Sebastián Gómez, who, despite his crippled legs, stayed with them to the end. That night they sang to keep their spirits up, and when they grew tired of harangues, discussions, and songs, they settled into little groups to get through the night as best they could. The last to rest was Miguel, who seemed to be the only one who knew what to do. He took charge of distributing water, transferring into receptacles even the water already in the toilet tanks, and he improvised a kitchen that, to everyone's amazement, produced instant coffee, cookies, and some cans of beer. The next day the stench of the waterless toilets was overpowering, but Miguel organized a cleanup and ordered that the toilets not be used: everyone should relieve themselves in the courtyard, in a hole that had been dug alongside the stone statues of the founder of the university. Miguel divided the group into squads and kept them busy all day with such efficiency that his authority went unnoticed. Decisions seemed to arise spontaneously from the groups.

"You'd think we were going to be here for months!" Alba exclaimed, delighted at the prospect of being under siege.

The armored cars of the police stationed themselves out on the street, surrounding the ancient building. A tense wait began, which would last for several days.

"Students all over the country, unions, and professional

schools are going to join us. The government may fall," Sebastián Gómez commented.

"I doubt it," replied Miguel. "But the main thing is to establish the protest and not leave the building until they sign the workers' list of demands."

It began to drizzle and darkness came early in the lightless building. They lit a few improvised lamps made of tin cans filled with gasoline and a smoky wick. Alba thought the telephone had been cut, but when she tried to use it it still worked. Miguel explained that the police had reason to listen to their calls, and he warned them how to conduct their conversations. In any case, Alba called home to let them know she would be staying with her comrades until victory or death, which sounded false the minute she said it. Her grandfather grabbed the phone from Blanca's hand. In a tone of voice she knew all too well, he told her that she had an hour to be home with a reasonable explanation for having stayed out all night. She replied that she could not leave, and that even if she could she would not think of doing so.

"You have no business there with all those Communists!" Esteban Trueba roared. But he immediately softened his voice and begged her to leave before the police came in, because he was in a position to know that the government was not going to let them stay indefinitely. "If you don't come out voluntarily, they're going to send the mobile unit in and drive you out with clubs," the senator concluded.

Alba peeked through a chink in the window that was covered with planks of wood and bags of earth and saw the tanks lined up across the street and a double row of men in combat gear, with helmets, clubs, and gas masks. She realized that her grandfather was not exaggerating. Everybody else had seen them too, and some of the students were shaking. Someone said there was a new kind of bomb worse than tear gas, that provoked diarrhea attacks terrible enough to discourage the bravest, because of the stench and the ridicule they caused. To Alba the idea seemed terrifying. She had to make an effort not to cry. She felt stitches in her stomach and supposed they were from fear. Miguel put his arms around her, but that did not console her. They were both exhausted and were beginning to feel the effects of the sleepless night in their bones and in their souls.

"I don't think they'd dare break in here," Sebastián Gómez said. "The government's already got enough problems to deal with. It's not going to interfere with us."

"It wouldn't be the first time they've attacked students," someone said.

"Public opinion wouldn't stand for it," Gómez replied. "This is a democracy. It's not a dictatorship and it will never be."

"We always think things like that only happen elsewhere," said Miguel, "until they happen to us too."

The remainder of the afternoon passed without incident and by nightfall everyone was more relaxed despite the prolonged hunger and discomfort. The tanks remained in place. The young people played checkers and games of cards in the hallways, slept on the floor, and made defensive weapons with sticks and stones. Fatigue was visible on every face. The cramps in Alba's stomach were growing stronger, and she thought that if nothing was resolved by the morning she would have no other choice but to use the hole in the courtyard. It was still raining outside, and the routine of the city continued undisturbed. No one seemed to care about another student strike, and people walked past the tanks without stopping to read the placards hanging from the university façade. The neighbors quickly became accustomed to the presence of armed police, and when the rain stopped children ran out to play with a ball under the streetlights in the empty parking lot that separated the building from the police detachments. At moments Alba felt as if she were on a sailboat becalmed at sea, locked in an eternal, silent wait, peering out at the horizons for hours. With the passage of time and the increasing lack of comfort, the high-spirited camaraderie of the first day had turned to irritation and constant bickering. Miguel inspected the building and confiscated all the food supplies in the cafeteria.

"When this is gone, we'll pay the concessionaire for it. He's a worker like anybody else," he said.

It was cold now. The one who never complained, not even of thirst, was Sebastián Gómez, who seemed as indefatigable as Miguel, even though he was twice his age and looked tubercular. He was the only professor who had stayed with the students when they seized the building. It was said that his crippled legs were the result of a burst of machine-gun fire in Bolivia. He was the ideologue who made his students burn with the flame that in most of them extinguished itself as soon as they graduated and joined the world they had once hoped to change. A small, spare man with an aquiline nose and sparse hair, he was lit by an inner fire that gave no respite. It was he who had christened Alba "the countess," because the first day of classes her grandfather had had the bad idea of sending her to school with his chauffeur and Professor Gómez had seen her arrive. By sheer chance his nickname had hit home; Gómez could not have known that in the improbable event that she should choose to do so, she could unearth the noble title of Jean de Satigny, which was one of the few authentic features of the French count who had given her his name. Alba did not resent his mocking nickname for her; in fact, on more than one occasion she had fantasized about seducing the stalwart professor. But Sebastián Gómez had seen a lot of girls like Alba and recognized the mixture of curiosity and compassion aroused by the sight of the crutches that supported his poor lifeless legs.

The next day went by without the mobile unit moving its tanks or the government giving in to the workers' demands. Alba began to wonder what the hell she was doing there; the pain in her abdomen was becoming unbearable and the need to take a bath with running water was beginning to obsess her. Each time she looked out at the street and saw the police, her mouth filled with saliva. By that point she had realized that her Uncle Nicolás's training was not nearly as effective in a moment of action as it was in the fiction of imagined suffering. Two hours later Alba felt a warm viscous liquid between her legs and saw that her slacks were stained with red. She was swept with panic. For the past few days the fear that this might happen had tormented her almost as much as hunger. The stain on her pants was like a flag, but she made no attempt to hide it. She curled up in a corner, feeling utterly lost. When she was little, her grandmother had taught her that everything associated with human functions is natural, and she could speak of menstruation as of poetry, but later on, at school, she learned that all bodily secretions except tears are indecent. Miguel noticed her shame and anguish. He went to the improvised infirmary to get a package of cotton and found some handkerchiefs, but it was soon clear that they were insufficient. By evening Alba was crying in humiliation and pain, terrified by the pincers in her guts and by this stream of blood that was so unlike her usual flow. She thought something must be bursting inside her. Ana Díaz, a student who, like Miguel, wore the insignia of the raised fist, observed that only rich women suffer from such pains; proletarian women do not complain even when they give birth. But when she saw that Alba's pants were a pool of blood and she was as pale as death, she went to speak to Sebastián Gómez, who said he had no idea how to resolve the problem.

"That's what happens when you let women get involved in men's affairs!" he roared.

"No! It's what happens when you let the bourgeoisie into the affairs of the people!" the young woman answered him indignantly.

Sebastián Gómez went over to the corner where Miguel had settled Alba, gliding up to her with difficulty because of his crutches.

"You have to go home, Countess," he said. "You're not contributing anything here. On the contrary, you're in the way."

Alba felt a wave of relief. She was too frightened, and this was an honorable way to leave that would allow her to return home without seeming like a coward. She argued a little with Sebastián Gómez to save face, but she almost immediately accepted the proposal that Miguel should go out with a white flag to parley with the police. Everybody watched him from the observation posts while he crossed the empty parking lot. The police had formed into narrow lines and ordered him through their loudspeaker to stop, lay his flag on the ground, and proceed with his hands behind his neck.

"This is like a war!" Gómez observed.

Soon afterward Miguel returned and helped Alba to her feet. The same young woman who had previously criticized Alba for complaining took her by the arm and the three of them left the building, stepping around the barricades and sandbags, illuminated by the powerful searchlights of the police. Alba could barely walk. She felt ashamed and her head was spinning. A police patrol came out to meet them halfway, and Alba found herself a few inches from a green uniform, with a pistol aimed directly at her nose. She raised her eye and looked into a dark face with the eyes of a rodent. She recognized him right away: Esteban García.

"I see it's Senator Trueba's granddaughter!" García exclaimed ironically.

This was how Miguel learned that Alba had not been entirely truthful. He felt betrayed. He deposited her into the hands of the other man, turned on his heel, and left, dragging the white banner on the ground, without even looking back to say goodbye, accompanied by Ana Díaz, who was as surprised and furious as he was.

"What's the matter with you?" García asked, pointing at Alba's pants. "It looks like an abortion."

Alba straightened her head and stared him straight in the eye. "That is none of your business. Take me home!" she ordered, copying the authoritarian tone her grandfather employed with everyone he considered beneath his social station.

García hesitated. It had been a long time since he had heard orders from the mouth of a civilian, and for a moment he was tempted to take her to the stockade and leave her there to rot in a cell, bathed in her own blood, until she got down on her knees and begged him, but his profession had taught him that there were men more powerful than he, and that he could not afford the luxury of acting with impunity. Besides, the memory of Alba in her starched dress, drinking lemonade on the terrace of Tres Marías while he shuffled around barefoot and sniffling in the chicken yard, and the fear he still had of Senator Trueba were more powerful than his desire to humiliate her. He could not bear the way she stared at him and he lowered his head imperceptibly. He turned around, barked out a brief instruction, and two policemen led Alba by the arms to a van. This was how she reached her house. When Blanca saw her, her first reaction was that the grandfather's prediction had come true and that the police had attacked the students with their clubs. She began to scream and did not stop until Jaime had examined Alba and assured her that she had not been injured and there was nothing wrong with her that a couple of injections and some rest would not cure.

Alba spent two days in bed, during which the student strike was peacefully terminated. The Minister of Education was relieved of his post and transferred to the Ministry of Agriculture.

"If he could be the Minister of Education without finishing school, there's no reason why he can't be the Minister of Agriculture without ever having seen a cow," Senator Trueba remarked.

While she was in bed, Alba had time to think back to when she had met Esteban García. Poring over her childhood memories, she remembered a dark-skinned boy, the library, the fireplace ablaze with enormous pine logs whose perfume filled the room, evening or night, and herself sitting on his knees. But that vision came and went quickly in her mind and she began to wonder whether she had dreamt it. The first definite image she had of him was later. She knew the exact date because it was her fourteenth birthday, and her mother had recorded it in the black album her grandmother had started when she was born. She had curled her hair in honor of the occasion and was out on the terrace in her coat, waiting for her Uncle Jaime to take her out to buy her present. It was very cold, but she liked the garden in wintertime. She blew on her hands and pulled up her coat collar to protect her ears. From where she was standing she could see the window of the library, where her grandfather was speaking with a man. The glass was clouded, but she recognized the uniform of a policeman and wondered what her grandfather could be doing with one of them in his library. The man had his back to the window and was sitting stiffly on the edge of a chair with a straight back and the pathetic air of a leaden soldier. Alba watched them for a while, until she guessed that her uncle must be about to arrive, and then she walked through the garden to a half-ruined gazebo. She rubbed her hands together to keep warm, brushed away the wet leaves that had fallen on the stone bench, and sat down to wait. Soon afterward, Esteban García encountered her there when he left the house and crossed the garden on his way toward the front gate. He stopped abruptly when he saw her. He looked all around him, hesitated for a moment, and then approached her.

"Do you remember me?" García asked.

"No . . . " She spoke doubtfully.

"I'm Esteban García. We met at Tres Marías."

Alba smiled mechanically. He stirred up bad memories. There was something in his eyes that made her uneasy, but she could not say why. García swept the leaves away with his hands and sat down beside her in the gazebo, so near that their legs were touching.

"This garden looks like a jungle," he said, breathing very close to her.

He took off his police cap and she saw that his hair was short and stiff, groomed with hair tonic. Suddenly, García's hand was on her shoulder. The familiarity of his gesture disconcerted the girl, who was paralyzed for a second but quickly drew back, trying to struggle free. The policeman's hand squeezed her shoulder, and his fingers dug through the thick cloth of her coat. Alba felt her heart pound like a machine, and her cheeks turned red.

"You're grown, Alba. You almost look like a woman now," the man whispered in her ear.

"I'm fourteen. Today's my birthday," she said hesitantly.

"Then I have a present for you," Esteban García said, his mouth twisting into a smile.

Alba tried to turn her face away, but he held it firmly in both hands, forcing her to look at him. It was her first kiss. She felt a warm, brutal sensation as his rough, badly shaven skin scraped her face. She smelled his scent of stale tobacco and onion, and his violence. García's tongue tried to pry open her lips while his hand pressed against her jaw until he forced it open. She imagined that tongue was a warm, slimy mollusk, and she was overcome by a wave of nausea, but she kept her eyes open. She saw the hard cloth of his uniform and felt the ferocious hands wrap themselves around her neck; then without interrupting the kiss, the fingers began to tighten. Alba thought she was choking, and pushed him with such force that she managed to get away from him. García got up off the bench, smiling ironically. He had red splotches on his cheeks and was breathing rapidly.

"Did you like my present?" He laughed.

Alba watched him disappear across the garden with enormous strides, then sat down and wept. She felt dirty and humiliated. Afterward she ran into the house and washed her mouth with soap and brushed her teeth, as if that could remove the stain in her memory. When her Uncle Jaime came to find her, she clung to his neck, buried her face in his shirt, and told him that she did not want a present, she had decided to become nun. Jaime gave one of his deep laughs that rose up from his stomach and that, since he was a taciturn man, she rarely heard.

"I swear I'm going to become a nun!" Alba sobbed.

"You'd have to be born all over again," Jaime replied. "Besides, you'd have to do it over my dead body."

Alba did not see Esteban García again until he was standing next to her in the university parking lot, but she could never forget him. She told no one of that repulsive kiss or of the dreams that she had afterward, in which García appeared as a green beast that tried to strangle her with his paws and asphyxiate her by shoving a slimy tentacle down her throat.

Remembering all that, Alba discovered that the nightmare had been crouched inside her all those years and that García was still the beast waiting for her in the shadows, ready to jump on top of her at any turn of life. She could not know it was a premonition.

Miguel's disappointment and rage at Alba's being the grand-daughter of Senator Trueba vanished the second time he saw her wandering like a lost soul down the corridors near the cafeteria where they had met. He decided that it was unfair to blame the granddaughter for the ideas of the grandfather, and they resumed their stroll with their arms around each other. Soon their kisses were not enough and they began to meet in the rented room where Miguel lived. It was a mediocre boardinghouse for penniless students, presided over by a middle-aged couple with a calling for espionage. They watched with undisguised hostility when Alba went upstairs holding Miguel's hand, and it was a torture for her to overcome her timidity and face the criticism of those stares that ruined the joy of her meetings with Miguel. She would have preferred to avoid seeing them, but she rejected the idea of taking a hotel room together for the same reasons she did not want to be seen in Miguel's boardinghouse.

"You're the worst bourgeois I know!" Miguel would say, laughing.

Once in a while, he managed to borrow a motorcycle and they escaped for a few hours, traveling at reckless speed, crouched low on the machine, with frozen ears and anxious hearts. They liked to go to deserted beaches in the winter, where they walked on the wet sand, leaving their tracks to be lapped away by the waves, frightening the sea gulls and gulping great mouthfuls of salt air. In the summer they preferred the thickest forests, where they could frolic as they wished as soon as they got away from hikers and boy scouts. Alba soon discovered that the safest place of all was her own house, because in the labyrinth of the rear rooms, where no one ever went, they could make love undisturbed.

"If the servants hear noise, they'll think the ghosts are back," Alba said, and she told him of the glorious past of visiting spirits and flying tables in the big house on the corner.

The first time she led him through the back door of the garden, making a path in the jungle and stepping around the statues that were covered with moss and bird droppings, the young man did a double take when he saw the house. "I've been here before," he murmured, but he could not recall when, because the nightmare jungle and dilapidated mansion bore only meager resemblance to the luminous image he had treasured in his mind since his childhood.

One by one the lovers tried out all the abandoned rooms, and finally chose an improvised nest in the depths of the basement. It had been years since Alba had been there, and she had almost forgotten that it existed, but the minute she opened the door and inhaled its unmistakable odor, she felt again the old magical attraction. They used her Uncle Nicolás's books, the dishes, the boxes, the furniture, and the drapes of bygone days to arrange their astonishing nuptial chamber. In the center they created a bed by piling together several mattresses, which they covered with pieces of moth-eaten velvet. From the trunks they took innumerable treasures. They made their sheets out of old topaz-colored damask curtains. They unstitched the sumptuous dress of Chantilly lace that Clara had worn the day Barrabás died, and made a time-colored mosquito net, which also protected them from the spiders that fell down unexpectedly from embroidering on the ceiling. They lighted their way with candles and ignored the rodents, the cold, and the fog from the other world. They walked around stark naked in the eternal twilight of the basement, defying the humidity and drafts. They drank white wine from crystal goblets that Alba took from the dining room, and made a detailed inventory of each other's bodies and the multiple possibilities of pleasure. They played like children. It was difficult for her to recognize in this sweet infatuated young man, who could laugh and romp in an endless bacchanal, the eager revolutionary so committed to the idea of justice that he took secret courses in the use of firearms and revolutionary strategy. Alba invented irresistible techniques of seduction, and Miguel created new and marvelous ways of making love to her. They were blinded by the strength of their passion, which was like an insatiable thirst. In their ambitious effort to possess each other totally, there were not hours or words enough to tell each other their most intimate thoughts and deepest memories. Alba stopped practicing the cello, except to play it naked on the topaz bed, and she attended classes at the university with a hallucinated look in her eyes. Miguel put off his thesis and his political meetings, because he and Alba wanted to be together every hour of the day. They used the least distraction on the part of the inhabitants of the house to sneak down to the basement. Alba learned to lie and dissimulate. On the pretext that she had to study late at night, she left the room she had shared with her mother ever since her grandmother died and set up a room on the first floor, facing the garden, so she could let Miguel in through the window and lead him on tiptoe through the sleeping house to their enchanted lair. But they did not meet only at night. Love's impatience was sometimes so unbearable that Miguel ran the risk of daytime visits, slinking through the bushes like a thief until he reached the basement door, where Alba waited for him, her heart in her mouth. They embraced with the desperation of a parting and slipped down to their refuge suffocating with complicity.

For the first time in her life, Alba wanted to be beautiful. She regretted that the splendid women in her family had not bequeathed their attributes to her, that the only one who had, Rosa the Beautiful, had given her only the algae tones in her hair, which seemed more like a hairdresser's mistake than anything else. Miguel understood the source of her anxiety. He led her by the hand to the huge Venetian mirror that adorned one wall of their secret room, shook the dust from the cracked glass, and lit all the candles they had and arranged them around her. She stared at herself in the thousand pieces of the mirror. In the candlelight her skin was the unreal color of wax statues. Miguel began to caress her and she saw her face transformed in the kaleidoscope of the mirror, and she finally believed that she was the most beautiful woman in the universe because she was able to see herself in Miguel's eyes.

That seemingly interminable orgy lasted more than a year. Finally, Miguel finished his thesis, graduated, and began to look for work. When the pressing need of unsatisfied love had passed, they regained their composure and were able to return to normal. Alba made an effort to take an interest in her studies again, and he turned once more to his political activities, because events were taking place at breakneck pace and the country was torn apart by a series of ideological disputes. Miguel rented a small apartment near the place where he worked, and this was where they made love; in the year they had spent frisking naked in the basement they had both contracted chronic bronchitis, which dampened somewhat the attraction of their subterranean paradise. Alba helped decorate the new apartment, hanging curtains and political posters everywhere she could and even suggesting that she might move in with him, but on this point Miguel was unyielding.

"Bad times are coming, my love," he explained. "I can't have you with me, because when it becomes necessary I'm going to join the guerrillas."

"I'll follow you wherever you go," she promised.

"You can't do that for love. You do it out of political conviction, and that's something you don't have," Miguel replied. "We can't afford the luxury of accepting amateurs."

His words seemed cruel to Alba, but it was several years before she was able to understand their full meaning.

🌶

Senator Trueba was already old enough to retire, but the thought had not even crossed his mind. He read the daily papers and muttered under his breath. Things had changed a good deal in the preceding years, and he felt overtaken by events that he had not expected to live long enough to have to confront. He had been born before the city had electric lights and had lived to see a man walking on the moon, but none of the upheavals of his long existence had prepared him for the revolution that was brewing in his country, right under his eyes, and that had everyone in a state of agitation.

The only person who did not speak about what was happening was Jaime. To avoid arguing with his father, he acquired the habit of silence and soon discovered it was far more comfortable. The only time he abandoned his Trappist laconism was when Alba went to visit him in his tunnel of books. His niece always arrived in her nightgown, her hair wet from the shower, and sat at the foot of his bed to tell him happy stories, because, as she put it, he was a magnet for other people's problems and irreversible disasters, and someone had to keep him posted about spring and love. But her good intentions clashed with her need to talk with her uncle about the things that preoccupied her. They never agreed. They shared the same books, but when it came time to analyze what they had read, their opinions were different. Jaime made fun of her political ideas and bearded friends, and scolded her for having fallen in love with a café terrorist. He was the only one in the family who knew about Miguel.

"Tell that spoiled brat to come and spend a day in the hospital with me. We'll see if he still wants to waste his time on pamphlets and speeches," he said to Alba.

"He's a lawyer, Uncle, not a doctor," she replied.

"I don't care. We need whatever we can get. Even plumbers would be a help."

Jaime was convinced that after so many years of struggle the Socialists were finally going to win. This he attributed to the fact that the people had become conscious of their needs and their own strength. Alba would repeat Miguel's words: that only through armed struggle could the bourgeoisie be toppled. Jaime was horrified by any form of extremism and held that guerrilla warfare is only justified by tyranny, where the only solution is to shoot it out, but that it would be an aberration in a country where change can be obtained by popular vote.

"Don't be so naïve, Uncle. You know that's never happened," Alba answered. "They'll never let your Socialists win!"

She tried to explain Miguel's point of view: that it was not possible to keep waiting for the slow passage of history, the laborious process of educating and organizing the people, because the world was moving ahead by leaps and bounds and they were being left behind; and that radical change is never brought about willingly and without violence. History confirmed this. The argument went on and on, and they became locked in a confused rhetorical exchange that left them exhausted, each accusing the other of being more stubborn than a mule. But in the end they kissed each other good night and both were left with the feeling that the other was an extraordinary human being.

One night at dinner, Jaime announced that the Socialists were going to win, but since he had been saying that for twenty years, no one believed him.

"If your mother were alive, she'd say that those who always win are going to win again," Senator Trueba replied disdainfully.

But Jaime knew what he was talking about. He had heard it from the Candidate. They had been friends for years, and Jaime often went to play chess with him at night. He was the same Socialist who had had his eye on the Presidency for the past eighteen years. Jaime had first seen him behind his father's back, when the Candidate rode the trains of victory in a cloud of smoke during the electoral campaigns of his youth. In those days, the Candidate was a robust young man with the angular face of a hunting dog, who shouted impassioned speeches over the hissing and heckling of the landowners, and the silent fury of the peasants. It was the era when the Sánchez brothers had hanged the Socialist leader at the crossroads and when Esteban Trueba had whipped Pedro Tercero García in front of his father for spreading Father José Dulce María's strange interpretations of the Bible among the tenants. Jaime's friendship with the Candidate was born by chance one Sunday night when he was summoned from the hospital to make an emergency house call. He arrived at the appropriate address in an ambulance, rang the doorbell, and was ushered in by the Candidate himself. Jaime had no trouble recognizing him, because he had seen his picture many times and he had not changed much since the time he had seen him on the train.

"Come in, Doctor. We were expecting you," the Candidate said.

He led him to the maid's room, where his daughters were attempting to help a woman who appeared to be choking. Her pop-eyed face was purple, and her monstrously swollen tongue was hanging from her mouth.

"She was eating fish," one of the daughters explained.

"Bring the oxygen that's in the ambulance," Jaime said, preparing a syringe.

He remained with the Candidate, sitting beside him next to the bed until the woman began to breathe normally and was able to get her tongue back in her mouth. They discussed Socialism and chess, and it was the beginning of a strong friendship. Jaime introduced himself with his mother's surname, which was the one he always used, never imagining that the next day the party's security service would inform the Candidate that he was the son of Senator Trueba, his worst political enemy. The Candidate, however, never mentioned this, and right up to the final hour, when they shook each other's hand for the last time in the din of fire and bullets, Jaime wondered if he would ever have the courage to tell him the truth.

His long experience of defeat and his knowledge of the people allowed the Candidate to realize before anyone else that this time he was going to win. He told Jaime this, cautioning him not to let anybody know, so that the Right would go into the elections sure of victory, as arrogant and divided as ever. Jaime replied that even if they told everyone, no one would believe it—not even the Socialists themselves—and as proof he told his father.

Jaime continued working fourteen hours a day, including Sundays, and took no part in the political process. He was frightened by the violent turn the struggle had taken, polarizing everyone into two extremes and leaving the center to a flighty, indecisive group that was waiting to see who the winner might be so they could vote for him. He refused to be provoked by his father, who seized every opportunity to warn him of the handiwork of international Communism and the chaos that would sweep the country in the improbable event of a victory of the Left. The only time Jaime lost his patience was one morning when he awoke to find the city plastered with angry posters that portrayed a full-bellied, lonely woman vainly attempting to wrest her son from the arms of a Communist soldier who was dragging him off to Moscow. It was part of a terror campaign organized by Senator Trueba and his co-religionists, with the help of foreign experts who had been especially imported to that end. This was too much for Jaime. He decided that he could no longer live beneath the same roof as his father. He closed the door to his tunnel, packed his clothes, and went to sleep at the hospital.

The pace of events escalated during the final months of the campaign. Portraits of the candidates were on every wall; pamphlets were dropped from airplanes and carpeted the streets with printed refuse that fell from the sky like snow. Radios howled the various party slogans and preposterous wagers were made by party members on both sides. At night gangs of young people took to the streets to attack their ideological rivals. Enormous demonstrations were organized to measure the popularity of each party, and each time the city was jammed with the same numbers of people. Alba was euphoric, but Miguel explained that the election was a joke and that whoever won, it would make no difference because you would just be changing the needle on the same old syringe, and that you cannot make a revolution at the ballot box but only with the people's blood. The idea of a peaceful, democratic revolution with complete freedom of expression was a contradiction in terms.

"That poor boy is crazy!" Jaime exclaimed when Alba told him what Miguel had said. "We're going to win and he'll have to eat his words."

Up until that moment, Jaime had always managed to avoid Miguel. He did not wish to know him, for he was tormented by a secret unconfessable jealousy. He had helped bring Alba into the world and had sat her on his knee a thousand times; he had taught her to read, paid for her schooling, and celebrated all her birthdays. Feeling like a father, he could not shake off his uneasiness on seeing her become a woman. He had noticed her change in recent years, and had deceived himself with false arguments, even though his long experience in taking care of human beings had taught him that only the knowledge of love could bring such splendor to a woman's looks. He had seen Alba mature practically overnight, leaving behind the vague shape of adolescence to assume the body of a satisfied and gentle woman. With absurd intensity he hoped against hope that his niece's infatuation would prove to be a passing fancy, because deep down he could not accept that she should need another man more than she needed him. Still, he could not continue to ignore Miguel. It was during this time that Alba told him Miguel's sister was ill.

"I want you to speak to Miguel. He'll tell you about his sister. Would you do that for me?" Alba pleaded.

When Jaime met Miguel in a neighborhood café, all his suspicion was swept away by a wave of sympathy, because the man across the table from him nervously stirring his coffee was not the petulant extremist bully he had expected, but a tremulous, sensitive young man who was fighting off tears as he described the symptoms of his sister's illness.

"Take me to see her," Jaime said.

Miguel and Alba led him to the bohemian quarter. In the center of town, only yards away from the modern buildings made of steel and glass, streets of painters, ceramists, and sculptors had sprung up on the side of a steep hill. There they had built their burrows, dividing ancient houses into tiny studios. The craftmen's workshops had glass roofs to let the sky in, while the painters survived in dark hovels that were a paradise of misery and grandeur. Confident children played in the narrow streets, beautiful women in long tunics carried babies on their backs or anchored on their hips, and bearded, sleepy, indifferent men watched the stream of life pass by from chairs they had set up on street corners or in doorways. Miguel, Alba, and her uncle stopped before a French-style house that looked like a cream cake, with cherubs carved along the friezes. They ascended a narrow staircase that had been built as an emergency exit in case of fire but that the numerous subdivisions of the house had transformed into the only means of entrance. As they climbed, the staircase turned on itself and wrapped them in the penetrating smell of garlic, marijuana, turpentine. Miguel stopped on the top floor before an orange door. He took out a key, turned it in the lock, and they went in. Jaime and Alba felt as if they had stepped into an aviary. The room was round, and capped by an absurd Byzantine cupola surrounded with windows, through which one could see all the rooftops of the city and feel close to the clouds. Doves had nested on the windowsill, adding their excrement and feathers to the spattered panes. Seated on a chair before the only table in the room was a woman in a ragged robe adorned with an embroidered dragon on its front. It took Jaime a few seconds to recognize her.

"Amanda . . . Amanda . . ." he whispered.

He had not seen her in more than twenty years, when the love they both felt for Nicolás was stronger than the love between them. In that time the dark, athletic young man with the damp slicked-down hair, who used to walk back and forth reading aloud from his medical textbooks, had become a man slightly curved from the habit of bending over his patients' beds. Though he now had grey hair, a serious face, and wire-rimmed glasses, he was basically the same person as before. But to have recognized Amanda, he must have loved her a great deal. She looked older than she could possibly have been, and she was very thin, just skin and bones, with a wan, yellow complexion and neglected, nicotine-stained hands. Her eyes were red and bloated, without luster, and her pupils were dilated, which gave her a frightened, helpless look. She saw neither Jaime nor Alba, looking only at Miguel. She tried to get up, but she stumbled and swayed. Her brother jumped to catch her, holding her against his chest.

"Did you two know each other?" Miguel asked in surprise.

"Yes, a long time ago," Jaime replied.

He felt it would be useless to discuss the past and that Alba and Miguel were too young to understand the sense of irreparable loss he was feeling at that moment. With a single brushstroke the image of the gypsy girl he had treasured all those years had been erased, the only love in his solitary fate. He helped Miguel lay the woman on the sofa she used as a bed and put a pillow under her head. Amanda held her robe with both hands, weakly trying to protect herself and mumbling incoherently. She was shaken by a series of convulsions and panted like a tired dog. Alba watched in horror. Only when Amanda was lying still, with her eyes closed, did she recognize the woman who smiled in the little photograph Miguel always carried in his wallet. Jaime spoke to her in a voice unfamiliar to Alba and gradually managed to calm her. He caressed her with the tender, fatherly touch he sometimes used with animals, until the woman finally relaxed and allowed him to roll up the sleeves of her old Chinese robe, revealing her skeletal arms. Alba saw that they were covered with thousands of tiny scars, bruises and holes, some of which were infected and full of pus. Then he uncovered her legs: her thighs were also tortured. Jaime looked at her sadly, comprehending in that moment the abandon, the years of poverty, the frustrated loves, and the terrible road this woman had traveled before reaching the point of desperation where they now found her. He remembered her as she had been in her youth, when she had dazzled him with the flutter of her hair, the rattle of her trinkets, her bell-like laughter, and her eagerness to embrace outlandish ideas and pursue her dreams. He cursed himself for having let her go and for all the time they both had lost.

"She's got to be hospitalized. Only a detoxification program can save her now," he said. "She's going to go through hell."

Translated by Magda Bogin

Eunice Arruda (Brazil)

THEME II

Deliberately
we use
all the erogenous zones
submitting

to the animals
that traverse the skin
submitting
to our disposition
undeserved
shaken
by car horns
by sudden rains confusing
the marker of a path already
travelled

Deliberately
between the sweat and the grunts
wet
the rite has been performed

Only then do we restore ourselves.

Translated by Paula Milla-Kreutzer

THEME III

I cannot resist words

I cannot resist
words hug me

like the madness of an octopus
the wandering of your tongue

I cannot resist
the breath of your mouth
flames
red like a throat
travelling its path
and the shadow
the body cannot resist
the deep dagger being born
words
being born

the warm trajectory
of your tongue
I speak
words chose me.

Translated by Paula Milla-Kreutzer

Leila Miccolis (Brazil)

THIRD POEM FOR MY LOVER

Your feminine side eroticizes me.
Beautiful, sensual and very dear are
certain delicious moments, when I face you
less as a man, and more like a girl:
when you massage your creams over your skin,
or put your apron on to cook,
or when you rub against me to enjoy
your endless pleasures,
or when your light and lesbian hands
fall over me like feathers.

DEMAND

I want my man
as much as he can
wet and humid
like a woman.

Translated by Paula Milla-Kreutzer

ILLUSION

Like all the others
she wanted to be unique,
she told me stories, affairs of her affairs,
talked about fears, madness, terrors
and of a future that would be ours.
Like all the others, many and diverse,
asked me a thousand questions about my past,
was jealous,
touched me lightly,
wanted to back out, thought better: acted,
like all the others
she laid with me, slept
with her legs between my knees
and dreamt about being multiplied
in my room of mirrors.

Translated by Paula Milla-Kreutzer

BEYOND DEATH

He left my body to the necrophiles
for them to pet me,
      to suck me,
      to cut me up,
      to penetrate me.
Once again they will come
Once again, I will not.

Translated by Paula Milla-Kreutzer

🔥 Ana Lydia Vega (Puerto Rico)

LYRICS FOR A SALSA
AND THREE SONEOS BY REQUEST

La vida te da sorpresas, sorpresas te da la vida.
—Rubén Blades

There's a holy feast day fever of fine asses on De Diego
Street. Round in their super-look panties, arresting in tube-skirt
profile, insurgent under their fascist girdles, abysmal, Olympian,
nuclear, they furrow the sidewalks of Río Piedras like invincible
national airships.

More intense than a Colombian buzz, more persevering
than Somoza, He tracks Her through the snaking river of derrieres.
He is as faithful as a Holy Week procession with his hey little fox
litany, his you're fine, you're lookin' good, those pants dress you up
nice, that's a lush woman, man, packed to load limit, all that meat
and me livin' on slim pickins.

And in fact She is a good looker. Brassiere showing
through, Bermuda triangle traced with every jiggle of her spike
heels. On the other hand, He would settle for a broomstick in a
baseball jersey.

Sssssay, fine asssss woman. He comes undone in sensual
hissing as he leans his mug perilously close to the technicolor curls
of his prey. She then kicks in the secondaries and, with her rear end
in overdrive, momentarily removes her virtue to safety.

But the salsa chef wants his Christmas ham and turns on
his relentless street song: what a chassis, baby, a walkin' pound
cake, raw material, a sure enough hunk of a woman, what legs, if I
were rain I'd fall on you.

The siege goes on for two biblical days. Two days of dogged
pursuit and unnerving ad lib. Two long days of hey, delicious, hey
honeycakes, I could light you up, she's an animal that woman, I'm

all yours, for you I'd even work, who are you staying in deep-freeze for, man-killer?

On the third day, directly in front of the Pitusa Five and Ten, and with the spicy noontime sizzle of sofrito in the air, the victim takes a deep breath, pivots spectacularly on her precarious heels and slam dunks one.

"Whenever you're ready."

Thrown from his mount, the rider does an emotional head-over-heels. Ready nevertheless to risk it all for his national virility, he alights on his feet and blurts out in telling formality, "as you wish."

At this point she solemnly takes over. A metallic, red '69 Ford Torino sits in the parking lot at the Plaza del Mercado. They get in. They take off. The radio howls a senile bolero. She drives with one hand on the steering wheel and the other on the window, with a couldn't-care-less air about her. He begins violently to wish for a seaside bachelor's pad, a kind of discotheque/slaughterhouse where he could process the grade-A prime that life sometimes drops in one's lap like free food stamps. But unemployment fuels no dreams and he is kicking himself, thinking if I had known about this ahead of time I'd have hit up Papo Quisqueya for his room, Papo is blood, he's Santo Domingo soul, a high-steppin' no-jive street sultan and we're thick with our chicks. Damn, he says to himself, giving up. Then, sporting his best soap opera smile, he attempts to sound natural giving directions.

"Head for Piñones."

But she one-ups him again, taking instead the Caguas Highway as if it were a golden thigh of Kentucky Fried Chicken.

The motel entrance lies hidden in the shrubbery. Guerrilla warfare surroundings. The Torino slides vaseline-like up the narrow entranceway. The clerk nods from a coy distance, gazing coolly ahead like a horse with blinders. The car squeezes into the garage. She gets out. He tries to open the door without unlocking it, a herculean task. At last he steps out in the name of Homo Sapiens.

The key is shoved all the way into the lock and they penetrate the entrance to the room. She turns on the light. It is a merciless neon, a revealer of pimples and blackheads. He jumps at the sight of the open black hand sticking out through the pay window. He remembers the interplanetary void in his wallet. An agonizing and secular moment at the end of which She deposits five pesos in the black hand, which closes up like a hurt oyster and disappears, only to reappear again instantly. Godfather-like gravel voice:

"It's seven. Two more."

She sighs, rummages through her purse, takes out lipstick, compact, mascara, Kleenex, base, shadow, pen, perfume, black lace bikini panties, Tampax, deodorant, toothbrush, torrid romance and two pesos which she chucks at the insatiable hand like so many bones. He feels the socio-historical compulsion to remark:

"It's tough on the street, eh?"

From the bathroom comes the rushing sound of an open faucet. The room feels like a closet. Mirrors, though, everywhere. Half-sized single bed. Sheets clean but punished with wear. Zero pillows. Red light overhead. He like freaks out at the thought of all the people that must have blushed under the loud red light, all the horny Puerto Rican thrills spilled out in that room, the orgies the mirror must have witnessed, the bouncing the bed has taken. He parks his thought at the Plaza Convalescencia, aptly named for the hosts of sickies who get their daily cure there, oh, Convalescencia, where the cool stroll of the street lizards is a tribal rite. It is his turn now, and it won't be campaign rhetoric he's spouting. He stands before the group, walking back and forth, rising and falling on his epic mount: She was harder than a mafioso's heart, bro'. I just looked at her and she turned into jelly right there. I took her to a motel, man. They hit you for seven pesos now just to blast a cap.

She comes out of the bathroom. Her goddess complex not undeserved. Not a stitch on her. An awesome Indian queen. Brother, there was more ass on her than you could put up on a movie screen.

"Don't you intend to take your clothes off?" thunders Guabancex from the pre-Columbian heights of El Yunque.

He turns to the task at hand. Off comes the undershirt. Off comes the belt. Down come the pants. She lies back, the better to grasp you. At last his underwear drops with the metallic weight of a chastity belt. Remote-controlled from the bed, a projectile closes the strip-tease act. He catches it and—oh, must we not blush—it is a condescending condom and an indisposable one at that.

In the Pine-Sol-saturated bathroom the stud ram engages nature. He wants to go into this in full warrior splendor. Retroactive cerebral functions are no help. Cracks spied through barely open doorways: zip. Social science teacher in black panties: zip. Gringo female sunning her Family Size tits on a terrace: zip. A couple feeling each other up inside and out in the back row at the Paradise Theater: zip. Stampeding women rubbed against and desired on the streets and freely deflowered in his mind; recall of memorized pages of Mexican porno rags; incomparable Playboy centerfolds, rewind, replay; the old hot and heavy war lingo: nail me, negrito; devastate me, daddy, melt me down, big man. But . . . zip. There's not a witch doctor alive who can raise this dead body up.

She is calling him. In vain Clark Kent seeks the Emergency Exit. His Superman suit is at the cleaner's.

From within a Marlboro smoke cloud she is saying her final prayers. It's all up to luck now, you might say, and she is on the threshold of life's own phenomenal cleansing ritual. Since Hector's wedding with that shit-eating white baby doll from Condado, having a hymen is a crime that drags her down. Seven years in a playboy dentist's hip pocket. Seven years filling cavities and scraping tartar. Seven years staring down gaping throats, breathing septic tank breath for a wink or a limp pass or a Tinkerbell tease or a hollow hope. But today the convent lets go. Today the vows of chastity take the tomato pickers' flight out. She changes the channel and tunes in to the cheap deal destiny has dealt her for this date: a plump little cork of a man, stiff-comb Afro, bandanna-red T-shirt and battle-weary jeans. Truly light years away from her glittering, dental assistant's dreams. But truly, too, the historic moment has come, is banging down the door like a drunken husband, and it's getting later all the time and she already missed the big ride once; there was Viet Nam and there was emigration and that left rationing in between, and statehood is for the poor, and you jog or you get fat though after all it's not the gun that counts but the shots it fires. So there it is, the whole thing, scientifically programmed right down to the radio that will drown her vestal cries. And then back to society sans tasseled debutante gown, and let the impenetrable veil of anonymity forever swallow up her portable emergency mate.

Suddenly there is a wrenching scream. She rushes to the bathroom. He is straddled and half-bent over the bidet, pale as a gringo in February. When He sees her he falls to the floor, epileptically writhing and moaning as if possessed. Dawning realization that She may have gotten herself involved with a junkie, an actual, hard-core dope addict. When the moaning reaches all but a death rattle, She asks if perhaps it wouldn't be wise to call up the motel clerk. As if by magic, his wailing ceases. He straightens up, maternally cooing and soothing his hurt tummy.

"I've got a stomachache," he says, giving her his mangy-dog-looking-at-kennelmaster look.

SONEO I

First aid. Mouth-to-mouth resuscitation. Caressing the crisis-stricken belly, She breaks into a full-blown rap on historical materialism and classless society. Vigorous dictatorship-of-proletariat rub-down. Party Program hallelujah chorus. First on a small, then a medium, then a large scale, He experiences a gradual strengthening of his long-napping consciousness. They unite. Intoning the Fifth International in emotional unison, they bring their infrastructures to shuddering excitation. Nature answers the call of the mobilized masses and the act is dialectically consummated.

SONEO II

Heavy-duty confrontation: Her on Him. She sits him down

on the bed, sitting cross-legged next to him. Inspiringly fluent, dazzlingly lucid, She tears a millennium of oppression to shreds; all those centuries of ironing, comrade, and all that forced kitchen work. She gets carried away while emphatically demanding genital equality. She gets carried away in her own eloquence, using her brassiere as an ashtray while emphatically demanding genital equality. Caught in the implacable spotlight of reason, He confesses, repents, firmly resolves to mend his ways and fervently implores communion with her. Their emotions stirred, they join hands and unite in a long, egalitarian kiss, inserting exactly the same amount of tongue into their respective bucal cavities. Nature answers the unisex call and the act is equitably consummated.

SONEO III

She gets dressed. He is still holding out in the bathroom. She throws his clothes to him. They split from the motel without a word to each other. When the metallic red '69 Ford stops at De Diego Street to unload its cargo, the holiday of rideable rear ends is still in full cinematic swing. Intense as a Colombian buzz, as persevering as Somoza and as shameless as the Shah, He falls basely back into it. And He's a rogue combing the streets again, a part of the endless daybreak litany that says bless my soul, brown Sally, my but do you move, baby, say, what do you eat to stay so healthy, those are some lamb chops, man, God bless rice and beans, a prime cut I'd say, Momma, watch out if I catch you . . .

Translated by Mark McCaffrey

Rosamaría Roffiel (Mexico)

GIOCONDA[1]

My vulva is a flower
she's a shell
a fig
velvet
she is full of scents flavors and corners
she's the color of a rose
soft
intimate
fleshy

When I was twelve she sprouted down
a cloud of cotton between my thighs
she feels vibrates bleeds gets angry gets wet throbs
she talks to me

Jealously between her folds
she guards the exact center of my cosmos
tiny moon that bursts into flames
wave that leads to another universe

Every twenty five days she turns red
explodes
screams
then I squeeze her between my hands
I whisper words of love to her

She is my second mouth
she's naughty
she frolics

---

[1]Another title often used for Leonardo DaVinci's "Mona Lisa." — Eds.

spouts
she drenches me

She likes tongues that think they're butterflies
solidary penises
the pulp of woman's plum
or simply
my own caresses

She's a panther
a gazelle
a rabbit
she plays the coquette if you spoil her
she closes violently if you offend her
she's my accomplice
she's my friend
the eternal smile of the pleasured woman.

Translated by Stephanie Lovelady

Excerpt from
AMORA

We are women, and we like it

I let the afternoon slip by, a cup of coffee before me. Around me, a steady murmur of voices, of children running between the tables like flies wounded by the light. I feel isolated, however. It is a pause in my day. A gift from time. Just for me. To recollect my life. To pinpoint my life cycles. The path traveled. My years of solitude, of feeling like a strange toadstool, different from any other woman I knew. Completely alienated from the domestic reality of my former schoolmates, from the longings for marriage and motherhood of my colleagues at work, from my neighbors' mediocre lives. I, the strange one. The silently maladapted. The one who never understood why she wasn't like the others. How long ago seems that October morning in 1977 when I heard the feminists speak out for the first time and I told myself—dazed by surprise— "But I am a feminist, and I didn't know it!" What bewildering joy to discover that there were women who lived like me, who shared my hopes, who spoke my language. What touching relief to find answers to questions that had been troubling me since my childhood. I attended my first meeting at Marta Lamas' like someone keeping an unavoidable appointment with the unknown. Terror, curiosity, nervousness, hope. There were fourteen of us. We started to talk about abortions, lovers, lost virginities. We grew intimate, candid. We drank red wine. We rocked with laughter, every so often someone would get up to pee. We felt deliciously perverse and marvelously free as we told each other things we wouldn't share with anyone else. Then I knew I was no longer alone. That I had found a new meaning for the word friendship. I began to wear the stigma of feminism with such pride! *What a pack of crazy old fools, hags, idle women. What a bunch of lesbians, of manhaters. What a band of ugly, bitter women.*

But, say what they may, the women of the future are going

to have much to thank us for, we, the pioneers in saying no, in thinking, in daring to live alone, to be independent, to run risks, to refuse to be sexual objects, to face a secular and patriarchal society with a new mentality.

Most of us are burdened with dreadful histories that not only have failed to annihilate us but from which we learned to draw our strength. Millions and millions of women being born to a new identity, searching within and outside ourselves, eager to attempt new ways of being, anxious for a more dignified and equitable relationship with a man or with another woman, knowing ourselves for the first time in our lives. The panorama of possibilities open to us has startled us, we can't believe our eyes. Some of us are perhaps terrified. But it is too late to stop. The process has begun and there's no going back. It becomes clearer every day: we are the force of the future, the engine driving our coming history, and men know it and tremble. Many men will share our dawn. The rest will resort to desperate measures that will only hasten their downfall. Those willing to renounce their privileges will build the new society by our sides.

For many people, feminist is synonymous with lesbian. I wish it were so! But, not all feminists are lesbians and—unfortunately—not all lesbians are feminist. If you just knew what a hard struggle it was to get many "feminist sisters" to accept lesbians in their own groups. God forbid if someone got us mixed up . . . It was quite a relief to them when the Mexican Homosexual Liberation Movement was organized. But people still hold on to that notion. And yes, some feminists are lesbians, that is, some of us are women who love other women, which only means that we too are people, one of the two genders of humanity, and look—what a coincidence!—we are born, we grow up, we reproduce and we die . . . just like the rest of the human race; we enjoy ice cream and tacos; oh infamy!, we have to work to pay the rent; we get beaten down on like Lupita D'Alessio; we take buses, jitneys, and even the subway; we belong to all religions, political ideologies and signs of the Zodiac, and, as Rita Mae Brown has said, we come in all colors and flavors. Yes, just like you, we ended up living on the planet Earth, in the twentieth century, and to top it off in the Federal District of Mexico, so some of us are a little neurotic, just like some of you. And it is true that—just like you—we sometimes plunge headlong into love affairs that are real melodramas in several acts. And the worst thing is that sometimes it's just like going out with a guy, or worse still, that we act like the guys. Oh, whoa!, one says all of a sudden, what happened here? Well, nothing, that no matter how feminist, how free, how well-intentioned we are, we are mired in clichés, in learned habits, in traps, self-sabotages, limitations, a drag and a half, in short.

Of course, we would have to learn to love differently. To exchange the Mexican *rancheras* and the *boleros* for our own music, invented by us and our girlfriends. How I would love to print a full-page ad in all the newspapers, something like an invitation to all lesbians still repeating the patterns of domination so common in heterosexual love relationships: let's love differently, without slashing our veins, without threatening to jump from a car on the funicular, without ending up throwing up in Garibaldi Square or snatching away our friend's girlfriend just to show people how fucking irresistible we're being nowadays, that is, let's not love like they say lesbians love, as if we were the female version of the Black Charro. Because, I say, so much publicity is given to love and then it ends up with our looking pale and with dark circles under our eyes, depressed, saying at the age of twenty-two that life is not worth living, and that all chicks are the same. But no, fortunately, life is worth a lot and we're not all the same. There are still some of us who think that love can be different, that it is not necessary to fall in love passionately in order to build a life as a couple, that there are other options besides cohabitation and possessiveness, that we struggle each day against jealousy, that we hold our friend's freedom and privacy highly, that we try to speak honestly so as not to allow room for resentment, in short, that we make efforts to make of our love an oasis to run to after a day of working for the government, of standing in line to take the Route 100 bus, of breathing lead and amoebas from seven o'clock in the morning.

For me, to realize I could love women was as important as it was for Columbus to discover America. And it isn't that I had bad relationships with men. Quite the contrary! I went out with the cutest guys, which I really enjoyed until way into my twenties. We would go bowling, to the movies, drinking, dancing to Barbarella's, out to eat tacos and to fool around. But as I got to know myself better, they would relate to me less and less, until the time came when the gaps between us were bigger than the fillings. By then, women had begun to shine in my universe. Ah, women! So crucial to my life, for better or worse.

My mother, who did not crumble to pieces when my father left her. Who, although she kept repeating that a woman needs a man in order to exist, demonstrated the opposite in practice.

My grandmother, to whom I owe, among other things, two of the most beautiful gifts I received during my childhood: the love of books and knowing how it feels to be the most important being in someone's life.

My sisters, who showed me with their example exactly how I didn't want my life to be.

Miss Marianne, my literature teacher, who sowed in me forever a passion for British poets of all centuries.

Those anonymous women, traveling companions in the Roma-Mérida and Mariscal Sucre routes, who taught me how to defend myself from feelers and masturbators, also anonymous.

Those colleagues who welcomed me so sweetly the first time I set foot in an office, at the age of fifteen, dying of fright. And those others who would later be my rivals, and thanks to whom I learned to raise my voice and demand my rights.

Doña Raymunda, spiritualist and my grandparents' neighbor in Veracruz, who talked to me for hours about how we must love every living being in this world and about how death doesn't exist because in reality we are souls dressed in bodies and minds.

Paola, who with her eyes full of fire and her tender lips awakened me to the possibility of loving women.

Eva, my first love relationship, with whom I lived for four years, and who was able to recognize and fulfill my longing to dis-

cover the mysteries of art and literature, who taught me to appreciate good films and theater, and to love classical music. Eva, who
wasn't able to understand that forever doesn't exist and turned the
last weeks of our love story into a true hell.

Marisa, my lover, my friend, my cosmic sister, my proudest
relationship. Seven years of living together with love and without
deceit. Why separate after passion subsides when there are so many
other things left? Only the physical distance that took her to her job
in Europe finally forced us to live under different roofs.

And all those other women I have loved, those whom I
fooled myself into believing I loved, those who were not able to love
me. I owe them my strength. Through them I learned my capacity
to love, and to cry. I learned the exquisiteness of passion. Their
presence is always with me, because they are part of my history.

This surely must be how goddesses love
Fresh moon water, with silver glints. Lace sheets. Shroud of
light. Mother-of-pearl bed. Two women. Two. Face to face in this
unrepeatable game which is love. Fever of desire, song in one voice.
Love dart nearing its target, sweet whisper. I let the afternoon
undress you, I let it consecrate your skin. You offer yourself like a
flower, like a giant wave. What an urge to kiss you! But I only look
at you, look at you . . . and I don't dare touch you. Your aroma surrounds me. I sense you, my love, I sense you. You have fire inside.
Time doesn't exist. Only this. A fusion of sighs, a tempest of
echoes. What drunkenness. What joy. A flight of turtledoves over
your body. A nest of larks your nest. Your flesh-colored grotto. I
yearn, I yearn for your womb, for the coral between your thighs. I
trace your contour with my eyes. I look at you a thousand times. I
look at you again and never grow tired. How many wetnesses flow
over us. Oh sweat that makes our flesh glow! Quietly, the silence listens to us desiring each other. From your shore, your breath reaches
me and bites me, excitedly. The afternoon is dyed with sap, with

bird-flowers, with the smell of sandalwood. Your tender sex invites me. So does your hair. Your nipples dare me. How I would like to fill my mouth with them! Come near, the sails of my love are ready to navigate to your deepest skin, to touch your essence. Come, let's love and love and love and love each other, and never stop. Your pupils sparkle with such tenderness. Our backs arch and tremble. So much wealth in a simple look. You finally shatter the space with your hand, you touch my lips lightly with your fingertips. You break Sleeping Beauty's spell. Desire overflows in an infinite swing. Our caresses unstring the night. The semi-darkness is a shawl that covers our shoulders. Outside, the wind blows history away. Under the sheets, a love belonging to the cosmos, two women love each other in a secret language, withdrawn from the world. In spite of everything.

Love is a many-splendoured thing
"Tell me how you realized that you could love women."

We are in Claudia's bed, facing the wooded landscape of a ravine. We have just made love. I hold her tightly in my arms, and she lets me love her.

"I already told you . . . Besides, that was a very long time ago."

"Precisely because it was, tell me! I didn't know you then."

"Well, here it goes: 'Once upon a time there was a little princess . . . ' "

"Amora, don't be such a clown!"

"Ok, ok, but only from the time I went to Cuernavaca with a colleague from work and, at a given moment, she stared into my eyes, held my chin and drew near me to kiss me, on the lips!"

"Yes, from that point."

"I thought I was going to have a fit. In a fraction of a second a flood of thoughts overwhelmed me. 'I'm sure she's a lesbian. What do I do now? Do I push her away? Do I hit her? Should I scream? Should I run out of here?' I didn't know how to react, but that wonderful part of me which tends towards a shockproof mental health, went into action. 'Lupe, my girl, aren't you the one going around proclaiming that you want to experience everything so that you don't have to hear about it? Well, this is part of everything!' It was as if I had fought an inner battle and well, I relaxed, I allowed myself to be kissed, I returned the kiss, and that was when . . . "

"When what?"

"When I started to feel very pleasant, very different things. My blood galloped through my veins, I felt a new warmth in my body, as if my skin were alive, separate from me, as if my lips had turned softer, I don't know how to explain it very well."

"And what else happened?"

"She undressed me very delicately and we made love. Well, she made love to me because I, apart from being a beginner, was in Nirvana. Everything was spinning around me!"

"How old were you?"

"Twenty two."

"But you had already made love to guys, right?"

"Of course! And I continued doing it long after, falling deeply in love with some."

"And why not anymore?"

"Less and less all the time, it's true. I have tried, but . . . emotionally, they're just children. They can't touch my soul! Although, as I've told you, I will be open to a heterosexual relationship till the end of my days."

"And when you had that incident with that girl, did you feel any guilt or conflict?"

"Never! Quite the contrary. I was levitating with happiness. I had the feeling I had uncovered a very important secret, that I had recovered half of the world."

"What a lucky one you are!"

"Norma says I must come from another planet because I don't react like earthlings do. But it's just that I thought: 'Anything that awakens such beautiful feelings in me can't be bad.' What madness! I was dying to embrace people in the streets and cry out: 'One can also love women!' Obviously, not only did I never do that but many years went by before I could tell anyone about it."

"I wish I could feel like that, but I can't. I'm scared. Sometimes I think that we're really just friends, but when we make love and you make me feel all this, I realize that I am fooling myself, that we are lovers. And my fear returns!"

"What are you afraid of, Claudia? Of what people will say? Of what you feel? Of what?"

"Of everything! But yes, mostly of what people will say."

"Claudia, life is not a gift but an option. Life is not about suffering from trying to do what others want you to do instead of what you truly want."

"I find sexuality to be the most conflictive aspect of all. "

"Sexuality has to do with life. It's an everyday thing, but it's been surrounded by so many taboos that we find it difficult to reconcile it with our eagerness to be coherent."

"What does it mean for you to be coherent, Amora?"

"To live according to your beliefs, not to allow any part of your self to be denied, to give your self every possibility to develop."

"But that is almost impossible."

"What matters is to be true to yourself, Claudia, to feel life around you, in spite of everything. And I swear to you, sweetheart, that no one can say that we're not trying, every day, every instant."

"Who's we?"

"Women of conscience, in our case, feminists."

"Amora, what really is feminism?"

" I suppose there are as many feminisms as there are women in the world. To me, it is a life project that restores to us our historical value. One should be the first to recognize one's own value, and with that as a foundation, demand the same recognition from the beings around you."

"It's an exhausting task."

"Of course it is! Do you think it's easy to have a conscience? It's a pain in the ass! And there's no going back! But one doesn't choose . . . "

"I sometimes wish I didn't know anything."

"If you like to live with clenched teeth, that's up to you."

"If you don't know anything you don't have to live with clenched teeth."

"Not necessarily. How many women without conscience bear situations that make them live with clenched teeth."

"It also frightens me to see that you and I see life in so very different colors."

"Ah, but it is the combination of colors that make up the most beautiful paintings."

"This is the closest thing to happiness I've ever known, I don't know why I'm so scared. It's stupid, I admit! I have spent years dreaming of a love like this, and now I'm scared."

"Great loves exist, Claudia. It's just a matter of learning to recognize them, of not fearing them when they appear in your life, because they don't always arrive in the shape one expected."

"Oh, Amora, you make me feel so good!"

Claudia kisses my neck. I melt. She brings her lips near my ear and says to me:

"Who loves you, Amora?"

"Well, to begin with, me . . . "

She bursts out laughing:

"Overtime! This is too much! This feminist works overtime!"

"And since she works so hard she's dying of hunger . . . "

We get up, half-dressed, wearing long t-shirts and no panties.

"Oh, Amora, I'm going to freeze my little tail off."

"Your what?"

"My little tail," she replies, covering her sex with both hands.

"Claudia, it is your vulva, your sex, your flower, your dove, your butterfly, something more . . . poetic!, how can you call it a little tail?"

"That's what they taught me as a child."

"I must admit you were luckier than I."

"Why?"

"Because back in Veracruz, boys had little birds and girls had little cockroaches."

"Really?"

"I swear to you. Imagine, growing up with the sensation of having a cockroach between your legs, and people still ask me why I'm in therapy!"

In a matter of minutes we move from the depths of our being to the simplicity of a couple of boiled eggs, bathed in a strange sauce that Claudia invents, mixing almost alchemical substances right before my eyes, eyes full of tenderness toward this tiny magician capable of bringing so many new flavors into my life.

We install ourselves back on the mattress. Claudia takes off her t-shirt and her breasts appear like two exotic fruits from some island lost even to geographical atlases. I make an effort to concentrate again on the food trays.

We turn on the television just as three moustached charros with guitar and hats sing the ballad of Rosita Alvirez:

> Hipólito arrived at the party
> and asked Rosita to dance.
> Since she was the prettiest girl there
> she didn't spare him a glance.
> "Rosita, don't you dare snub me,
> they'll notice if you do."
> "Why should I care about all that,
> I will not dance with you."
> He reached down for his holster
> and drew his pistol out,
> and into poor Rosita
> he fired three fatal shots.

"Dead for being a tramp!," Claudia concludes.

"Not at all! Dead for daring to defend her right to choose

which man to dance with."

"Dead for being a feminist then!"

"Let's just say that's a very *sui generis* interpretation."

"Why? You don't like my explanation? Rosita Alvirez, first Mexican feminist to die in the line of duty."

"The very first, I don't know about that. Can you imagine all the anonymous dead women in this country, assassinated for having dared contradict our national *charros*?"

"I see your point. There should be a monument to them like that of the unknown soldier."

"Of course! In honor of the unknown rebellious woman, that is, of all those women who dared say no."

"And just for that the motherfuckers slapped the hell out of them!"

"Yes, ma'am. Although that is not a very feminist way to talk."

"What should I say then? The fatherfuckers?"

"Father? Lord no! What sense does it make to say fatherfuckers when in Mexican society fathers are best known for not being around. Anyone can say to me *fuck your father* and I couldn't care less. My parents divorced when I was six years old and he completely forgot that he had contributed to the procreation of five human beings. You tell me if that has any power to insult me. Not at all!"

We turned off the tv set and went back to cuddle in our nest. Now it's my turn to let myself be loved. I start to respond and we make love once more. We loved each other for a long while, until I dozed off in Claudia's arms. I don't know how much time has gone by. Suddenly, I recall the time, and with my lips glued to her neck I say:

"Sweetheart, do you realize that we have spent close to forty hours in this room?"

"Humm . . . I love our anarchy," she says as she stretches out.

And she adds:

"Oh, Amora! Sometimes I think that I could live with you."

She remains thoughtful, sighs and asks:

"What would it be like to live together?"

Waxing poetic (and silly), I sit on the bed, think for a moment, and say:

"Humm . . . if I lived with you, I would rise before the sun, and before I pushed the sheets away, I would leave my prints on you as if you were made of sand. I would bring you carnations for breakfast and would spy on you through the bathroom keyhole to see you commune with the water. We would have our own code, we wouldn't fall back on habits and grudges, we would walk around the house barefoot, embracing each other with each glance. We would drink wine or tea before the fireplace, while it rains outside. And I would feel outrageously happy as I watched you discovering all the cardinal points of your womanhood."

Claudia watches me, enraptured.

"Oh, Amora, there's no doubt about it: love is a many-splendoured thing!"

Translated by Lizabeth Paravisini-Gebert

❦ Nemir Matos

I SOAR ON THE WINGS . . .

I soar on the wings of your cunt at high tide
to the sea mastered by the embankments of your body
I soar to the sourcespring of water
I soar on the petals of your cunt
        to the blossom of the marigold
I soar to the seed
        to the secret cycle of life and death
and of the seed
        to the stem
        to the bud
        to the open flower
        to the dry petal
        to the womb of the new seed which as it falls
        impregnates the earth and grows anew
I soar to the eternity of movement
to the very center of time
to the vortex.

Translated by Lizabeth Paravisini-Gebert

Matilde Daviú (Venezuela)

THE WOMAN WHO TORE UP THE WORLD

> " . . . From the May Flower will come the bread, the May Flower
> will produce the water that they carry in their katún. Then it
> will come to pass that they will begin to stain their lips with the
> women and will summon the May Flower with their hands, dur-
> ing the Katún, with a sideways glance . . ."
>
> —7 Ahau
> (The Book of Chilam Balam)

The woman who tore up the world and the man who burnt
it left the bar together. He gave her a flower and she smiled com-
plaisantly. Then they entered the cavern, passing from darkness
into the dim interior. The man who burnt the world threw himself
onto the uncovered bed, hid his face between his arms, and punc-
tured the air with his first drunken snores. He entered a dreamless
sleep. The woman remained dressed, and in an effort to impose
wakefulness, maintained a love dialogue, or at the very least a philosophical discussion. She approached the bed where the man snored.
She caressed his ears with the tip of her tongue and bit his neck
softly. She enjoyed playing the role of temptress unveiling all her
cards. She felt capable of unbridled seduction after all for the first
time. Uninhibited, in an outburst of freed sexuality, she decided to
awaken the man. At first, he responded to the kisses and caresses,
but strength abandoned him, and he again sank into a deep, dreamless sleep. The woman gave up slowly and, rationalizing the drunk
man's behavior, withdrew without bitterness. Feeling her way, she
walked to the desk, turned on the night lamp, looked for paper and
pencil, and sat down at the table. When she was about to trace the
first strokes of her lines, she found herself startled by a key word
caught between two pillars: a jar of vitamins and another one of
Optalidon. She halted her initial stroke as her thoughts shifted

from writing to reading. She picked up the two jars that supported the letter and started to read. She skimmed the first paragraphs, the first page, and continued to read her lover's description of Carnival. Halfway through the page she stopped abruptly: an inconceivable anger shook her. The man continued sleeping dreamlessly. The woman who tore up the world continued to read avidly and the evidence jumped out at her. In the letter the man had gone overboard crudely describing memories of a past sexual encounter. The woman felt disgust, abandoned her reading, and gave herself over completely to a vaginal and cerebral fury. She looked with disgust at the mound on the bed and became convinced he was unworthy of her. All the beauty of the love act had suddenly become repugnant. She rose from the chair and sat on the edge of the bed. She managed to turn the man's body with great effort and when he faced her, she slapped his face. The man did not react; he slept like a log. Insisting on violence, she hit him even harder. The woman who tore up the world had two ways of striking his face: with the back of the hand for situations that called for a dignified response, and with the palm of the hand for punishment. This time the woman used both methods. She was unable to wake him, and overcome by a wild fury, she rose from the bed and began to pace the room. She felt abused in the innermost recesses of her womanhood; she felt used, torn in her center. Something atavistic exploded in her solar plexus. She felt and lived man's neglect of his most divine essence. She rebelled against venal love lacking poetry. She felt like an invaded land, and began to prepare her defense.

She looked for scissors and went directly to the world that was his, with the aim of extracting Latin America. The man continued to sleep. With great care, she cut out the Atlantic coast, the Caribbean and the Pacific Coast. As she removed America, her anger slowly turned to sadness. She had to separate it from the rest, to avoid its contamination by the sexual enslavement of the Western world. Let the other continents sink, she did not care. She wanted to save America in order to save herself. For that reason she put it in her pocket, and tore up the rest . . . Isn't it possible to live happily and carelessly in the most transcendental acts?

She returned to the desk and began to throw all the roses in the room out the window. She again sat at the desk, and overpowered by a profound sadness, she settled down to await daybreak. It would be another day with America safely in her pocket. She would wait for the man to open his eyes and discover the disappearance of the other continents. She discovered in herself a tiny belly laugh, and allowed it to carry her away. The myth of Huehanna returned to life: the happy ones, the contented ones and the ones who knew how to sing to everything, all were saved in that woman's pocket. In a gesture of absolute scorn, she threw the other pieces of the world in the bottom of the waste basket.

It was nine o'clock when the sun entered the man through his swollen eyelids. She remained in her warrior position. She observed his heavy awakening and his routine morning greeting. Lost inside herself she replied between clenched teeth: "contaminated." The man looked at the empty wall, looked to the sides and searching in anguish questioned the woman. The woman who tore up the world refused to give a single word in reply.

The war had been fought in Silence . . .

Translated by Carmen C. Esteves

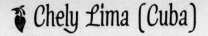 **Chely Lima (Cuba)**

CARNAL INVENTORY

You are throbbing to a tenacious rhythm, imperceptible,
in a throat that yields to my teeth.
                             Turn over, rub your fruity cheek
against the sheets.
Centimeters below, your mouth plays at quivering
                         and letting go,
butterfly of blood, oyster anointed with honey.
And then the sunbronzed prairie of your back
where invisible animals graze
                        and wander to drink at your waist.
Fierce waters converge at the chiaroscuro line,
the mysterious border of your buttocks
what better pillow for my forehead when you lie
                        face down,
what smoother mattress for my waist
when you sleep with arms open allowing
                        my etching hands
to gird your torso,
as they burn with the arrow tips of your
                        nipples.
Apollo resides in your bared legs
and in your pleasurable thighs there is an antediluvian
                        taste that summons the tongue:
secret passages close up: sibyllic passages
                        open
under the pubic grasses that offer those who can
                        follow
entry to the abode of the fires:
there an ivory boar suns herself on the paired
                        fruit
and still takes the winding staircase to the grotto
                        of no return.

Chely Lima

Now the fish sleeps in the palm of my hand
clamped within the rings of an ancient amphibian.
                    Sleep,
await the hour of bewilderment.

Translated by Margarite Fernández Olmos

🦉 Ana Istarú (Costa Rica)

III

This treatise testifies
honestly
that modesty and its dream
cannot a better master find
than the peaceable haven
of the vagina
and to me it assigns
a virginal
and lasting peace.
This the treatise attests.
As a Latin and thus sweet and truly
inclined
to a chaste tension of the behind.
And with no harm
seemingly done
by the intentions pure
of so many curates.
The bridegroom is pleased,
the father is appeased
that in Central America
one always finds
his daughter virginal and asexual.
This treatise relates
how the male dominates
and impregnates
in America, Central
and Panamanian.
And from this phallic
omnipotence
my working woman's resistance

defends me.
Because I take the tips of my breasts,
little bells
of the sharpest iron
and banish
this punctual hymen
that muzzles me silent
with machista violence
and a long list
of colonial inheritance.
I delete this treatise from the skulls,
with the wrath of quetzal
I annihilate it,
with military reserve
I bite and pulverize it,
as with a corpse, as hesitant and withered
I kill it and kill it again
with my sex open and red,
cardinal cluster of my happiness,
from this America incarnate and inflamed
the Central one, my America of rage.

Translated by Heather Rosario-Sievert

XI

My clitoris sparks
into the whiskers of the night
like a petal of lava,
like a tremendous eye
assaulted by bliss
attacked and counter-attacked by pleasure
with delicate juices,
feverish salamanders.
The uterus forgets
its soft habitation. It unravels
the chords of space.
Man, my pubis
traverses you, fiery and open.

Translated by Heather Rosario-Sievert

XII

I am the day.
My left breast is the dawn.
My other breast is the setting sun.

The night I am.
My sex drank in the shadow
black vineyards, peaches,
the storm.

The robust rose of the wind,
silk made flesh in my ovary.

Translated by Heather Rosario-Sievert

XVI

This nuptial night
I am my balcony.
Window I am
With no attire save that of love.
And when the day
knocks on the window pane
I shall dress myself in my bridal sheet.
A balcony I am.
To display the ever-so-white bedsheet
through the window,
after this nuptial night.
Without a single bitter nervure,
without purple pins,
without an island or cotton
in which the pain can lodge itself.
White and pure
I am my balcony.
Goodbye blood.
Goodbye blood and its darkness.
For naked and covered
with my wedding sheet
I am armed.
And through the streets of Spain
and to my tired America I go,
displaying my white cloth,
white vagina. White love.
Because on this nuptial night I am my balcony.

Translated by Heather Rosario-Sievert

XVII

The sun is born between your legs,
and raises with the effort
of a minor god
the tower of your body,
as solemn as he, and as light.
His golden fist
is erecting your penis
(the envy of the archangel
without a sex to depend on)
until reaching the top
of the lip where you sweeten
your drop of maleness
and sustain it,
tied up like a ship
anchored in its sperm.
You will navigate an echo in my womb.
I will be the rain, something I will create
during the flight
grabbing fast to your loin.
And then, what tidal peace
as you baptize
the vessel of my deepest essence.
Your sun. Your sun. Your sun.
My dark well.

Translated by Daisy C. De Filippis

XIX

An expanding moon
rides between my legs.

On its thighs the steed
turns golden, the rising sun.

For husband dove,
the heavy Plum.

This wife that I am
the sea shell.

The darkest hare
in my man ascends.

Horizon inhabits me
of guava and curvature.

The axis of his body
of my body is the axis.

An ebony in two branches,
an inky vine.

An expanding moon
rides between his legs.
On my thighs the steed
turning golden, the rising sun.

Translated by Heather Rosario-Sievert

Ana Istarú

XX

The night was torn
through its flour sack.

Your hair was the shadow
that unraveled the string.

Footprints of snails
moisten
the rosy peak
of my two calves.

I am bathed
in sap and wounded grass.

Under an Ilian roof,
bone of white essence,
my disk of happiness
blazes.

Translated by Daisy C. De Filippis

✿ Daína Chaviano (Cuba)

EROTICA I

What will he think of me
this man caged in shyness
what mouth of musty sounds
would be able to compound it into particles
falling to pieces
on my breasts subjected and open
what would he do if
                        in a moment
I were to hurl at him the link that opens my legs
or an erotomanic smile
in what unerring manner can I erase
certain ways of burying him deep into me
the misguided breath
when I look and I imagine him
face downward on me
I lady godiva on the fortunate loins
what solid way of submerging myself into his southern accent
while he watches and imagines me
                        clinging to his mane
like a tree of sun or
        a conquered beast
                red habit of threading myself
what events will his hands knit
get to boil
                        between
my former history and that which will come after him
how to raise up the necklace of compliments
he set aside
                only for me
what phallic peoples will rise up from my knees

to achieve their assault on the heavens
from this giant with lust of suicide
at the edge of the avalanche
but noting his destiny
                              sword compass against all
                              the predictions of the game
towards the central furrow of my hips

Translated by Heather Rosario-Sievert

MEMO FOR FREUD

In the center of the lake was an island
full of castles inhabited by ants.
Each rainy night
came the warriors to spawn
their spears of light
that I frightened away by the cries of a vampire.
Slowly I stretched out on the grass
and you rolled over me.
Over and again you plunged a smooth stake
                              into my vulva
Like a silver nail
                         and you smiled,

I don't know why
when I fall in love I have nightmares.

Translated by Heather Rosario-Sievert

EROTICA IV

It smells here of pent-up sex
        butterfly of incense covers us,
large drops of sugar on your tongue
falling in crazy spirals of walnut
        to your belly.
As you grow
you search for my sea animal
        and remain
ship anchored in the bay,
well of hard flesh
        submerged inside me.
    Marsupial
I shelter you in my womb until night,
my legs of lime wall you in
and on the peak of the world
        I discover
the fearless trot of the herd.
        I am the stanchion
        and you the foundation:
explosion shouting at the four fires
the exemplary rain that is born
of this sweetest beast in my hips.
Like a river I fuck you in the open bed.
An enormous house in your arms
        I imagine.
To your croup I return
To your croup
    of a riding breed in full flight.
I am the one who possesses you.
I am the one who proposes
        kiss by kiss
a revolution.

Translated by Heather Rosario-Sievert

Pía Barros (Chile)

FORESHADOWING OF A TRACE

Lick my knees, entreaty and devotion me, these thighs, tongue to tongue, lick the eager arch of my pelvis, subdue me, suck me, lick all my desire and aching, go up along my belly, higher, let your skin quiver as it grazes mine, hold me, bite my shoulders and tremble, let the fear invade you, that fretful longing, examine the secret trace of my pores, yearn for me . . . I will kiss your eyes, will bite the corners of your mouth, I will let you tremble in a masculine swoon, I'll draw my nails down the long descent of your back to plunge my head into your groin, I'll rub my face across your anguish and I shall have to hold you up by force as your knees flex involuntarily, no, you must not yet, not yet; and then, very slowly, my nipples will make their way up your belly, higher, going higher, but you will not hold me, you'll be weeping and I'll be powerful, invincible before you and you will not be able to take me, now that you are so wounded, you will bend your knees and weep over your trembling desire, still quivering, defeated . . . then, and only then, will I embrace your head to my pelvis, then I'll descend to where you are, I'll deploy my open thighs and give asylum to your anguish of sea and sands that will break on my powerful coasts, since by now it must be clear to you, now that the face of time has revealed itself to you, now that any trace of me is both indelible and unattainable.

Translated by Amanda Powell

A SMELL OF WOOD AND OF SILENCE

"You seem different this morning."

"Because I dreamt about seagulls," she said as she jumped from the bed to toast and eggs, steaming coffee and the daily ritual of shared breakfasts. She didn't listen when he said:

"How strange, you have green grass between your fingers . . ."

It started as a game to make the laundry less numbing. She began dreaming of hands that emerged from the sheets in search of her breasts. Hands that ought to be large, rough, bony and unkempt, with long fingers, that would touch her painlessly, vigorous hands raising and lowering her nipples, outlining her tingling skin, traversing her body.

She smiled on discovering that the washing machine had quit a long time ago, and she chased away this drowsiness, pouncing upon the sheets and covers that she would pin up still perturbed by that caress.

At times, as Ismael was sleeping, she would close her eyes in the semi-darkness, and let the hands carry her away. In turn, she would seize them to show them the secret traces of her pores and her trembling pleasure.

Ismael would drink his coffee as usual, immersed in the newspaper, but he noticed she looked ethereal and more beautiful than ever. Life was secure and he felt complete.

One afternoon as the heat stifled and made her dream about lakes in winter, she began to want some narrow hips with small, tight buttocks to dig her fingernails into; she wanted dark pubic hair to obscure the outline of the genitals.

He found her sleeping on the rug, her clothes in disarray and her lips partially opened and moist. Leaving his briefcase on the desk, he desired to make love to her that very instant, but he held himself back. This image appeared so virginal and she so delicate, that he refused to invade her and sat smiling for a long while, watching her sleep with such abandon, so sweetly, with her face made childlike by her dreams.

But she was licking hips, kissing buttocks, digging in her nails.

He didn't worry about her pale countenance until much later, when he noticed the obsessive way she dedicated herself to sleep. She seemed to be seeking every moment for a chance to close her eyes and when the house began to flaunt its neglect he asked her to see a doctor, for he'd heard that excessive sleep was a symptom of anemia. The tests came out negative and he didn't mention it again.

Autumn arrived and now she wanted him to be tall, not too tall, but enough so that in an embrace she could bury her face in a chest that would make her feel vulnerable. She passed long hours feeling him with her nude body, raising and lowering her nipples as if to outline his flat belly. She adored the extremely lean build she had given him in her dreams and she liked to imagine that his bones left their trace on her stomach. Little by little sleep was becoming the art of never being discovered and she liked to arrange sheets of different colors to cover herself and get away, far away, where privacy offered a refuge in which to proclaim her fantasies.

One time in particular the vertical rain over the city seduced her and the window opened her wider until she could imagine the countryside and the horses getting drenched in the distance. Wintertime kept her drowsy and the rain chipped at the landscape. It was then that she gave him a face and, shaken, she had the thought that from this moment on she was being unfaithful. The idea was jolting because he didn't exist, he was just many pieces of a various someone, fragments of attraction that made her guilty of nothing save the contents of her dreams. Liberated and eager she smiled and wished him a green, horizontal gaze with thick, dark eyebrows; and she felt saved, because she realized that he stayed far off, on the other side of the threshold, where it was possible to invent his salty skin that she could lick little by little, without constraint, until she could seize that skin, make it hers, go back over it.

Ismael began to keep watch over her sleep, to see the thin brown man smiling at him through the pupils of her half-opened eyes. He knew she was going to that man, that he was waiting for her . . . but soon she could close the tunnel of her lashes completely and leave Ismael on this side, defenseless, aching, and laughing at himself, while she tangled herself in the sheets and smiled in a distant and alien way.

"What took you so long?" he asked, tall and enigmatic, as she dreamed him to be.

It was hard for her to fall asleep, she responded, embracing the body that smelled of wood and of silence.

She knew that on this side everything was her own, that he would love her achingly and shamelessly, his soul filled with horses. Obligations, guilts, schedules were left on the other side.

The morning surprised them as she wanted it to, their bodies entangled, and he said, Don't leave yet, and began kissing her, searching for answers on her nipples, for questions on her buttocks, and she was getting dressed and walking to the door of the cabin, and he was following her laughing and boyish and was tumbling her down to the grass and making love to her with a joyful penetration, where the seagulls of time burst from their fingers and the orgasm came with the heavens in their eyes and she grabbed a fistful of grass to keep from feeling like she was dying, face to face with the bewilderment of a bird that flew over them, and the hoarse, deep laughter, that flowed uncontrollably, full, vibrant.

Ismael's hand on her shoulder had broken the threshold, and he said,

"You seem different this morning."

"Because I dreamt about seagulls."

Ismael watched her. He waited for her to sleep and he tried to see through the barely opened space of her groggy pupils where they were making love, where she was looking. The cabin, the lake and the sea were their hideaways; small barren islands where dreams were anchored leaving him vulnerable, defenseless. Ismael came across small objects that she had forgotten and brought with her across the threshold: a few grains of sand, weeds, a little paper boat, a reminder of winter in the heat of summer, or the blades of wild glass that were tangled in her hair when she woke up. He had grown accustomed to inspecting the sheets, painfully searching them for traces, humiliated by the fog that he didn't know how to fight, hiding the evidence from someone else's dreams.

She slept, fitful or ethereal, spending almost all her time on the other side of the threshold. In the house, dust piled up under the furniture and dirty dishes spilled their contents in various parts of the kitchen.

The rain made her close her eyes anew. "Come," she heard from far away. He was biting her briefly, licking her, bending her, subduing her. She wanted to return to the dreams of seagulls, but each bite hurled her towards strange images, a mouth screaming in the darkness, a partial smile half-opened by a cigarette, a man's shoes on the grass . . . , the tongue and teeth chafing her nipples launched her entirely into an enraged sea and the urgency of her desirous skin into a flaming hell that dried her mouth and scrawled her own silhouette, the silhouette of a voyeur spying on the game . . . his hand and his green gaze crawled over her skin and she slowly opened her thighs calling him, with an ancestral smell that she didn't recognize as her own, and the cabin became a fissure in the rock that scratched her back and the sea was there, roaring, lapping her calves which she raised to straddle the upright man whom the ocean seemed to be trying to knock down with its waves and foam, roaring, his buttocks and her legs intertwined around his back where her nails clung trying to mark, to leave a trace, and the man assailed her, making her eyes cloud over and leaving a thin line of moisture between her lips.

This time she couldn't hide her scraped back, the teeth-marks on her hips. Ismael didn't smile anymore, but he didn't ask questions. He was afraid he wouldn't be able to face the answers. There was no one to blame.

Little by little she grew thinner and now she didn't even go through the farce of getting out of bed. It was useless for Ismael to lift her head to coax her eyes open and make her swallow a few spoonfuls of soup. She was over there, in her delirium, making an offering of her fingers and her possessions, "because I am in you, my flesh is what carries you away, come on, lick me, let your green pupil slide over the water . . ." The fever came on slowly, one day when the sheets grew damp with the traces of two sweaty bodies. Those bony and translucent fingers could barely raise themselves to gesture for a glass of water. The fever began little by little to saturate her hands, her forehead, and gradually carried the dreams far away.

"Ismael," she yelled in the dark, "I can't dream, help me."

Ismael was frightened by the anguish that made her voice hoarse. But later, some time after, he smiled and quit giving her the medicine.

In her delirium, she asked him to help her remember, to recall the lake and those eyes and how I formed his chest, Ismael, how big were those hands that grasped my hips to thrust himself inside me, help me Ismael. This afternoon there would be swings and we would be high, high, we'd be kites and laughter and our skins would be called by their own names there, Ismael, there, where guilt has no stature and the birds can never be lost birds . . .

But Ismael just brought water to her lips and smiled.

"Everything will be fine, I promise you, everything will be fine once again."

She struggled desperately with herself, trying to clutch his hands, his hair, something that would return her to the threshold, while the fever began to smudge the contours of the cabin, the smile of the man, the rough hands that grazed her while caressing, the smell of wood and of silence.

Ismael help me.

Everything will be fine.

She cried, far away, the anguished voice blurring in the call, "Sleep, dream of me once more" but it was no longer a voice, it was just the memory of having heard some voice and the horror and emptiness and hips and shoulders and green gaze became diluted until it all disappeared.

After that, there was only a long silence and the end of winter, while the fever lowered and a wordless pallor began to take possession of her body.

Sleep surprised her with its emptiness and found her powerless to dream of him again.

Ismael opened the window to change the stale air of the past few months and she felt that the air was carrying away the final vestiges of the memory.

The window was only a wide frame displaying buildings and streets and cement.

She refused to struggle; it was useless. In this abandonment the sheets became numbing stains once again, to which she could never restore the smell of wood and of silence.

Translated by Elizabeth Chapman and Amanda Powell

🖤 Ángela Hernández (Dominican Republic)

HOW TO GATHER
THE SHADOWS OF THE FLOWERS

"Voyage of voyages with a hundred returns / capricious voyages / testimony of sighs / returns without turns / time in bouquets / and in my brow a sacred zeal to fade away / perhaps to return."

We found this text under the mattress and, like the rest of them, it seemed intended to provide us with clues to understand her. An impossible enterprise for us who had known her and loved her as a common girl, as the eldest sister, for whom our parents reserved certain privileges.

Faride was the only one of us to attend a private school (Papa got her a scholarship to an evangelical institute). The rest of us went to public school. When she finished high school she started working as a cashier in a supermarket; she remained in that job for six months. One day, surprisingly, she quit. Mama accused her of acting unconscionably, a judgment ratified by my father's recriminating glances. They both employed every possible means to extract from her the reason for her self-dismissal. She had not been laid off, nor had she had any difficulties in balancing the register every day, nor any trouble with any customer. It was not until after many weeks of siege that she said: "The supervisor kept pawing me." Nobody bothered her about it again. Two months later she began to work in a fabric shop. That's how she was, unaffected, serious, and reserved. I have brought you some photographs, but I must return them right away. My mother has forbidden us to touch her belongings.

From the very first glance the photographs captured my attention; I was intrigued above all by the well-defined combination of white and black features in one face: thick lips, very fine nose, long and kinky curls. In her eyes you caught a glimpse of an expression as dual and marked as the lines of her profile; there was in them a latent force: a vague expres-

siveness, *a black blaze behind a deceiving curtain of void. From that day on, the image of her seductive gaze has been an obsessive burden in my brain. After that I would stay with José after class to hear more details.*

The women of my family marry before they turn twenty. My grandmother married very young; my mother followed the tradition, and Faride got married a few months before turning eighteen. I don't think she had a good idea of what marriage meant; I'm not even sure whether she was happy or not, but I do remember her clearly, distressed and nervous, untiringly knitting tablecloths and bedcovers the year before Raúl left for the United States. Not that she had much choice. Faride supported the household. They had two children and had been married four years and he still had not found a steady job. When she returned to our house with the children, she seemed sad and somewhat relieved.

I have turned this information over and over in my mind, trying to understand the meaning of the events that took place in José's house. I haven't found anything that points to Faride having been subject to any special circumstances in her childhood and adolescence. There were nine siblings, who received the same upbringing and grew up in the same house. Three of them, including Faride, were born in the central mountains, but that doesn't make them different. The two eldest brothers seem to have nothing in common with her; José, the sixth child, whom I know best, is as normal a young man as they come.

Industrious and conscientious, when she moved back into the house Faride continued working in the shop and knitting tablecloths and bedcovers in the evenings and weekends. Her friends would say to her jokingly: "Aha! knitting while she awaits her husband, like Penelope," and she would reply with a smile: "I knit to eat, not to deceive myself."

In some ways, in some small things, my sister's behavior was different from that of other people. She showed no special interest in her physical appearance. She never wore lipstick or eye makeup. Her wardrobe was very simple; she made her own clothes of light fabrics and pastel colors; lemon yellow and lilac predominated in her apparel. I was the oldest of the siblings still living at home; I was then just past twelve; I don't remember ever seeing her angry at me; she never lectured me, nor did she offer advice on any subject. But these details of behavior don't make anyone special; least of all in our house, where chattering and long conversations between adults were extremely rare and where everyone preferred to keep to themselves; my mother listened to the radio; my father played dominoes; my older brothers cruised the streets; Faride knitted.

We got along very well with her and the children; life followed its natural course and none of us, not even our parents, had noticed the gradual transformation taking place within our sister; it was with great surprise that we witnessed the unexpected eruption of the world brewing within her. It happened at breakfast:

"He'll help me, this one will indeed help me, Mama. This man is really worth it. He is beautiful like a sun. He smells of May, he tastes like mint washed by a rain shower. He's not rich, nor young; he's not even heroic. But he's incomparably loving. He carries me to bed every day, and you should see what a bed, soft like a song filtered through water. He only needs a glance to understand me; he knows what I yearn for just from sensing it."

We couldn't quite understand her words. Not even Papa and Mama seemed to understand, since they were looking at her with puzzled expressions on their faces.

"The house has burst into flower in the few days we have spent together. Flowers assumed gigantic proportions with every minute of love. Violets and poppies growing deliriously; fennel and sunflowers and red-wine-colored hollyhocks like open umbrellas. It's like a jungle now. The orchids climb the walls, forming very elegant nosegays, they barely let you see anything through the glass. The whole house is made of transparent glass. At first I was embarrassed; someone could see us when we did things in bed. Then I realized that the house was alone in the world. Swarms of bees embroider honey hives around the stalks of the carnations, green crickets and fireflies gather pollen to build their homes. Ah, the hollyhocks fascinate me with the red-wine blood exquisitely retained in their corollas! Please advise me: What can one do with a garden gone out of control? What would we do if the flowers continue to climb to the ceiling and manage to conceal the sun? He could abandon me. He knows the garden grows only for me. What tragic pleasure! What sweet mortification!"

We remained silent. We couldn't understand her speech, but it fascinated us; Mama and Papa looked at her in astonishment. She got up, washed her hands, took her purse, and left.

The children delighted in our daughter's stories as if they were fairy tales. We got very agitated; we had never heard Faride talk about men, least of all in such insolent terms. We went over the details of the past week, and not finding anything extraordinary to justify her words, we decided to question her when she returned.

She didn't come back until eight o'clock that night, and didn't even allow us to approach her: "I'm dying to sleep," she said as she threw herself onto the bed between her children without changing clothes. She was snubbing us for the first time in her life, and the disrespect of her action poisoned our evening.

The correspondences between their description of Faride's words and her writings were remarkable. The papers she left in her own handwriting share a similar tone. In one and the other the central mystery derives from the comparison between her discourse and her slight intellectual training. Where did these figurations come from? Was it perhaps a peculiar type of schizophrenia? Sometimes her brother worries me; more than by vocation, he has chosen this career with the hope of solving her enigma, and perhaps he's only moving further and further away from the clues.

We had been watching for her when she came in and sat next to me at the table. She seemed peaceful, cheerful; there was a disconcerting clarity in her eyes; two drops of dew hung from her pupils. A serenity and happiness which I felt spreading through my body.

I shuddered, my hands shook, when I saw her approach. A presentiment oppressed my heart. I saw the six-year-old girl with a wide ribbon holding her hair, the lively girl who grabbed my legs and whom I pushed away with a slap; the angel of light who kissed me, licked my lips, hugged me, caressed my breasts, and whom I pushed away, annoyed because two younger children demanded my attention; the insistent girl that got under my skirt wanting to play, and whom I spanked because I had too much work and her moving bothered me; the little one who at dawn cuddled at my feet hoping to remain unnoticed, and whom I would put back to bed screaming at her to be quiet. The one who would take care of her little brothers and sisters so I would love her more, the one who asked me to let her suckle when I breast-fed her little brother, the one who exasperated me with her cajoling, when it was already too late. The same face, the same ribbon, the same laugh, the same eyes. I would have wanted to hug her, but too much time and distance had passed between the two of us.

"I gave him a shell of twelve colors. Uf! it was so hard to find. It was between rocks, in a big hollow. I placed a strong tree trunk across the hollow, hung from it and walked with my hands to where the treasure was. It is the size of a teacup. The colors spring from the outside and then spread to the inside. It is so curious, so many colors emerging from a dark little knot."

She lowered her voice, as if she were speaking to herself; then she continued, excitedly.

"He loved my gift. *C'est très joli, comme la vie*, he said to me."

My mother contained herself. Who is he? she asked her. Faride looked at her, puzzled, and replied naturally: "The director of the Oncology Institute.

"I never imagined he would be so beautiful. When he laughs, and he's almost always laughing, he leans back, chair and all. His laughter soars to the sky like bubbles of music coming out of a flute. I feel like sucking his mouth, I feel like eating him with lettuce and carnations. His teeth look moist. His laughter flows from inside, as if a glass of water flowered in his throat."

Mama blushed; Papa was uncomfortable in his chair; we were enjoying the story.

"He has requested me as his assistant in his operations, in the radioactive treatments and the laboratory. I tell him I know nothing of diseases and healing. He soothes me with his beautiful laughter; you'll learn, we'll teach you. We spent long dead hours, no, better still, living, gloriously living hours seated in two wooden chairs, on the rocks, by the sea. The others were far away. The rocks jutted out of the sea, we sailed on an indigo air several meters above the water."

Then, deep in thought, she commented to herself: "This special man makes me forget cancer." She devoured her breakfast and left hurriedly. We remained there talking about cancer. For some of us it was a bumblebee with horns, to others a plant with white spots. Unable to agree, we asked Mama. Anguished, she replied: "It's many things at the same time."

My husband and I were troubled. We had educated Faride as a good Christian and didn't recognize her in these daring speeches. We even came to suspect that she was keeping bad company, but anyway, people don't change just like that, from one moment to the next.

"They're dreams. Did you notice today? They're only dreams."

"She believes they're real. This is very unusual. She'll go telling those filthy stories around. They'll say she's a tramp. The husband working in New York and she living with other men."

"People who know us won't take her words seriously."

On Monday Mama woke us up early; she made us have breakfast and get ready for school in a hurry. Before we left, however, she couldn't prevent our overhearing our sister telling her in the kitchen:

"Mama, the young ones are darlings. His name is Andrés and Lucía introduced me to him at her party. Fire at first sight! One look and we were captivated. It's understandable: tender, passionate, soft, with his big green eyes, he's like a big son between my legs."

I found the piece of paper on the nightstand in her room; it was in her handwriting, and the contents seemed to refer to the story of the shell and the doctor. I woke her up very early, dawn had not yet broken. I took her to the kitchen, I wanted to speak to her without interruptions. Maybe the paper would clarify something, maybe her stories were nothing more than ideas copied from some disturbing book. What is this? I asked her.

"Can't you see? I wrote it night before last: I am a relative of the stones / of the delicate waves of the coast / of the fragile horizons / the ever winding and unwinding snails / rocking in the vigils of their chiaroscuro moves / with their easy melodies / with their sonority of distant sea / with their peaceful and oblivious song / with mother-of-pearl winding and unwinding around submarine lines / drinking them like wine, like salt, like elementary milk."

She had repeated from memory the words on the piece of paper; she half-closed her eyes and continued to recite, as if she were reading something written inside her lids:

"Wet and surprised / like a newborn / I can barely touch myself / I did not take the sun, there was no time / nor did I learn my tongue / nor did I detect the clues to my surroundings / I lie on myself / drowsy and timid / my textures are tender / in this my very embryo / sometimes I renew myself."

I felt a tingle down my spine. I didn't dare interrupt her, it wasn't my daughter talking.

"To exist and not to be / is a miracle / to be the frontier to the undecipherable / equidistant to acceptance / a wisdom on the margin of precepts / a lucid candor / a hidden golden vertebra / a lace made of spinning violets / forming a violet heart."

Almost voiceless, I said: Faride, my daughter, what is happening to you? I didn't even dare touch her, I sensed her distant and alien.

"Nothing is the matter, Mama."

"Where do you get these stories from?"

"What stories?"

"The ones you've just told me, the ones from breakfast on Saturday and Sunday."

"They're not stories. I wrote that poetry fifty years ago. It's mine. I don't tell stories, I never could learn any."

"Are you telling me that these are truths, reality?"

"What is the truth, Mama? What is reality?"

"The truth is the truth, the same truth you learned when you were a child. Reality is that you're twenty-three years old. You couldn't have written anything fifty years ago. Tell me the truth; you never lied."

"I'm not lying."

"Don't drive me to despair. Trust me; tell me what's happening in your life."

"I trust you. Nothing is happening to me; I am well."

"Tell me then, why are you inventing these extravagant stories so detrimental to your good name?"

"What extravagant stories?"

"These fantasies of men and love affairs so different from your reality as a serious woman."

"What is reality, Mama?"

"Reality is eating rice and plantains, giving birth to a child, working, seeing clearly what things are like!"

"And what are things like?"

I didn't insist anymore; this senseless conversation was driving me mad.

The next day, she sat at the table, giddy. The children had left for school. One of our older children was with us. I had asked him to be there, knowing that Faride respected him almost more than she did her father, she feared him more. From the time she was very young we entrusted her care to her brother. His presence, however, didn't inhibit her.

"It was a beautiful, but at the same time, boring trip; two months at sea, seeing sky, seeing blue and more blue, seeing the same people, the unseasonal birds hovering over our heads. But it was worth it. My mother's friends were waiting for me, with a bouquet of flowers and open arms. I went with Ferita to register at the university. I took only two courses: botany and history, because I first must grow used to the city and my new friends, before I throw myself completely into my studies. I get my teachers confused; they are so white, so similar. God made white people's skin with the same roll of fabric. Yesterday we went to see Unamuno's *Shadows of Dreams*. The theater is very elegant, and so are the people. After the performance we went to my apartment, we drank wine and beer, we danced, and rolled on the floor."

"Enough!" I said with anger and sadness. My oldest son only commented: "What is she talking about?" We had to practically push him out of the house by force, he was furious and wanted to beat her up. According to him, Faride had become a trollop and two or three good blows would straighten her out. She didn't seem surprised, and when we returned she even added:

"The trolley cars, the buildings, the beautiful paintings in the museums, the Graf Zeppelin, the romantic friends reciting verses in the parks."

The narratives at breakfast became routine. They sent us away from the table, they made us run out to school, they separated us from her and her belongings, managing thereby to sharpen our curiosity. We spied on conversations, searched her purse, and eluded Mama's and Papa's watchful eyes to be with her. Mama thought that Faride's ravings were a passing thing, attributing them to lack of news from Raúl. In effect, there had been no news from him since he had left. Mama had gone to the group that had organized the trip, but they said they weren't responsible for people after they took them over. Papa considered Raúl a scoundrel; he wasn't interested in his whereabouts, and even less in his fate. That Saturday, Faride came in to the kitchen, trembling: there was a somber expression on her face. Papa and Mama were alarmed.

"It was alive, the desiccated bird, the prehistoric desiccated bird sent to me by my friend from India was alive. It chased me into the rice bog, into the labyrinth of caves in San Juan, between my legs. It seemed dead when it arrived through the mail, but it was alive. An atrocious bird, sticky, with long legs and long sharp goads instead of feathers. It was humid and dead and moved. I don't know what to do with it. I tried throwing it out the window only to find it again under my bed. Ten times I took it out of my room and it would return to my side, like an amulet reeking of death, and it is in my room, and it holds its viscous skin to my face. Oh God, it has made me throw up my insides!"

Papa and Mama listened to her in consternation. Even we, spying through the gaps in the kitchen wall, were profoundly impressed. She suddenly changed her expression and laughed:

"Ah, but what a beautiful little house. He sent it to me as a gift. It came in the mail today. It's not taller than my legs, but it has a thousand little doors, all pink, all painted in a different pink. A thousand shades of pink on the façade. When you open a little door, you find a three-verse poem and a painting which explains that year's history. A thousand years of Indian history in a thousand paintings and a thousand poems. In the last little door, the one in a pink so intense it approaches the orange of red-tinted clouds, is the Salt March and the Peace Poem: Peace, salt, autumn splendor / they are within us and together they will sprout / like a water spring that blinds certain fires."

When we, intrigued, asked her about the little house, she told us that she would show it to us later. In India, she told us, children didn't use books to study history, but little houses like these. Through millennia, Hindus have learned the exceptional art of miniaturizing trees and history.

On Faride's birthday her colleagues at work organized a little party for her, to which they invited us. We went to the store in the afternoon, after the shop closed, feeling apprehensive. To our surprise, the celebration proceeded quite normally. The shop owner gave her a certificate commending her for her exceptional performance as a salesperson; he also gave her a small gold chain, exhorting her to keep up the good work with her usual cordiality and efficiency. Her co-workers loved and admired her, as we could attest to.

At home, however, the modifications in her conduct were marked. She knitted less and spent long periods of time in silence.

She didn't waste any chance to play. She would get lost in the ring around the rosie, pocket full of posies, look who's here Punchinella, Punchinella, Miss Mary Mack Mack with silver buttons all down her back back; she ran and jumped with boundless energy, and none of us could catch her when we played tag. Papa and Mama rested easy when they saw us like that. But a turn in the situation agitated the entire household, and from then on our parents didn't even bother to hide their anguish from us.

It was Sunday. Papa was playing dominoes with a group of friends, in front of the house. Faride, euphoric, started to turn around the playing table, jumping as she held the edges of her skirt, opening it like a fan. She sang out the words, heaping them onto each other in an easy flowing laughter.

"My lover returned from the crystal house. He has brought me his riddles once more. This time I will guess the answers. The glass house is celebrating tonight, all the windows have been opened and the rooms are bursting with full moons. We are going to Moscow to ride the Ferris wheel. He amuses himself with the trapeze artists. Together we built a sculpture to the tenderness of the panda bear / Providence shines like a firefly in the Caribbean Sea / with the fishermen on the golden beach / at dawn / we encircle its waters / with boreal ribbons / we wove a basket / that knows about Ithaca / through eternal ice / we go animatedly / on expeditions / silver camels / carry us on their rumps / through snowy peaks / so clear / so beautiful / that in their translucency / time melts / and the soul dissolves."

From that moment on, our household was in an upheaval. Faride would tell her rapturous stories to anyone who would listen. Some people would come to our house and incite her to talk so as to feed the rumors circulating around the neighborhood. Mama and Papa quickly gathered together some money and took her to a psychiatrist.

He examined her, and submitted her to different tests. He tested her reflexes, laid logical traps for her; they spoke for more than an hour. Faced with our bewilderment, he told us she was undoubtedly sane, and that he found her to be an intelligent and cooperative young woman. We narrated to him the events of Sunday and of the days before. He asked us to understand her youth and her ideas. The dreams of each generation differ, he insisted. I insisted on his hearing her in front of us, thinking that perhaps she had pulled the wool over his eyes. We called her in and I asked her to read one of her poems. She then proceeded to recite with great spontaneity, looking us in the eye:

"Populations of stars uninhabit the sky to hurl themselves at my heavens / matrixes of fresh bubbles / pay deaf ears to their original water springs / and make a watery bouquet in my sex / juice of virgin meadows / squeezed by sheer will / form the blood of my wanderings / I am with them / a game of love / a born traveler."

The doctor expressed that that poetry confirmed his diagnosis: Faride was intelligent and original, and advised us to let her be. We left his office even more baffled; no one said a word on our way back.

Her dreams gained ground as the days went by. It was hard to wake her up in the morning. Sometimes she would wash up, have breakfast in the kitchen, and return to bed. We would wake her up again by shaking her roughly. She would do two or three routine chores and then return to bed to continue her interrupted sleep. When we forced her to get up and kept her from returning to bed, as I lectured her on her lack of responsibility toward work and of the importance of her salary to the family's finances, she would walk through the house as if it were a stage and she the leading actress, playing a role known only to herself.

Sometimes, sitting upright in bed, she examined her surroundings as if she didn't recognize anything. She walked by inertia, repeating to us previous dialogues. Pensive and inexpressive, it would take her up to three-quarters of an hour to cross the line that divided her two realities.

We did all we could to isolate the neighbors from the atmosphere of our house. Our older children would entertain visitors in front of the house, taking chairs out to the sidewalk and engaging in conversation almost on the street. I abstained from going out. I went only to mass on Sunday and I tried to do so with the greatest discretion: I was terrified of questions. We forbade the children to enter Faride's bedroom. After repeated excuses, we had to admit that she wouldn't return to work, and so we informed the shop owner. But all our efforts did nothing more than unleash more rumors. The neighbors' assumptions were like knives in my heart. As far as they were concerned Faride was pregnant, Faride had had a botched abortion in a back-alley clinic, Faride had an unstoppable hemorrhage, Faride had gone mad and walked naked through the house making pornographic gestures, Faride was rotting with cancer, her face had been eaten up by maggots, and therefore we had locked her up.

Our friends asked us in school if it was true that our sister smelled bad, if we were having another little brother or sister, how many men had given her children; they asked us if we would get sick just like her. Faced with that rosary of rumors, Mama drastically changed policies. She opened doors and windows, invited the neighboring women to the house for coffee, canceled the orders that kept us away from our sister, allowed her children to sleep with her again, and no longer prevented her from going out into the yard.

The friends and neighbors saw her walk the sidewalk, water the eggplants planted in the yard, and frolic with her children. They took turns spying on her, since she would let herself be seen only once in a while. Some ended up attributing to her a passing illness or a harmless dementia. They also agreed, however, that her physique did not betray any ailment whatsoever. They saw her like she looked then: her profile more defined, her cheeks rosy and with a profound calm always peeking through her eyes.

Every once in a while I would sit down to watch her sleep. Certain discoveries had awakened in me hopes of a cure. Watching her fixedly, I noticed the movements of her eyelids and the slight stretching of her lips when the familiar voices of the market women offered their pigeon peas, coriander, and oregano for sale. She didn't seem disconnected from the prattle of children playing baseball in the neighborhood park. If my daughter was not completely rooted in this reality, neither was she in the other.

Mama's hopes soon began to fade. Faride's residence on this side of reality diminished progressively, until it was reduced to the narrow space of no more than an hour. Then she would awaken completely, drink a glass of water, bathe and perfume herself. She would talk briefly with Mama and Papa, and would romp with us for a while, demonstrating a complete command of her two diverse time frames. When she was asleep, she lay totally submerged in a deep tranquility; when she was awake, she was nimble and clear-sighted.

One day she awakened all of us with a frantic cry. It was a calm dawn in April, fresh and fragrant. I will never forget it. Standing around her bed, we heard her last words.

"I have found the solution!! Kiss me all of you!! Kiss me and hold me in your arms because I have found the solution!! Now I know how to irrigate a garden that won't stop growing, how to gather the shadows of the flowers, how to prevent their concealing the sun, and how to walk diagonally across the instants."

She went to sleep definitively. She slept for exactly six months. Pale, on her back, smiling: her heartbeats began to fade. At the end she looked like a beautiful dream dressed in pink, a dream that our parents refused to bury.

I don't know why the family opted for the diagnosis of madness. The notion that it was a singular form of dementia, still unexplored by psychiatry, is taking root in José; his career plans are driven by the desire to deepen the investigation of the case.

The one exception is the mother, for whom the daughter was possessed by a woman from the past; her eagerness leads her to think that José, sometimes, is possessed by Faride's spirit. They alone knew her intimately, having witnessed every detail of the most intense moments of her extraordinary behavior; but they could be mistaken, however, and it could perhaps be a mere matter of poetics.

Translated by Lizabeth Paravisini-Gebert

Biographical Notes

EDITORS:

MARGARITE FERNÁNDEZ OLMOS is professor of Spanish at Brooklyn College of the City University of New York. A recipient of a Ford Foundation Fellowship and a Postdoctoral Fellow of the National Research Council, she has lived and studied in Europe and Latin America. Professor Fernández Olmos has lectured extensively on contemporary Latin American literature and written for such journals as *Studies in Afro-Hispanic Literature, Revista/Review Interamericana, Hispania, Revista Iberoamericana, The Lion and the Unicorn, La revista canadiense de estudios hispánicos, Revista de crítica literaria latinoamericana, Heresies,* and *Third Woman,* as well as for several anthologies on Puerto Rican literature. She is the author of a book on the Dominican writer Juan Bosch, *La cuentística de Juan Bosch: un análisis crítico-cultural* (1982) and co-editor with Doris Meyer of *Contemporary Women Authors of Latin America: New Translations* and *Introductory Essays* (1983). Her most recent book is a collection of essays on contemporary Puerto Rican literature, *Sobre la literatura puertorriqueña de aquí y de allá: aproximaciones feministas* (1989).

LIZABETH PARAVISINI-GEBERT, former associate professor of Caribbean literature at Lehman College of the City University of New York, is currently associate professor in the Department of Hispanic Studies at Vassar College. Professor Paravisini has written on contemporary Caribbean, American, and Latin American fiction, and on popular culture, for such journals as *Obsidian, Plural, Clues, Callaloo, Sargasso, Cimarrón, Anales del Caribe,* and *The Journal of West Indian Literature.* She has contributed chapters to several anthologies, including *Comic Crime, Spanish American Women Writers: A Bio-Bibliographic Sourcebook,* and *History of the Literatures of the Caribbean.* Her translations have appeared in *Cimarrón* and *Her True True Name: An Anthology of Writings by Caribbean Women.* She has edited Ana Roqué's 1903 novel *Luz y sombra,* and is editor of *Green Cane and Juicy Flotsam:*

Short Stories by Caribbean Women (with Carmen Esteves), Subversión de cánones: la escritora puertorriqueña ante la crítica (in press), and The Complete Poems of Phyllis Shand Allfrey. She co-authored Caribbean Women Novelists: An Annotated Bibliography and is completing a literary biography of Dominican writer and politician Phyllis Shand Allfrey.

AUTHORS:

MARJORIE AGOSÍN (United States/Chile, 1955) was born in the United States of Chilean parents. She grew up in Chile, where she lived until the age of fifteen. She has lived in the United States since 1970. Agosín considers herself first and foremost Chilean, and maintains close contacts with her Latin American roots. Agosín's poetic work includes Chile: gemidos y cantares (1977), Conchalí (1980), Silencio que no se deja oír (1982), and Hogueras (1986).

DELMIRA AGUSTINI (Uruguay, 1886-1914) is considered to be one of Latin America's most unique Modernist poets. Before her premature death at the age of twenty eight, Agustini published three collections of poetry: El libro blanco (1907), Cantos de la mañana (1910), and Los cálices vacíos (1913). Her erotic expression in characterized by "the tragic dichotomy between the erotic voracity of the male and her feminine passion presented as an aesthetic constructive force."

ISABEL ALLENDE (Chile, 1942) published her first novel, La casa de los espíritus, in 1982 to immediate international acclaim. Shortly afterwards, her second novel, De amor y de sombra (1985) would also find itself on international best-seller lists, and would be translated as well into numerous languages. Allende has worked for years as a journalist. She claims that the inspiration for La casa de los espíritus was her need to tell the story of her country and of America while in political exile from Chile after the fall of the Allende government. El plan infinito (1992) is her most recent novel.

ALBALUCÍA ÁNGEL (Colombia, 1939) is the author of

five novels and a collection of short stories *¡Oh gloria inmarcesible!* (1979), named after the Colombian national anthem. Her novel *Estaba la pájara pinta sentada en el verde limón* (1975) earned her the distinction of being the first woman to win the Colombian National Prize. Other works by Ángel include *Los girasoles en invierno* (1970), *Dos veces Alicia* (1972), *Misiá Señora* (1982), and *Las andariegas* (1984).

EUNICE ARRUDA (Brazil, 1939) published her first collection of poetry in 1960, *É Tempo de Noite*. It was quickly followed by six more: *O Chao Batido* (1963), *Outra Dúvida* (1963), *As Cosas Efémeras* (1964), *Invençoes do Desespero* (1972), *As Pessoas, as Palavras* (1976), and *Os Momentos* (1981).

PÍA BARROS (Chile, 1956) has written poetry and short stories. Her first book, *Machismo se escribe con m de mama*, appeared in 1989, and was quickly followed by a highly-regarded collection of short stories *A horcajadas* (1990). Barros conducts literary workshops for women in Santiago under very repressive political conditions and has been arrested on several occasions.

GIOCONDA BELLI (Nicaragua, 1948) is a poet whose political consciousness was formed during the Somoza regime and as a result of her active collaboration with the Sandinista movement. Her second collection of poems, *Línea de fuego*, won the 1978 Casa de las Américas Prize in Havana; her first, *Sobre la grama* (1974) appeared while Belli was in political exile in Costa Rica. Belli's most recent work is *Truenos y arco-iris* (1982).

MARÍA LUISA BOMBAL (Chile, 1910-1980) is an acclaimed novelist and short story writer. Her novel *La última niebla* (1935) is an avant-garde precursor of the Latin American novel of the 1960s; Carlos Fuentes has called her "the mother of us all." Her works, which also include the novel *La amortajada* (1938), present a unique and intriguing view of feminine experience.

JULIA DE BURGOS (Puerto Rico, 1914-1953) wrote poetry characterized by her defense of the working class and of her feminist and nationalist ideals. Her three collections of poetry are *Poema en veinte surcos* (1938), *Canción de la verdad sencilla* (1939), and *El mar y tú* (published posthumously in 1954). She is recognized as a forerunner of contemporary Puerto Rican feminism, and her work is credited with helping to undermine the male-oriented aspects of traditional Puerto Rican culture and with broadening the range of Puerto Rican literature to include women's experience.

ROSARIO CASTELLANOS' (Mexico, 1925-1974) impressive list of publications includes two novels, *Balún-Canán* (1957) and *Oficio de tinieblas* (1962); three volumes of short stories, including *Álbum de familia* (1971); four collections of essays and criticism, among them *Mujer que sabe latín* (1973): several plays, chief among them *El eterno femenino* (1975); and a dozen books of poems. Her work is marked by her concern with the many varieties of domination prevalent in Latin American societies. The strong feminism of her work is unusual in Latin American literature.

DAÍNA CHAVIANO (Cuba, 1957) represents the younger generation of innovative Cuban women authors who dare challenge the secondary literary roles assigned to women. Her unpublished manuscript of poems *Confesiones eróticas y otros hechizos*, received Honorable Mention in Mexico's "Concurso Plural" in 1984. Among her other works, which include science fiction, are: *Los mundos que amo* (1980), *Amoroso planeta* (1983), *Historias de hadas para adultos* (1986), and *Fábulas de una abuela extraterrestre* (1988).

MATILDE DAVIÚ (Venezuela, 1946) has studied literature, languages, and anthropology. Her first collection of short stories, *Maithuna* (1978) received critical recognition for its impeccable style and its intensely personal and compelling themes. She has also published a collection of novellas, *Barbazúcar y otros relatos* (1977).

ROSARIO FERRÉ (Puerto Rico, 1942) has published *Papeles de Pandora* (1976), a collection of fiction and poetry, *Fábulas de la garza desangrada* (1982), a collection of poetry, *Maldito amor* (1986), a novel, and several volumes of literary criticism. Her highly-acclaimed work has consistently explored the role of women in Puerto Rican society, questioning the feminine stereotypes common in Latin American culture and pointing to their roots in the class system.

BEATRIZ GUIDO (Argentina, 1925) is the author of numerous short stories and novels, several of which have been filmed by her husband, Argentinian director Leopoldo Torres Nilsson. Her work often centers around the psychological plight of a young adolescent girl coming to terms with a politically and sexually repressive society, and present a critical vision of Argentinian reality. Her novels include *La casa del ángel* (1955), *La caída* (1956), and *Fin de fiesta* (1958).

ÁNGELA HERNÁNDEZ (Dominican Republic, 1954) was trained in chemical engineering, but has worked primarily as a researcher and activist on women's issues. Known primarily as a poet and essayist—she has published two volumes of poetry and numerous essays and articles on feminism and women's rights—Hernández published her first collection of short stories, *Alótropos*, in 1989 to immediate and enthusiastic critical acclaim. "Cómo recoger la sombra de las flores" won the 1988 Casa del Teatro Prize. Her work is characterized by the poetic richness of her prose and by her blending of the vivid details of the external world with a poet's understanding of the fantastic world of the imagination.

ANA ISTARÚ (Costa Rica, 1960) won the singular prize for poetry awarded in 1982 by EDUCA (Editorial Universitaria Centroamericana) for her collection *La estación de fiebre*, a work of highly erotic verses. Other collections by Istarú include *Palabra nueva* (1975), *Poemas para un día cualquiera* (1977), and *Poemas abiertos y otros amaneceres* (1980).

ILKE BRUNHILDE LAURITO (Brazil, 1925) is a poet and professor of literature in São Paulo. Laurito has also participated in the production of television programs on Brazil for the BBC in London. Her collections include *A Noiva do Horizonte* (1953), *Autobiografía de Mãos Dadas* (1958), *Janela de Apartamento* (1968), *Sol do Lírico* (1978), and *Genetrix* (1982).

CHELY LIMA (Cuba, 1957) has received numerous literary prizes for her boldly creative work which includes poetry, novels, film and television writing, children's literature, and the first Cuban rock opera. Her published works include *Monólogo con lluvia* (1982),

Espacio abierto (with Alberto Serret, 1983), and *Terriblemente ilumi-nados* (1988), a collection of poems that received the Union of Cuban Artists and Writers Award in 1985.

NEMIR MATOS (Puerto Rico, 1949) began writing poetry in the 1970s, publishing her work in literary journals. Her collections, *A través del aire y del fuego pero no del cristal* and *Las mujeres no hablan así* appeared in 1981. The latter work, particularly, revealed Matos' feminist concerns and her experimental and direct use of erotic language.

MARÍA LUISA MENDOZA (Mexico, 1931) is a journalist by trade, adept at fusing fiction and non-fiction in a highly personal style. She has published two novels, *De Ausencia* (1984), from which the selection included in this anthology is taken, and *Con él, conmigo, con nosotros tres* (1971), a semidocumentary work character-ized by the use of free association and colloquial language.

LEILA MICCOLIS (Brazil, 1947) is a lawyer and founder of Editora Trote. Her writings include works of poetry, prose, and essays. Among her publications are *Impróprio para menores de 18 amores* (with Franklin Jorge, 1976), *Silencio Relativo* (1977), *Respeitável Público* (1980), *Maus Antecedentes* (with Paulo Véras, 1981), and *Muita Poesía Brasileira* (1982). Miccolis' works have appeared in anthologies in Brazil and abroad.

SILVINA OCAMPO (Argentina, 1903) is a poet and short story writer whose work is marked by a disquieting eroticism dis-played in fictional works where passions are their own laws. Her fic-tion often presents everyday reality as a manifestation of the mar-velous and the fantastic. She has published numerous collections of prose and verse, including *Viaje olvidado* (1937), *Autobiografía de Irene* (1948), *Las invitadas* (1961), and *Amarillo celeste* (1972). Ocampo, sister of famous writer Victoria Ocampo, has also collabo-rated with Jorge Luis Borges and her husband, Argentinian author Adolfo Bioy Casares, in several literary anthologies.

CARILDA OLIVER LABRA (Cuba, 1923) has been a lawyer, librarian, and art instructor. Her fragile and nostalgic verses celebrate the joys of everyday reality. Oliver Labra's published volumes include *Preludio* (1943), *Al sur de mi garganta* (1949), *Canto a la bandera* (1950), and *Calzada de Tirry 81* (1987).

RENATA PALLOTINI (Brazil, 1937) studied law and philosophy before turning to work in the theater. A writer of poetry and drama, her plays have been performed in Brazil and abroad. Pallotini's books of poetry include *Acalanto* (1952), *Livro de Sonetos* (1961), *A Faca e a Pedra* (1965), *Antología Poética* (1968), and *Cantar de Meu Povo* (1980). Her collection of short stories *Mate é a Cor da Viuvez* was published in 1975.

CRISTINA PERI ROSSI (Uruguay, 1941) writes poetry, novels, and short stories. Her books include *Los museos abandonados* (1968), *La tarde del dinosaurio* (1976), *Descripción de un naufragio* (1975), and *Diáspora*. The latter is a daring and ironic collection of poetry which blends eroticism and social critique. Her collection of homoerotic poetry *Evohé* exemplifies the erotic stance of her work. Peri Rossi has lived in Barcelona since 1972.

ALEJANDRA PIZARNIK (Argentina, 1936-1972) published eight books of poetry before her suicide in 1972. Among them are *La tierra más ajena* (1955), *La última inocencia* (1956), *Los trabajos y las noches* (1965), *Extracción de la piedras de la locura* (1968), and *Nombres y figuras* (1969). Pizarnik displayed a surprising, unrestrained imagination in her work, which is characterized by her unsettling view of reality and a macabre fictional landscape.

ELENA PONIATOWSKA (Mexico, 1933) has sought to give voice in her works to the marginalized and the politically voiceless. A journalist by trade, she has received high praise for her courageous and innovative testimonial works, among them *La noche de Tlatelolco* (1971) and *Hasta no verte Jesús mío* (1973). Poniatowska's fictional work includes a collection of short stories, *De noche vienes* (1987).

ROSAMARÍA ROFFIEL (Mexico, 1945) is a poet, journalist, and author of the first openly lesbian novel published in Mexico, *Amora* (1989). She has published a testimonial work based on her experiences in Nicaragua, *¡Ay, Nicaragua, Nicaragüita!* (1987), and a collection of poetry, *Corramos libres ahora* (1986).

CLEMENTINA SUÁREZ (Honduras, 1906) has published numerous collections of poems, among them *Corazón sangriento* (1930), *Los templos de fuego* (1931), *Engranajes* (1935), and *El poeta y sus señales* (1969). She is known for her strong, sensual poetry that examines the many meanings of being a woman.

LUISA VALENZUELA (Argentina, 1938) has worked as a journalist and newspaper editor in her native Argentina. She has published several novels and collections of short stories, all characterized by her highly personal and ironic view of reality. Her publications include *Hay que sonreir* (1966), *Los heréticos* (1967), *El gato eficaz* (1972), *Aquí pasan cosas raras* (1975), *Cambio de armas* (1982), and *Cola de lagartija* (1983). Her script "Clara," based on her novel *Hay que sonreir*, won an award from Argentina's Instituto Nacional de Cinematografía. Valenzuela has lived in the United States since 1979.

ANA LYDIA VEGA (Puerto Rico, 1946) is one of Puerto Rico's most promising and productive authors. Vega captures the tone and rhythm of contemporary Puerto Rican culture in her collections of short stories and her essays. Her publications include *Vírgenes y mártires* (with Carmen Lugo Filippi, 1981), *Encancaranublado y otros cuentos de naufragio* (1982), winner of the Casa de las Américas prize in Cuba, and *Pasión de historia y otras historias de pasión* (1987). Vega has recently edited a collection of essays by contemporary Puerto Rican authors, *El tramo ancla.*

CECILIA VICUÑA (Chile, 1948) began her university studies in her native Chile and continued them in Great Britain. Her poems have been published in journals in Latin America, Europe, and the United States, as well as in several collections: *Sabor a mí* (1973), *Precario/Precarious* (1983), *Luxumei o el traspie de la doctrina* (1983), *PALABRARmás* (1984), and *La Wik'uña* (1990). Vicuña currently lives in New York, and is the editor of Palabra Sur, a series of Latin American literature in translation published by Graywolf Press.

Bibliography

BIBLIOGRAPHY OF ORIGINAL WORKS
IN SPANISH AND PORTUGUESE

Delmira Agustini, "Otra estirpe," "La copa del amor," "Íntima," "Batiendo la selva," *Poesías completas*. Barcelona: Editorial Labor, 1971. pp. 217, 145-146, 139-140, 120.

Julia de Burgos, "Armonía de la palabra y el instinto, " "Río Grande de Loíza," *Poemas*. San Juan: Instituto de Cultura Puertorriqueña, 1964.

Clementina Suárez, "Sexo," "VI," "Conjugación," *Con mis versos saludo a las generaciones futuras*. Tegucigalpa: Ediciones Librería Paradiso, 1988. pp. 29-30.

Carilda Oliver Labra, "Me desordeno, amor, me desordeno," "Discurso de Eva," *Calzada de Tirry 81*. La Habana: Editorial Letras Cubanas, 1987. pp. 22, 112-116.

María Luisa Bombal, *La última niebla*. Barcelona: Editorial Seix Barral, 1988. pp. 17-25.

Beatriz Guido, *La casa del ángel*. Buenos Aires: Emecé Editores, 1954. pp. 154-175.

Silvina Ocampo, "Albino Orma," *Los días de la noche*. Madrid: Alianza Editorial, 1970. pp. 95-97.

Rosario Castellanos, "En el filo del gozo," "Ninfomanía," *The Selected Poems of Rosario Castellanos*. St. Paul, Minnesota: Graywolf Press, 1988. pp. 56-58, 72.

María Luisa Mendoza, *De Ausencia*. México: Joaquín Mortiz, 1984. pp. 95-106.

Alejandra Pizarnik, "Palabras," "En esta noche, en este mundo," "La muerte y la muchacha," *Textos de sombra y últimos poemas,* selección de Olga Orozco y Ana Becciú. Buenos Aires: Editorial Sudamericana, 1985. pp. 11-12, 67-69, 72. "Acerca de la condesa sangrienta," *El deseo de la palabra,* pp. 20-22.

Elena Poniatowska, "La felicidad," *De noche vienes.* México: Ediciones Era, S. A., 1987. pp. 66-70.

Ilke Brunhilde Laurito, "Genetrix I," "Genetrix III," "Genetrix V," and "Genetrix VI," *Carne Viva.* Olga Savary, ed. Editora Anima, 1984. pp. 176, 177, 178.

Luisa Valenzuela, "La mala palabra," *Revista Iberoamericana* 51 (julio-diciembre 1985): 489-491.
"Juguemos al fornicón," *El gato eficaz.* México: Joaquín Mortiz, 1972. pp. 68-71.

Rosario Ferré, "Fábula de la garza desangrada," *Fábulas de la garza desangrada.* México: Joaquín Mortiz, 1982. pp. 16-22. "Arroz con Leche," *El medio pollito.* Río Piedras, P. R.: Ediciones Huracán, 1977. pp. 27-30.

Marjorie Agosín, "Mi estómago," "Lo que somos," and "Pene," *Nosotras: Latina Literature Today,* María del Carmen Boza, Beverly Silva, and Carmen Valle, eds. Binghamton, N. Y.: Bilingual Review Press, 1986. pp. 10, 51, 58.

Cristina Peri Rossi, "El testigo," *Cuentos eróticos.* Barcelona: Ediciones Grijalbo, S. A., 1988. pp. 151-152.
"Ca Foscari," *Poesía feminista del mundo hispánico.* Ángel Flores y Kate Flores, eds. México: Siglo XXI Editores, 1984. pp. 247-248.

Renata Pallotini, "Mulher Sentada Na Areia," *Muito Prazer*. Márcia
    Denser, ed. Río de Janeiro: Editora Record, 1980. pp. 80-84.
    "Recado de Estio," *Carne Viva*. Olga Savary, ed. Editora
    Anima, 1984. p. 310.
    "O Meu Prazer," *Carne viva*. p. 311
    "Depoimento Cruel No. 2," *Carne Viva*. p. 312.

Albalucía Ángel, *Estaba la pájara pinta sentada en el verde limón*.
    Barcelona: Editorial Argos Vergara, S. A. 1975. pp. 181-184.

Cecilia Vicuña, "Amada amiga," *Poesía feminista del mundo hispánico*.
    Ángel Flores y Kate Flores, eds. México: Siglo XXI Editores,
    1984. pp. 263-269.

Isabel Allende. *La casa de los espíritus*. Barcelona: Plaza y Janés
    Editores, 1982. pp. 283-200.

Eunice Arruda, "Tema II" and "Tema III," *Carne Viva*. Olga Savary,
    ed. Editora Anima, 1984. pp. 117, 116.

Leila Míccolis, "Tercero Poema para o Namorado," *Carne Viva*. Olga
    Savary, ed. Editora Anima, 1984. p. 202.
    "Ilusâo," *Carne Viva*. p. 203.
    "Para além da Morte," *Carne Viva*. p. 203.

"Ana Lydia Vega, "Letra para salsa y tres soneos por encargo,"
    Vírgenes y mártires. Carmen Lugo Filippi y Ana Lydia Vega.
    Río Piedras, P. R.: Editorial Antillana, 1981. pp. 81-88.

Gioconda Belli, "En la doliente soledad del domingo", *fem* 50
    (Febrero 1987): 17.

Rosamaría Roffiel, "Gioconda," *Corramos libres ahora*. México:
    Ediciones FEMSOL, 1986.
    Amora. México: Editorial Planeta, 1989.

Nemir Matos, "Vuelo en la aleta . . . ," *Compañeras: Latina Lesbians (An Anthology).* Juanita Ramos, ed. New York: Latina Lesbian History Project, 1987. p. 139.

Matilde Daviú, "La mujer que rasgó el mundo." *Maithuna.* Caracas: Monte Ávila Editores, 1978. pp. 91-95.

Chely Lima, "Recuento carnal," *Terriblemente iluminados.* La Habana: Ediciones Unión, 1988. pp. 91-95.

Ana Istarú, "III," *La estación de fiebre.* San José: Editorial Universitaria, 1986. p. 16.
"XI," *La estación de fiebre.* pp. 26-27.
"XII," *La estación de fiebre.* p. 27.
"XVI," *La estación de fiebre.* pp. 31-32.
"XVII," *La estación de fiebre.* pp. 32-33.
"XIX," *La estación de fiebre.* pp. 35-36.
"XX," *La estación de fiebre.* p. 36.

Daína Chaviano, "Erótica I," from the unpublished manuscript *Confesiones eróticas y otros hechizos.*
"Memo para Freud," from *Confesiones eróticas y otros hechizos.*
"Erótica IV," *fem* (Febrero-marzo 1986): 45.

Pía Barros, "Prefiguración de una huella," *A horcajadas.* Santiago de Chile: Mosquito Editores, 1990. pp. 11-12.
"Olor a madera y a silencio," *A horcajadas.* pp. 19-26.

Ángela Hernández, "Cómo recoger la sombra de las flores," *Alótropos.* Santo Domingo: Editorial Alas, 1989.

ACKNOWLEDGMENTS

"On the Edge of Pleasure" and "Nymphomahia" copyright 1988 by the Estate of Rosario Castellanos. Translation copyright 1988 by Magda Bogin. Reprinted from *The Selected Poems of Rosario Castellanos* with the permission of Graywolf Press, Saint Paul, Minnesota.

"Rio Grande de Loiza" by Julia de Burgos from *Inventing the Word: An Anthology of Twentiety Century Puerto Rican Poetry* edited by Julio Marzan. Copyright 1980 by Julio Marzan. Columbia University Press, New York. Translated from the Spanish of Julia de Burgos by Grace Schulman. Translation reprinted from *The Nation* with the permission of Grace Schulman.

"The Bloody Countess" by Alejandra Pizarnik from *Other Fires: Short Fiction by Latin American Women* by Alberto Manguel. Copyright 1986 by Alberto Manguel. Reprinted by permission of Clarkson N. Potter, a division of The Crown Publishing Group.

Excerpt from *The House of the Spirits* by Isabel Allende translated by Magd. Bogin. Translation copyright ©1985 by Alfred A. Knopf, Inc. Reprinted by permission of the publisher.

"How to Gather the Shadows of the Flowers" by Angela Hernández from *Green Cane and Juicy Flotsam: Short Stories by Caribbean Women* by Carmen Esteves and Lizabeth Paravisini-Gebert. Copyright 1991 by Carmen Esteves and Lizabeth Paravisini-Gebert. Reprinted by permission of Rutgers University Press, New Brunswick, New Jersey.

"In this Night in this World" and "The Lady of Pernambuco" from *Alejandra Pizarnik: A Profile*, edited and with introduction by Frank Graziano. Translated by Maria Rosa Fort and Frank Graziano with additional translations by Suzanne Jill Levine. Copyright 1987 by Frank Graziano. Reprinted by permission of Lobridge-Rhodes, Durango, Colorado.

"Beloved Friend" by Cecilia Vicuña from *Rolling Rock Review*. Translation by Anne Twitty. Reprinted by permission of Anne Twitty.

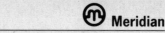

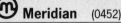